To Ginny
You should never have
left me at Communique!
I forgive you now (just)!

A MATTER ×
OF LIFE AND
DEATH

PAUL CARROLL

Matador
9 Priory Business Park,
Wistow Road, Kibworth Beauchamp,
Leicestershire. LE8 0RX
Tel: (+44) 116 279 2299
Fax: (+44) 116 279 2277
Email: books@troubador.co.uk
Web: www.troubador.co.uk/matador

ISBN 978 1780883 16 8

British Library Cataloguing in Publication Data.
A catalogue record for this book is available from the British Library.

Typeset by Troubador Publishing Ltd, Leicester, UK
Printed and bound in Great Britain by
Clays Ltd, St Ives plc

Matador is an imprint of Troubador Publishing Ltd

For Nathalie

AN ENDING

There was no point at which she thought her journey was taking a dramatically different course. Sure, she felt on the edge of death, but that's what every high was like.

The sonic boom as the heroin alerted her mu receptors to the pleasure and peace ahead seemed familiar. The seductive warmth kindled in the pit of her stomach spread through her somatosensory cortex ushering in an intense euphoria. The dragon chased; the dragon caught.

Her limbs heavy, her mouth dry, she lay down on the concrete floor and coiled into a foetal position, subconsciously strapping herself in for her voyage across the sea of tranquility. A welcome, nodding descent into dreamy and relaxed contentment. It felt… good.

As her central nervous system went out of its way to cater for the needs of its VIP guest she abandoned herself to the growing drowsiness, only momentarily breaking free of her torpor to register the reality of her surroundings.

She felt no alarm; she experienced no pain. There was no excessive sweating, panting or flailing to act as a warning. No panic. It felt… as before.

As her heartbeat and breathing slowed, she slipped out of consciousness. She felt… nothing. Out of the blue and into the black.

It was a squalid end. An overdose, pure and simple; her final moments of existence spent in a scruffy Manchester city centre car park running alongside the Rochdale canal. Her death caused some consternation, but not an excessive amount. The police officer who attended the early morning call, just about to knock off his shift, barely managed to suppress his irritation at the poor timing of it all. The workers in the office block above the car park where she was found tut-tutted at the inconvenience as they were temporarily barred entry to their workplaces as the scene was secured. The car park attendant who discovered her body would be sent on a counselling course by his employer to help cope with the shock.

Who was she? That, they'd never find out. Just a poor, young, homeless junkie with no means of identification. No one to report her missing, or to claim her. There being no suspicion of foul play, equally there was little imperative to spend time on an exhaustive investigation.

Few appeared interested in her fate other than those whose mornings had suffered a temporary diversion because of it, and even then the story quickly faded from their minds. Nobody was ever to determine where she'd come from, her family background, or what circumstances had brought her life to this lonely and intemperate close. She wouldn't be mourned, nor would she be missed.

It was a life of scant consequence.

Or was it?

CHAPTER ONE

Instant Karma

The press conference started dead on eleven o'clock. As Farren Mortimer peered over the heads of the assembled media he could see through the windows of the conference room to the carefully manicured gardens of The National Archives in Kew beyond. The rain was teeming down into the ornamental lake; the skies were suitably lachrymose on this cold, grey and miserable All Saints' Day.

Farren launched into his carefully prepared sound bite: 'In creating this new landmark date in the UK annual calendar, our intention is that everyone should have the opportunity to celebrate the life of a loved one, to remember and cherish the memory of family members and friends who are no longer with us.'

Farren Mortimer, the head of AMOLAD and the government's 'bereavement czar', was marking the one-year countdown to the inaugural People's Remembrance Day, the new autumn bank holiday date for England and Wales. Not everyone was happy with this decision. When, the previous year, the People's Remembrance Day – or PRD for short – was first announced a number of employers, large and small, had complained about the cost of another day off for their workforces. Tourism chiefs had derided the 'boost to tourism' the government assured them the new bank holiday would provide. 'In November?' they trilled.

Right-leaning newspapers had campaigned for the new bank holiday to be linked to Trafalgar Day at the end of October when the country could celebrate Horatio Nelson's, and the nation's, triumph over European adversaries some two centuries before. While this idea had garnered considerable support within the Cabinet, accusations of overt jingoism finally led to the decision to unfreeze, if only fractionally, the collective stiff upper lip with which the English and Welsh, if not the Scots, embraced the taboo subject of death.

To most people though, it was just another day off.

Farren delivered the rest of his party piece, and invited questions from the media throng. This was the bit he liked best. Any fool could be coached to deliver a statement, but for Farren the Q and A was where it really came alive, where he could dazzle with charm, sincerity, fortitude or wit depending on the requirements. His days spent pitching campaigns as an advertising executive provided an ideal training ground.

'Who has the first question?' said Farren, eager to engage.

From the floor, the warm up enquiry: 'A number of religious groups, not to mention leading agnostics, have voiced concerns over the essentially Christian theme chosen for the new bank holiday, being so clearly anchored to the dates of All Saints' and All Souls' days. What relevance does PRD really have in a multi-cultural Britain?'

'*A banker to start with,*' thought Farren before sharing his message of reassurance and inclusivity, and delivering a brief history lesson taking in the Day of The Dead and the ancient Celtic festival of Samhain.

'The British Legion is up in arms that, being so close to Remembrance Sunday, PRD will confuse people and impact on their fund raising. What do you have to say about that?'

'Look. I think that PRD will actually complement and reinforce the British Legion's own sterling efforts, for which the entire country is extremely grateful,' replied Farren. 'I have every confidence in the public's ability to differentiate between what are essentially personal and national commemorations. Next?'

Farren could keep this up all day if he needed to, but he still had the obligatory photo shoot to fit in before the lunchtime broadcast deadline. Fifteen minutes later Farren was posing in front of a giant herb garden where, spelled out in regimentally arranged rosemary, the legend of 'People's Remembrance Day' could be clearly captured by the photographers who had been ushered to the first floor balcony above the atrium. *'There's Rosemary, best for remembrance'* as all Shakespeare students, and googling PRs, well knew.

Darren Smith took five steps back, screwed his eyes up into a squint, and peered at the four A1 cardboard panels taped to the studio wall. He had just spent two hours cutting, slicing and fashioning the boards with his Stanley knife. *'Mint,'* he laughed to himself as he stepped forward to make a few final adjustments to his new stencil.

Not that anybody had ever heard of non-conformist street artist Darren Smith; his alter ego, Smudger, on the other hand, was an altogether different proposition. Darren had used the pseudonym Smudger to tag his graffiti executions from the very beginning of his street art career across London. Obviously, as an illegal street artist, it was *de rigueur* to work

3

under an alias but as Smudger developed his art and became bolder he also recognised that there were a number of benefits to be gained from concealing his true identity under the mantle of an anonymous anti-hero.

As his notoriety grew, and people expressed an interest in actually owning his works, Smudger installed an agent and his course was set: the more clever, outrageous and anti-establishment he could be, the more he would appeal – and sell – to the burgeoning brigade of middle class art collectors. He would be the embodiment of the rebellion that still burned in their bellies despite their selling out to the man a long time before.

Smudger didn't mind being a standard-bearer for Generation Y. He played the game, zealously masking his real name to help play up his image and engaging in a series of inspired PR pranks to burnish his notoriety. Asking prices for his work would climb in direct correlation to each new stunt he pulled, which is why Smudger was so preoccupied today. Only too aware of a double target of government hype and exploitative commercialism (someone else's – not his own) Smudger was putting the finishing touches to his anti-AMOLAD and PRD opus.

Quickly spraying across the closely set panels in first black and then red aerosol paint, he carefully unpeeled the four pieces of card from the wall. As he stood back for the second time, he broke into a self-congratulatory smirk as he studied the finished work. Looking back at him was a giant stencilled image of the Grim Reaper, holding a shopping basket in his hand. Underneath were the words: 'Add to basket. All major credit cards accepted.' By morning, with the aid of his crew, the stencil would be emblazoned on the walls of a number of London cemeteries, burial grounds and memorials.

Back at AMOLAD's head office, Jon Bell was watching Farren's performance on the one o'clock news. Jon rolled his eyes as Farren earnestly told journalists 'I'm glad you asked me that,' and 'that's a good question.' Still, Jon had to hand it to Farren that his softly enunciated northern vowels lent a distinctive and curiously reassuring air to his pronouncements.

Jon suppressed a blush of pride as the on-the-scene reporter referred to Farren as 'Mr Eulogy', a nickname that Jon himself had invented. Jon's final flourish for the profile boosting moniker had been to seed it via a friendly journalist to make the euphemism look warm and merited rather than self-styled. Now the rest of the media used it without question. Farren Mortimer *was* Mr Eulogy.

Jon's career with AMOLAD had been stellar, fast track and meteoric all rolled into one. Landing a job working in the marketing team at the high-flying AMOLAD had turned out to be only the start. Under Farren Mortimer's 'meritocracy' system, within two years of joining the business Jon found himself promoted to the role of Operations Director for the group.

As Farren's number two, he was primarily in charge of managing the PRD project for AMOLAD and, in addition, was preparing for tomorrow afternoon's board meeting. He was also, deep down, harbouring resentment that his boss was doing the press conference, not him.

'Right, let's get down to it,' said Farren, which was his normal way of getting a meeting started. The board was gathered at AMOLAD's magnificently appointed offices, a converted church in Clerkenwell dubbed 'The Steeple'. Farren had bought the deconsecrated church on the back of his first five years of trading. His architect had retained the stained glass windows of the church and made extensive use of reclaimed stone, iron and wood features throughout to create a spectacular working space as well as an architectural paean to commercial success.

Now, some ten years after launching AMOLAD, Farren was employing over 350 staff at The Steeple and across Life Centres in twenty-six UK towns. The organisation that had put the 'fun' into funerals with its online Forever in our Minds cyber cemetery and its pioneering biovid films to commemorate the life of the deceased was on a roll. Death had never been more alive and kicking in its profit-making potential.

Farren's financial director, Graeme Porter, covered point number one on the agenda – the accounts update. His summation of the month's sales figures, year-to-date progress, performance versus forecast analysis and year-on-year comparisons were all carefully laid out in a comprehensive report complete with spreadsheets and performance graphs. After fifteen minutes of facts and figures, Graeme proudly brought his presentation to a close. 'A number of high-water marks achieved there. Remarkable.'

'Yes, outstanding, everyone, well done,' echoed Farren.

Next, Jon cleared his throat and raced through the operational items on the agenda at a clipped pace – due to the profile PRD would create, the development team was pushing on with new and innovative bereavement services and products for the coming year and things couldn't be in better shape. They were also liaising closely with the government team on the marketing and promotion of PRD. Farren, together with Graeme and AMOLAD's IT director Peter Stevens, nodded their assent at the positive news emerging from Jon's lips.

6

As Farren trotted briskly through the coverage of yesterday's PRD press conference, a young IT manager slipped quietly into the room, proffered a quick apology, and knelt down next to Jon and Peter to convey his urgent tidings. A handful of printouts were pressed into Jon's hands and he peered intently at them for thirty seconds or so, his mouth drawn into a tightly wound pucker.

'Going to need to interrupt there, Farren,' interjected Jon. 'We appear to have a slight *problemette* on the horizon.'

'Problemette?' For a second, Farren couldn't be sure if Jon sounded alarmed or pleased at the inferred predicament. 'What is it?' he enquired.

'Our friend Smudger has been at it again,' replied Jon.

'I thought that had been handled this morning?' said Farren, assuming Jon was referring to the Grim Reaper episode.

'No, it's not the stencil stunt. He's managed to hack our mainframe, and has been doctoring, well should I say, defacing, random entries. Look.' Jon placed on the table the handful of printouts from the Forever in our Minds website the IT manager had just given him. At first glance they looked like fairly standard entries but as Jon pointed to various details, the extent of the hacking started to become clear.

Where a picture of a Mr Henry Woodcock had been formerly posted at the head of an in memoriam listing, this had now been substituted with a less than flattering photo of a penis and a large pair of testicles, bedecked with a pair of sunglasses. The addition of a cigarette tucked under the dangling member completed the bizarre impression of a face.

'Jesus Christ,' said Farren as he turned the page first one way, then the other.

'There's more,' said Jon, thrusting the next page under Farren's gaze, 'which is potentially even more damaging.'

Farren looked at the next listing, for a Mrs Edith Callaghan. 'What am I supposed to be looking for?' he said after a brief hiatus.

'Look at the ads,' urged Jon. 'He's switched them.'

Farren studied the ads, one for free fire alarms, one for mini fire extinguishers, and one for Zippy cigarette lighters. He looked again at Edith's entry: 'Sadly taken from us in a tragic house fire. May her light never be extinguished.'

'How the hell did he get into the mainframe?' demanded Farren. 'Have we checked the other pages?'

'We're doing that now, Farren,' replied Peter. 'If we get any calls from affected parties, customer services will advise them that their entries have had to be temporarily removed for technical reasons – just while we see how much damage he's managed to do.'

Farren quickly assessed the situation. He couldn't allow Smudger to control the agenda. 'Who has seen these?' he asked. 'I mean, have they been reported or circulated on the net or on Twitter by anyone yet?'

'Nothing yet, apparently,' said Peter, 'but we're on it. The trolling sweep picked this up half an hour ago and the team immediately pulled the pages.'

'In that case,' said Farren, 'we have to beat Smudger to the punch. Leak a rumour that a rogue hacker has tried to get into our mainframe, but was stopped by our firewall before he could do any damage. Then, when we're asked to comment, we'll concede that it's true, and that we've traced the hacker's location to a university site. That way, if Smudger tries to claim he did it people will think he's just trying to hijack someone else's stunt. If any images get circulated we'll say they're obvious spoofs. Add the usual "this is an attack on everyone who has suffered a bereavement etcetera" and we can hopefully minimise any impact.'

'Should we actually be drawing attention to it?' asked Graeme. 'Maybe it won't get out.'

'No, Farren's right,' said Jon. 'Smudger will try to boast about what he's done; there's no doubt about that. If we get our version out ahead of his, he can't bleat that it's not true – it *will* look like he's trying to claim the credit for something that he didn't do. Having a nerdy student trying to play a one-off joke is much better for us than being seen to be under siege from a nutcase with a mission.'

'Good,' said Farren. 'Well, we're just about done, so let's get this sorted as soon as possible – don't let that pillock get away with it. Oh, and double, double check the security of the mainframe – full code refresh, the lot.'

Farren sat back in his lavender coloured swivel chair as his colleagues left the room. He could have done without Smudger casting a shadow on their business dealings, yet again. He just didn't get this Smudger at all. At first, when he'd pulled a couple of stunts taking the rise out of AMOLAD, Farren had feigned indifference – he didn't want to be seen as being unsympathetic to a rebellious, creative soul because, after all, wasn't he one himself?

In any event, Smudger's first AMOLAD inspired pranks generated a lot of publicity that Farren claimed had boosted awareness of their services. Farren had even surreptitiously bought a couple of Smudger's works, congratulating himself on his sense of irony. But the irony was beginning to wear thin, and Smudger was now getting to be a problem. What was his motivation? Why was he persevering in his attacks? Why didn't he move on to another target? Yes, Smudger was really beginning to piss Farren off.

Just then, there was quick rap on his office door and Jon reappeared. 'Sorry – just thought we should add to the minutes an AOB that the new Christmas biovid gift vouchers are going great guns.'

PRD minus 364 days.

CHAPTER TWO

'Til I Die

Two hundred miles north, in their modest semi-detached home in the leafy Manchester suburb of Didsbury, Farren's adoptive parents also had death on their minds. Agnes Mortimer sat at the bedside of her husband, Ernest, trying to suppress the thought, God forbid, *'when will he be relieved once and for all from this suffering?'*

Married for over sixty years, Agnes quietly reflected on the unfairness of Ernest's ailments and the impact inflicted on his formerly robust frame. Where Ernest had once struck an imposing presence in any room he cared to walk into, he could now slip under the door like a wisp of smoke.

It was only a matter of time before his illness, an incurable inflammatory condition called adhesive arachnoiditis, exacted its final toll, with little respite in prospect for either Ernest or his resolute and devoted carer.

At least Agnes had cheerful news for Ernest. 'Farren just called. He's on the television this evening being interviewed, so I thought we could watch that after tea?'

'He's very popular all of a sudden,' said Ernest. 'He's been on a lot this last week.'

'I think it's that remembrance thing he's doing. There's been a lot of coverage.'

'What's he on?'

'The early evening programme, you know, with that Irish presenter you like.'

'Well, we can't miss that,' said Ernest. 'At this rate, we're going to have to start making appointments to see him.'

To the west of Didsbury, up Barlow Moor Road and across the arterial causeway of Princess Road, undertaker Michael Morrison was as yet unaware of the potential for impending business from the Mortimers. Michael and the four generations of Morrisons who preceded him had been ferrying the good people of South Manchester to their final resting place for well over one hundred years. Today, at Southern Cemetery, the firm's tally would be increased by two more unfortunate souls. Michael was presently between the day's funerals; one down, one to go.

Despite his outward mien of decorum, serenity and dignity, Michael was a troubled man. The family business, of which he was now the sole heir and survivor, was, to coin the sort of crude expression Michael himself would never use, 'dying on its arse'.

It wasn't that people had stopped expiring – far from it. However, during the 80s and 90s traditional family owned and independent funeral businesses had started to be swallowed up by two mega-corporations intent on cornering the cadaver market. They were difficult to compete with given their ability to invest in marketing and their hard-nosed determination to buy leads from hospitals, churches and care homes. In Michael's father's latter years, Morrison Family Funeral Services had begun to see its business become more and more squeezed.

If that wasn't bad enough, when Michael's turn came to

take over the company a new phenomenon, seemingly inspired by the death of Princess Diana, started to hit Michael even harder in the pocket – the rise of Farren Mortimer's AMOLAD and his new gimmicks for 'celebrating life'. Now, as well as the big conglomerates body snatching his customers, Michael had to contend with this irreverent upstart who was diverting money people used to spend on profitable extras such as headstones and best quality caskets further away from his grasp. Michael's business, and his sanity, was entering a terminal phase.

In his professional capacity Michael was of course no stranger to Southern Cemetery, and as he often did when he was preoccupied he now found himself heading down towards plot I R/C. There, at the grave of Mrs Violet Charlotte Byrom whose headstone pronounced had died in 1881, Michael paused briefly and allowed himself a brief reverie. Then, collecting himself, he turned abruptly and strode back to the cemetery gates for the second interment of the day.

Journalist and TV presenter Kieran McDonaghy, as he did virtually every minute he wasn't on air, sat fiddling with his iPhone, checking his Twitter feed, scanning his Facebook page and keeping an eye on his email accounts. Kieran was getting the heads up from one of the researchers about that evening's interview subject, Farren Mortimer. What angle should they take? Not that it would be a challenging confrontation – *Feet Up* was very much a family programme with a celebrity-led, light entertainment bent. Kieran had ambitions to do meatier stuff, but he was still on his way up and was grateful to have landed this high profile berth as his first real TV job.

The Dublin born son of a publican had roared his way

through the fourth estate to this brink of superstardom. Leaving school at the age of 16, Kieran landed himself a junior reporter's job on a Dublin weekly by dint of his charm, work ethic, productivity and low wages. Having cut his teeth in the world of journalism, Kieran's next stop was London, where a succession of promotions saw him, at the age of 24, installed as the showbiz correspondent at the Daily Tablet. He landed the post in somewhat amusing circumstances. His predecessor, having been poached by a rival tabloid, was told by the irate editor of the Tablet that 'any idiot could do the showbiz job': cue Kieran's elevation, mainly because he happened to be the first person to walk past the editor's desk. No matter, Kieran had the time of his life schlepping with the starlets, stooges and sycophants whose aspirations aimed no higher than a cursory namecheck in Kieran's *Connected* column. As his twinkling brogue and his chiselled televisual features began to be noticed further afield he found himself being invited to screen test for *Feet Up*. He didn't waste the opportunity. Once embarked on a TV career Kieran diligently continued to write regular columns for a variety of print publications, launched his own blog, and also became an early adopter of Twitter, building up a growing audience for his 140 character missives. Kieran was only just getting started.

The previous Monday's edition of *Feet Up* had covered the news announcement of PRD, opting for a straight comment to camera from the man who was formally in charge of the new bank holiday – the Parliamentary Under Secretary for Social Responsibility, Nigel Adlington MP. Today, Kieran's editor had decided there was still life in the story and wanted a look at changing attitudes to bereavement in the UK as exemplified by charismatic entrepreneur Farren Mortimer.

'What do you have?' Kieran asked the researcher – actually an intern working unpaid for six months to boost her CV – sat in front of him.

'Well, he's not married, and I can't seem to find any major girlfriends in his past,' was her opening observation.

'And, this is relevant to bereavement, because…?'

Sensing she'd not made the best start to her meeting with Kieran, the intern cut to the middle of her notes. 'Well, he's from Manchester, went to Leeds University where he did English, and after that he moved to London to work in advertising. Apparently, it was while he was working on the Fond Farewell Funerals account that he started to get ideas that would later lead him to start AMOLAD.'

'Much better,' said Kieran. 'Give me an example of what inspired him back then – what was the catalyst, the launch pad?'

Relieved their exchange was now back on solid ground, the intern confidently dealt the next fact to Kieran. 'The Funerals Top Ten. That's his; that's what kicked it all off.'

'And the Funerals Top Ten is…?'

'Well, basically, it's a list of the top ten songs played at funerals every year, and it became an annual press highlight for Fond Farewell.'

'Like *Knock on Wood, Smoke Gets in Your Eyes,* that sort of thing?

'I think it was more *My Heart Will Go On* and *Candle In The Wind* from what I read.'

'So how did that help sell anything?

'Well, it made people think about their funerals in advance – not just the songs, but other details too. Fond Farewell were offering a pre-planning service, so it was good for business.'

'I see. So, *Candle in the Wind* – is that the Diana connection?'

'It was obviously influential. The aftermath of Diana's funeral and the response to ideas like the Funerals Top Ten eventually persuaded Farren to jack in his job at the agency, because he could sense that there had been a sea change in attitudes to death and bereavement – at least that's what he's claimed in interviews since. Apparently, before Diana we didn't as a nation indulge in open and public grieving, is that right?'

'I'll have to pass on that, but I'll take your word for it.'

'Anyway, he started out with an online in memoriam site called Forever in our Minds where people created their own commemorative tributes to loved ones. It was novel at the time, but he was clever too because he linked in loads of commercial partners like florists, solicitors selling wills, life insurance companies and even undertakers who spent a lot of money on advertising.'

'And he didn't crash and burn with the other dotcoms?'

'No – he missed the first real wave, so learned the lessons, I guess.'

'Then what?'

'Well, the past decade has just been one new idea after another. The next big money spinner was biovids, where they do a video of the deceased's life. It's like a pop promo – you give them loads of stills, video clips and favourite music tracks and they edit them all together. They're played at funerals and families buy copies to give out to mourners.'

'Ah, yes, seen those. Interesting concept.'

'Yes – and easy to produce with a handful of templates and a few Apple Macs. Then they persuaded people to buy these at what they called "pre-need" stage. They sell loads because people want to get it right, and actually see it themselves.'

'The ultimate vanity project. I must ask him if he does discount.'

'And the latest big seller these days is memorial services for Joe Soap.'

'I'm sure he doesn't market them as that.'

'No, obviously. His pitch is that it's not only celebrities who deserve a memorial service – everyone should have one. The beauty of this for AMOLAD is that they create a second sales wave because they suggest these should be held around three months after the funeral. Everyone's in a lighter mood by then and, well, celebratory rather than mournful.'

'And he sells more copies of the biovids on the back of it as a result?'

'Not just biovids – he's set up a division called A Life Remembered for these memorials and you can actually book the venue, catering and entertainment through them.'

'Ingenious – a mark up at every turn. What else is he flogging?'

'The overall merchandising range is vast now; big Memory Archives – books to keep artefacts from someone's life in, a Departure Lounge service to get your will and personal affairs in order – all they do is sub it out to law firms who give them a kick back – and Bliogs where you can record your life, or your kids' lives, online from cradle to grave. It's mega.'

'Who's anti-AMOLAD? What's the tallest tree in his forest of pain?'

'There's a few, but they've not really been able to stop him. The church – virtually every religion – is "uneasy" about

AMOLAD's popularity; they think it's too commercial and moving death away from faith and belief to like, reality show schmaltz. And undertakers hate him – they reckon he's taking money out of their pockets because people are spending with him what they used to spend through them. Course, they can't openly attack him as it's the consumer's choice so they bang on about "sensitivity" and "vulnerability" of the bereaved in the main.'

'What about attacks on AMOLAD like the Grim Reaper stunt last week?'

'Hard to say. That was the street artist Smudger by all accounts, who's had a go at them before. But Mortimer always laughs stuff like that off and says he's grateful for the publicity. There's some really good stuff on Twitter as well – do you follow @wappinglie?'

'No, but I am aware of her reach and influence. One more thing – AMOLAD – where does that name comes from?'

'It's an acronym for A Matter of Life and Death – you can tell he's a former ad man, can't you? And that's pretty much everything I've dug up.'

'Good. "Maverick adman plugs into zeitgeist of conspicuous mourning to drag world of caskets, chrysanthemums and cremations into the 21st century". Think I've got it.'

Nigel Adlington MP, the Parliamentary Under Secretary of State for Social Responsibility, was scurrying back to his apartment keen not to miss Farren Mortimer plugging PRD on *Feet Up*. As he fished inside his briefcase for the front door key, his BlackBerry rang. The wife. He immediately put the handset back inside his jacket pocket.

Nigel had enjoyed a busy day, the sort of busy day that

comes with success, with progress, with recognition. He was in a state of near elation as he entered his two-bedroom *pied a terre* with its view of the Thames; his first action on entering was to toss his case on to the kitchen work surface so he could check the contents of the fridge. Perfect – a nicely chilled bottle of Puligny Montrachet stood to attention in the door rack, ready to offer itself up in recognition of Nigel's achievements.

His BlackBerry buzzed. An answer phone message from his wife, Emma, back at the family home in Cheshire. No need to spoil the mood by listening to that now – there was a cork to be pulled, a slow motion recall of the day's events to relish, and victories to be saluted before having to make the duty call back.

Nigel savoured the wine as he reflected on his recent run of good fortune. Firstly, the press coverage and reaction over the past week for the countdown to the People's Remembrance Day had been favourable. That morning Nigel had been thrilled to receive a 'well done' from the Secretary of State in recognition of his championing the concept and making it happen. Secondly, he'd learned after lunch that the law firm in which he remained a major partner had won a huge clinical negligence case that had been dragging on for over 30 months; his cut of the settlement would pay the school fees for his sons Adam and Teddy for another year.

That afternoon, in a skittish mood and urged on by his young, testosterone charged special adviser, Nigel had extended an invitation to road safety charity campaigner Annie Brooks to attend his offices for an exploratory meeting. How Nigel and his adviser had sniggered at the prospect of seeing former model and footballer's wife turned self-styled people's champion at close quarters – a little bit of light relief in a busy work schedule to which he could look forward.

The best news of all though had arrived just as he was planning an early escape for the evening; Nigel was informed in a phone call that the Party wanted to major on social responsibility at its Spring Forum in five months' time, and Nigel had been handed a significant role on the conference planning committee.

Still twenty minutes to *Feet Up*. *'Cheers, to me!'* was the toast as he turned up the volume on the CD player for his celebratory anthem. The aptly named XTC sang *Making Plans for Nigel*.

'Turn your head to the right. Chin up a bit. Now look back towards the lens.' The photographer issued his directions as if advising a lost tourist. His subject, Annie Brooks, was no stranger to the camera but even she recognised that this was the most prestigious shoot she'd ever done. The former model, now the wife of a moderately well known Championship League footballer, fixed her gaze to the lens of the Hasselblad 503CWD pointed in her direction.

'Serious, like you mean business,' came the photographer's new command. 'Now sternly down the lens and raise your index finger like you're warning someone. The pointing finger, yes.'

The founder of the safer street speed charity HASTE (Help Arrest Speed Through Education) did as she was bidden as the shutter whirred. Today, this photo shoot for the Clarion newspaper; in her handbag a copy of an email, received just before she left the office, inviting her to a meeting with the Parliamentary Under Secretary of State for Social

Responsibility to discuss her campaign. HASTE was taking her places she would have thought impossible a year earlier.

Finally, after three and a half hours, the photographer declared a wrap. The shoot was only supposed to have taken an hour, but what with adjusting lighting levels, attending to hair and make-up, three costume changes, and the photographer's behind the camera consultations with the art director, they'd overrun quite considerably.

Annie hurried over to the giant computer monitor to check the various images that were already being sifted into a final selection palette. Annie was slightly taken aback, and not a little pleased, to see a succession of rather sophisticated images of herself on view. Yes, this was certainly a bit different to her previous efforts in front of the cameras.

'This is the one, I reckon,' said the art director as he dragged a head and shoulders JPEG across the screen and dropped it into the digitised template located in the centre of the screen.

Staring back at Annie was a detailed mock up of a car sticker, branded with both the Clarion and HASTE logos, featuring a message from a decidedly sultry looking Annie to the driver of the car behind: '*I like men who take their time.*'

Clearly, the Clarion felt that women drivers never exceeded the speed limit.

PRD minus 357.

CHAPTER THREE

Soul on Fire

It was Christmas week and Agnes Mortimer hesitated in the hallway as Father Wilcox gathered his coat and scarf. 'He hasn't got long, has he, Father?' she whispered.

The parish priest, well used to handling situations like this, effortlessly slipped into his litany of comfort. 'Agnes, he's weakening, but his soul is ready. You must be strong for him and for yourself in the final phase.'

Father Wilcox was an increasingly frequent visitor to the Mortimer household as Ernest's condition deteriorated. The Church was a constant presence in the Mortimers' lives, perhaps not surprisingly given their backgrounds and upbringing. Knowing it was a Tuesday morning and that the priest was due, Ernest had raised himself from his sickbed and, with some assistance from Agnes, shaved and dressed so he could receive the priest in his living room; it was a sign of 'respect'.

Father Wilcox had been in the parish for five years and knew the Mortimers not only as stalwart members of his congregation but also as a decent and kindly couple who had been most welcoming when he arrived to replace the previous incumbent of some thirty-five years. Knowing people don't like change, he'd worked hard to build his relationships with his parishioners and was now beginning to think he was getting his feet under the table.

Agnes was right about poor old Ernest – he didn't look like he had long left, and Father Wilcox suppressed a thought that it would be interesting to see how Ernest's funeral plans may eventually progress given the occupation of the Mortimers' son, Farren, who had made quite a name for himself with his high profile AMOLAD antics. Wilcox and his fellow diocesans were only too aware of Farren's agenda changing ideas and most were not in favour – far from it. Still, no reason to trample on Mr and Mrs Mortimer, or Mortimer himself whom Father Wilcox had met twice on his home visits. God would provide.

As Father Wilcox left, he reminded Agnes to call him if he was needed and told her that he'd visit again next Tuesday. In the interim he knew he'd see Agnes at church – there were two masses that week, one on Christmas Day and one on the Sunday. The 'anything needed' was of course extreme unction, which Father Wilcox calculated would be called for before the Spring given the chronic state of Ernest's health and the resignation of the doctors and specialists in trying anything further to arrest his condition. All Father Wilcox could do now was help to make Ernest spiritually ready for God to receive him.

Agnes closed the door, and went back to Ernest. 'He's a lovely man, isn't he?' she said. 'Now, would you like to stay down a while, or go back to bed?'

'Do you know,' replied Ernest, 'I think I will go back to bed, love.'

After a further hour patiently spent getting Ernst back upstairs, out of his trousers, shirt and tie, into his pyjamas and settled down in bed, Agnes finally found herself back in the kitchen. Over a cup of tea and a tuna and cucumber sandwich, Agnes reflected, yet again, on how Ernest's life was to finally play out, and where it would leave her when it did.

The illness Ernest had fallen foul of really was the most rotten luck anyone could have imagined. Ernest, a short and stocky man, had always boasted a robust and hearty constitution, but in his late fifties, helping a friend build a garden wall one weekend, he had been over-ambitious with the brick-hodding and had suffered a slipped disc as a result. Despite the pain Ernest remained positive and good-humoured, saying that the National Health would sort him out. Eventually, he had an operation to correct the prolapse and it was here when his problems really started. One of the membranes that surround and protect the central nervous system, the arachnoid, became severely inflamed due to the invasive spinal surgery, resulting in the formation of scar tissue and adhesions causing the spinal nerves to glue together. This outcome wasn't apparent immediately as it took time for the extremely painful and debilitating symptoms – neuralgia, numbness and tingling, reduced bowel and bladder control and difficulty in standing, sitting and walking – to accelerate and for an accurate diagnosis to emerge.

That this happened was a million to one chance; it was an extremely rare outcome of such surgery. The only way to deal with the illness was to manage the impact on Ernest's body as effectively as possible with the most powerful of pain suppressants. It was, as Ernest told the claims consultant chasing his particular ambulance, 'an act of God, not the fault of the health trust.' He also told him: 'Now bugger off, you parasitic little worm.'

That was Ernest all over, and part of the reason why Agnes had been attracted to him in the first place. She'd not had to look far to find him. Her first encounter with Ernest had been at a local dance following his demob from the Royal Navy and romance and marriage had followed quickly. They walked down the aisle at St Mary of The Angels & St Clare's Catholic Church in Levenshulme on 20 November 1947, the same day Princess Elizabeth married Philip Mountbatten. This coincidence could be interpreted as being deeply romantic, patriotic, or possibly just plain indifferent to the royal cause. At least Ernest, by then working on the Rich Tea production line at the McVities factory on Crossley Road, was in an advantageous position to beat rationing when it came to cobbling together a wedding cake.

Agnes, nee Doherty, rarely strayed more than four miles from the Levenshulme epicentre where, the daughter of Irish immigrants, she'd began her life and been brought up with siblings Charlie, Mary, and Paddy. Her entire existence was enacted within this narrow geographical radius. Even her job for thirty years as a switchboard operator for the Post Office only took her the short bus ride into Manchester city centre.

With two jobs between them the newlyweds looked set fair for a comfortable enough life together. The only sadness was that it soon became apparent that Agnes was struggling to get in the family way, and despite their best efforts, Agnes and Ernest eventually had to come to terms with the fact that their union wasn't going to be blessed with children.

The married couple continued to share a happy loving relationship, but would never be free of the void to which barrenness had so cruelly condemned them. Ernest suggested adopting, or even fostering, but Agnes put her foot down – she felt it would compound her failure, rather than assuage it. And that's how they continued for the next twenty-five years or so, content in each other's company, but both knowing that it could have been so very different.

Then, in September 1973, at the age of 49, Agnes had a dramatic and unexpected *volte-face* when she and Ernest adopted a young boy, not yet two weeks old. What brought about this significant change of heart and mind? The brief answer? The Catholic Church. Possibly because she was approaching her 50s, maybe worn down by the nagging and incessant feeling of deprivation that childlessness had visited upon her, Agnes had a crisis of faith. For a devout Catholic of her generation this was serious news indeed for Father Culshaw, the local parish priest who regularly took Agnes' confession.

Over many months of personal counselling, Father Culshaw desperately tried to bring Agnes back into the arms of the Vatican. It became clear to the priest that the pain of childlessness, and the self-denial that prevented Agnes from adopting or fostering, had brought her to this pass. One day, presented with an altogether different problem, he came up with a solution that was to have a lasting impact on both Agnes' and Ernest's lives, and also on that of the young boy who would go on, in later life, to set up AMOLAD.

There's no doubt that Father Culshaw took his role of priest, pastor and shepherd very seriously indeed. He had learned over the years that a degree of pragmatism was as essential to getting results as the Holy Scripture. When confronted with the harrowing tale of a young mother in the care of the St Teresa's Home for Mothers and Babies in Salford, Father Culshaw had a flash of inspiration that could possibly solve two problems.

The mother, a student, had given birth to the boy in early

September, and she had been very difficult indeed according to the nuns who ran the home. The infant was destined for adoption, and the young mother in question had agreed to this course of action. Yet despite knowing this, or possibly because of it, the mother was found crouched over the one-week-old baby boy one night with a pillow in her hand in the act of attempting to suffocate the child.

Even by the standards of the Mothers and Babies home, this was a shocking episode, not to mention a lucky escape for all concerned. Father Culshaw, visiting another young mother from his parish on that very evening, found himself in the middle of the rumpus.

The unfortunate mother was immediately committed to a mental institution, and it would be some time before she would exit its grim, institutional grip. While the nuns fussed around the baby, Fred, thankfully recovering from his ordeal, Father Culshaw had an idea. Enquiring of the head nun, Sister Immaculata, whether Fred had been allocated adoptive parents yet, he received the reply that he was due to be processed the following day. The priest's brainwave was that Fred could fill the child-sized hole in Agnes Mortimer's life, reminding her that God is not only great and good, but ever thinking of his flock. Like the nuns, he knew that such a move would be in the best interests of the child. And that's how, in this mysterious way, Fred became the bait that lured Agnes back to the Church as well as satisfying a lifetime of want.

Did Agnes look for such a bounty, or even welcome it? Of course, she was shocked when Father Culshaw arrived later that evening to tell her of this divine intervention. She certainly harboured grave misgivings over her ability to become a mother, particularly as she was getting on in years. Also, even if she did say yes, didn't you have to have all sorts of tests to become an adoptive parent?

Father Culshaw allayed all of her fears. 'Just try it, Agnes, and I'll sort out the authorities. God has listened to you, and here is his reply. In any case, you can change your mind between the fostering and adoption phases which I'll help you with.'

Overwhelmed with compassion for the plight of the poor little mite, Agnes felt the call had to be answered, if only for a short period while something more permanent could be organised for the child. As for Ernest, he made a mental note to increase his weekly contribution to the collection plate on account of this unexpected gift. Once Agnes and Ernest took delivery of Fred four days later, there was to be no turning back. God's apostle worked his Jesuitical ways and within six months the fostering gave way to full adoption. Agnes and Ernest remained ignorant as to the identity of the child's real mother, but fully understood that the father was unknown and that the single young mother, unable to cope, had freely given up the child for adoption to ensure a better life for him.

In order to start with a completely clean sheet, the Mortimers immediately decided that the name of Fred had to go, replacing it with Farren in honour of Agnes' Donegal roots, as well as a nod to the country singer Faron Young who featured hugely in Ernest's record collection. Faron's *If You Ain't Lovin' you Ain't Livin'* was a particular favourite at the christening.

Life was blessed, the Mortimers were a real family at last, and all the years of emptiness were swept away in an instance as young Farren became the centre of their universe. Being on the cusp of fifty didn't deter the Mortimers – the child gave them a fresh lease of life and he wanted for nothing as he grew, and grow he did into a fine young man with a bright future ahead of him.

As the age gap between Agnes and Ernest and the other children's parents at school began to become apparent to Farren, his parents determined that he needed to know about his adoptive status, so with the help of Father Culshaw they broke the news to Farren when he was ten years old. Of course, they could tell him nothing of his real parents except that his father was unknown and his mother dead (Father Culshaw thought that this explanation was for the best), so Agnes and Ernest were his true parents and Farren was not to worry about it. And Farren didn't – well, not all of the time anyway. No mention was made of the unfortunate smothering attempt on the young child, not surprisingly as Father Culshaw had decided that this information would remain off limit to the Mortimers from day one.

Having dispensed with the technicality of disclosure, everybody moved on. Both Agnes and Ernest were retired by the time Farren went up to university in Leeds, and both parents could look back on the happiest part of their marriage in rearing young Farren. And hadn't Farren done well? Neither Ernest nor Agnes could believe his rapid rise to prominence and fame, and the success of his business. While they were proud of his achievements, they had to confess to a certain puzzlement over the popularity of his ideas, and how he managed to keep dreaming up such concepts. They would watch Farren on television, and assiduously collated press cuttings on him into a huge scrapbook that Agnes had bought. They were a little upset when Farren's impact on popular culture was attacked in some quarters as being ungodly and gimmicky, but they could square that with their religious beliefs, and in any case, it was just the modern way of things.

Farren hadn't let success go to his head – in their view, he was still kind and considerate and eager to look after his parents. Farren had offered to buy them a new house in Cheshire for their retirement; silly goose – as if they'd leave their home in Didsbury. Farren also was most insistent in getting the best possible medical opinion and specialists to address Ernest's condition. Ernest held out for a while, stating that there was nothing wrong with the National Health but as his health continued to deteriorate, he relented and undertook a series of tests at the Alexandra Hospital in Cheadle. All to no avail.

As Agnes sat in the kitchen pondering over her half-eaten sandwich, a tear rolled down her cheek. In contemplating and reminiscing over her life with Ernest she felt no bitterness, no anger; she was just sad that the end was in sight. All of her memories seemed so vital, real and recent to Agnes. Not remote, not lost, but within touching distance, and likely to be invoked with familiar intimacy at the merest smell, sound or image. For Agnes, the past wasn't a foreign country, it was as important a part of the present as the lunch that lay unconsumed on the table before her and the conversation she had just finished with Father Wilcox.

She stirred herself. The Christmas shopping wasn't going to buy itself, and she had plenty to do ahead of Farren's return home to share Christmas dinner with his parents, almost inevitably for the last time.

PRD minus 313.

CHAPTER FOUR

You Gotta Move

Christmas came a day early for Annie Brooks. She'd spent two hours getting ready for her meeting with Nigel Adlington, the Parliamentary Under Secretary of State for Social Responsibility who had invited her to 'share her work' with his office. There was no doubt about it, Annie's career with HASTE was 'motoring' as she told her husband, Championship footballer Stuart Brooks. 'Motoring' was, of course, an inappropriate expression to use in the context of an anti-speeding group, which is something Annie's image consultants got to grips with at the first opportunity. They also delicately pointed out that 'career' wasn't strictly accurate or reflective of her struggle for justice. So today Annie was advancing her mission for change, which, while it had already made significant progress to date, still had much to achieve.

That Annie found herself waiting at Millbank for an audience with the government's advocate for social responsibility was like a fairytale come true for her, although she couldn't admit to that either – she was here to advance the cause. Other people catapulted into the public spotlight through dint of circumstance may have been daunted by such a prospect, but Annie wasn't the timid type, far from it; she couldn't wait to impress her views on the junior minister. More importantly, she was relishing the prospect of briefing the media afterwards on their meaningful discussion.

Annie was an unlikely human rights campaigner. As an ex-model, married to a moderately successful footballer, she had never done anything of this nature before, but when the torch was passed to her, she had grasped it. And it wasn't as if she had asked for that torch to be handed over, no; however, once fate had intervened she knew she had to follow the calling.

The calling in question was to make the nation's streets safer from speeding motorists who endangered lives every day through their reckless, antisocial and irresponsible disregard of urban speed limits. Annie knew this on good authority because Annie was a victim. Or rather, her son Donny was a victim but that amounted to the same thing where the sacred umbilical cord between parent and child is concerned.

On first being married, Annie had harboured concerns about being a mother but had kept these thoughts from Stuart who was cock-a-hoop at the prospect of being a dad. In reality, Annie didn't mind motherhood too much once she got her figure back within two months of the birth. The nanny was a considerable help, and Annie was still able to enjoy a busy social life, both with the network of football WAGs she'd joined as well as with Stuart. Being a mother, and married to a footballer, she no longer had to work, which was just as well, as the number of bookings she was receiving pre-marriage didn't even constitute a trickle. OK – married life was a bit tame, a bit boring, but it could be worse, and she did get to appear on a *Dinner's at Eight* TV special where she and Stuart pitted their at-home culinary and entertaining skills against three other 'B' celebrity couples, finishing in a creditable third place.

Then Annie's life embarked on a dramatically different course when her son, by now four years old, was involved in an accident on the way to his reception class one morning. It must be said, straightaway, that no blame could be attached to the nanny – quite the opposite in fact as her presence of mind and quick reactions enabled her to pull Donny back from of the path of a speeding car when they were crossing the road just outside the school. The driver had come out of nowhere, doing 55 miles per hour in a 30 MPH zone. Despite the quick thinking of the nanny, Donny was clipped and sent soaring clean over the pavement, landing atop the holly hedge surrounding the cosmetic surgery hospital opposite the school. Luckily, the ambulance services, alerted by a number of parents also dropping children off, arrived quickly and Donny was whisked to hospital for emergency treatment. Annie was oblivious to all of this drama as she was having a fitness session in her home gym with her personal trainer. It took the nanny, police and teachers almost an hour to contact her to tell her the grim news, and Annie wasted no further time in getting to the hospital.

Fortunately the boy wasn't fatally injured, but did suffer serious leg and arm fractures and lacerations; while he was lucky to be alive, he did now face a considerable period of convalescence. At least the police later caught the driver, who hadn't stopped, and threw the book at him for dangerous driving, leaving the scene of an accident, failure to report an accident, and for being over the limit (at 8.40am in the morning). Justice was done when he received a 12-month driving ban and a small fine following his barrister's explanation that he'd been suffering from stress at home and at work.

The accident acted like a clarion call to Annie. She

complained to anyone who would listen about lawlessness on the roads threatening our kids' lives, and demanded to know why nobody did anything about it? Suddenly it struck her, why, *she* could do something about it by helping to promote vital messages about road safety to a wider public. After all, not only was she a victim, she also had a profile as a footballer's wife that she could use selflessly for the greater good.

After first finding a replacement carer for Donny following her sacking of 'negligent' nanny number one, Annie set about her new lease of life as a road safety campaigner and found that getting into the local news pages and on to regional TV and radio bulletins was in fact a doddle for an attractive looking woman with a minor celebrity status.

Annie loved the attention; she felt more alive than ever as she soaked up the coverage but at all times she was careful to remind herself that she was doing it for her family, and for others less fortunate than herself. However, the biggest development came when Stuart asked the PR company working for his club to help Annie 'take the campaign to the next level' – on a purely pro-bono basis, of course. As it was an offer they couldn't really refuse, they agreed and, as it turned out, did a remarkably good job.

Before poor little Donny could once again walk without the aid of crutches, Annie found herself the figurehead and face behind a new registered charity called HASTE (Help Arrest Speed Through Education), which had the luxury of being supported by some well known footballers and a leading tyre brand company (who figured that this was a perfect platform on which to demonstrate their tyres' traction capabilities as well as underlining their peerless corporate social responsibility credentials).

Annie was now 'hot' in media terms enabling her PR campaign team to pull off its next major coup in persuading the Clarion newspaper to partner HASTE in a speed awareness campaign.

Annie revelled in her fame, and soaked up the 'respect' she was earning from the nation's parents. She was also earning a not inconsiderable lifestyle out of the charity too – obviously not a salary, just essential expenses for everyday items like five-star hotels, first class travel, personal grooming and wardrobe. Nothing could be left to chance where the HASTE message had to be delivered – lives were in the balance.

HASTE punched well above its weight. After some quickly arranged media and presentation skills training (Phase II – more 'gravitas') Annie's PR campaign team, by now on a healthy fee, decreed that the time was right to make waves at government level, and sought a meeting where common interests could be explored. They obviously pitched it just right, as Annie now found herself on the verge of her greatest triumph to date.

After a five minute wait Annie and her campaign manager, who had come along to notate the exchange from HASTE's point of view, were summoned to a meeting suite where Nigel Adlington and his special adviser were already situated. Pleasantries were made and coffee served before Nigel cut to the chase. 'I must say, Mrs Brooks, that it really is a pleasure to meet you. Perhaps you could tell a little more about HASTE and your aims?'

Annie, well prepped by this time, launched into her plaintive appeal on behalf of parents everywhere, topping it with her carefully prepared mantra: 'The time has come for better driver education backed up with tougher sentences. That's what HASTE is all about.'

Nigel, normally not known for his patience, listened to her intently, but the words weren't really going in as, although feigning interest with a succession of head tilting manoeuvres, he was more interested in the magnificent cleavage that Annie's demure but well cut silk blouse was straining to contain. Fighting the distraction, Nigel jumped in during the first pause for breath from Annie. 'I must say, Mrs Brooks, that you appear to have been unflinching in the pursuit of your cause. Road safety, particularly in the suburbs, is a major concern for the government.'

'But how can you help us, Under Secretary?' enquired Annie before Nigel could continue. 'I mean, can we expect your support for HASTE in any tangible way?'

Nigel was impressed at the directness of the blonde vision sat across the table from him – normally a meeting would be enough for most visitors, but this one wanted action and wasn't afraid to ask for it. 'Absolutely, Mrs Brooks, in fact a number of ideas have popped into my head as you have been talking, and I think that if you would allow me and my team to give this some further consideration, there may well be ways we can address this common aim in tandem.'

Annie wasn't letting up though. 'Without wanting to appear ungrateful Under Secretary, I was rather hoping we could reach some form of consensus on the way forward today. Be in a position to at least announce that the government is prepared to look at our work in more detail, or explore how our recommendations may fit into future legislation?'

Nigel hadn't been expecting this; he'd only got her along as a result of a dare from his aide. Mrs Brooks was certainly pushy and she undoubtedly held an allure for men of a certain age making Nigel feel strangely compelled not to let her down. 'Well, we don't want to rush these things, but, please, do be reassured that I am prepared to help. In fact I have something very specific in mind, which I will be able to share with you as soon as I've been able to check some minor details with colleagues. Do bear with me; I'm sure you won't be disappointed.'

Nigel was thinking on his feet, a normal state of affairs for a politician, and suddenly he had the answer – a platform address for Mrs Brooks at the Party's Spring Forum, the news of which he would present to her in a personal call in the first week of the new year. Nigel was a goner; in his desire to please her and to see her again he'd made an instant decision and laid it on a plate for her, just like that. And Annie knew what he was thinking as he yielded before her – she recognised the signs well, having studied them half of her life.

'Under Secretary, I don't know what to say. That sounds very exciting.'

'I'm sure it's nothing less than your work to date has warranted, Mrs Brooks.'

'Oh, please, Under Secretary, do call me Annie.'

Yes, he and Mrs Brooks could certainly do business together.

PRD minus 311.

CHAPTER FIVE

Angel

On a cold mid January day with sleet falling in sheets, Kieran McDonaghy sat, as per usual, twiddling with his iPhone. He was in The Eagle on Farringdon Road awaiting his agent's arrival for lunch, and calculated he had time to squeeze some tweets off. Taking the top off his glass of Blonde Leffe, @kieranmcdonaghy let his 55,331 followers know: '*Pub lunch with agent. Cracking new project under wraps. More to follow!*'

As Conrad Callaghan, his agent, arrived Kieran left @kieranmcdonaghy land behind for once – this was to be a focused business lunch. Conrad had been busy on his client's behalf, and Kieran wanted to know how he had fared on his latest pitch that morning.

'We're on,' said Conrad by way of introduction. 'Now, let me get a beer before I tell you any more.'

It was the news Kieran had been waiting for, and he clenched his fist and punched his partner's shoulder in celebration. 'You bastard! Fantastic! Get me another Leffe too.'

Once furnished with drinks, Conrad ran down the deal. 'It's a seven-parter, being made for the Beeb by Baccarat Productions. It's called *Made Men*, and each programme will look at the story behind a British entrepreneur "who is changing the landscape of 21st Century Britain with his business ideas de dah de dah de dah." We have to do a pilot first, but that's only a formality for the BBC – they reckon nothing can stop the whole seven going ahead. We start shooting in the late spring/summer, for autumn broadcast.'

Kieran took it all in. '*Made Men*? What about women entrepreneurs?'

'Well, if the researchers come up with one, I'm sure they'll consider it, but come on, you're not going all Pankhurst on me are you? Besides, if this flies, you can do *Made Women* next year!'

'Oh, I'm not complaining! What about the readies?'

'It's a great fee for your first series, don't worry about that, but the main thing is that this is exactly where you want to be. Get this one right, and you could be a serious face on TV for years to come. I'll have you on *The Next Question?* and a royal wedding yet. Jesus, I'll even have you on a royal funeral.'

'Who've they got in mind for the subjects?' asked Kieran.

'Who cares?' replied Conrad. 'Men who've made it I guess – who gives a toss? I'm sure they can come up with seven and that's all we're going to need. Anyway, what's more important now is what we're going to have for lunch. I'm starving after all this hard work. Pass me that menu.'

Kieran felt elated, his mind whirring over the possibilities. Not just whether to have the bife ana steak sandwich or the piquant Napoli sausages with tomatoey beans, but on the vast landscape that had just opened up before his professional career – in the field of opportunity it was ploughing time again. *Feet Up* was great, of course it was, but this was the kind of serious stuff Kieran had lusted after, where he felt he could really perform and develop his own broadcast personality rather than just being charming eye candy for the nation's housewives. *Made Men* was going to be stand-out TV. *Made Men* would make him.

Pausing only for a swig of his Red Bull, Smudger was a study in concentration as he bent over the 27 inch Thunderbolt Apple display on his studio desk. Delighted by the publicity from his last foray against AMOLAD Smudger was working on his latest ruse. On the screen before him was an A5, sixteen-page booklet template, copied from an AMOLAD 'A Life Remembered' memorial celebration. On the desk in front of him lay copies of running sheets for the memorial booklet designed for the pop star Little Mo who had died of a drug overdose the previous October. Little Mo was to be given the ultimate 'A Life Remembered' send-off in two days' time with a massive party at The Round House in Chalk Farm, and Smudger was going make sure that the memorial booklet became a collector's item.

Smudger had spotted which printer AMOLAD used for these memorial booklets some months ago, gleefully discovering that spoils and running sheets of jobs in progress were dumped in with the normal rubbish in the waste disposal containers outside. Very sloppy. Not that Smudger had jumped at the first opportunity to filch material; he'd been waiting for a big one, and they didn't come much bigger than Little Mo.

Working with three of his associates, Smudger and his team pealed with laughter as they spent the entire day composing their own memorial booklet, complete with naked photo-comped photographs of Little Mo, made up stories on her as yet undiscovered recordings, glowing tributes from all the men (and women) she'd slept with, and a sorrowful tale of how her drug dealer was now going to have to cope with the sudden crash in his personal economy. There were also rather playful re-imaginings of Little Mo's album covers. Smudger would print 500 copies of the scurrilous facsimile, and his hoodie team would pay two or three lads off the street to distribute half of them at the memorial before disappearing. The balance he'd hold on to until their value soared.

Across in Covent Garden, at J. Sheekey's, Jon Bell was being seated. As a rule, Jon didn't do lunch, but on this particular day he hadn't been given an option. Opposite him sat Becky, his wife, who had demanded Jon meet her during her trip to the January sales.

'This is nice, isn't it?' said Becky. 'We really should do this more often. You're always so busy. I'm sure they can spare you for two hours. The place won't fall down without you, will it?'

In fact, despite what Becky said, she was convinced that AMOLAD would fall down without the steadying hand of her hyper-talented husband. Jon rolled uneasily in his chair. He had things to do, and this unwelcome intrusion into his schedule would only add to his anxiety to cross off all the items on his 'to-do' list for the day.

'Shall we skip the starter and go straight to the main?' he said as he tried to attract the attention of the waitress to take a drinks order.

'Don't be stingy,' came the reply. 'Come on, what's the rush? I'm going to enjoy my lunch. And we're going to have a bottle of wine too.'

Sensing defeat, Jon reluctantly conceded, despite feeling a rising tension at the prospect of the open-ended lunch that now stretched out before them. He knew he shouldn't be feeling like this, and should be paying more attention to his wife who took such a pride in him. Besides, what was he thinking of, trying to get out of lunch with his wife so he could work? No, get a grip. Today, he'd put Becky first and take his time. Well, until 2.45pm at the latest.

Jon's entry into AMOLAD was the perfect recruitment tale. Disenchanted with his career prospects at the red-hot London digital agency he'd worked at and coming across an early execution of Farren's ideas at the funeral of a colleague killed in a motorbike accident, Jon had decided to get in touch with the up and coming company. Discovering that Farren hated recruitment consultants and wouldn't use them, Jon had crafted his own biovid treatment that, thirty years into the future, looked back on his achievements for AMOLAD. This he had sent to Farren with an appeal to employ him. Farren was impressed by this original approach, and even more overwhelmed when he met Jon, who came armed with a refreshing balance of enthusiasm, solidity and ambition.

Possibly reinforcing the adage that most bosses try to recruit in their own image, Farren had found plenty of additional plus points to like about Jon; he was a no-nonsense northern lad like him (well, from Derby), had a degree in the Arts (Social Sciences) and his favourite band was Radiohead whom Farren had booked while Ents Sec at University. However, what really convinced Farren to employ him were the reasons Jon gave for wanting to quit his agency life to come and work for AMOLAD – his recognition that working in an agency with staid, conservative and dim-witted clients (and most clients fitted that description) was ultimately a fruitless pursuit for a true achiever – he was being held back. Farren thought it could have been himself talking. *When can you start?*

Jon hit the ground running, but Farren spotted early on that Jon was wasted in marketing – he had never come across anyone as organised, efficient, and dependable in his whole life. Jon was so in tune with Farren's needs, thinking and foibles, before long he was bringing fully formed ideas to him, solving problems with the minimum of fuss, and leaving no stone unturned in his desire to help make AMOLAD the best business in the world.

So, shortly after his 30th birthday, Jon found himself in his dream job, the newly created position of Director of Operations at AMOLAD, and earning more money than he could ever have envisaged (for Farren was very generous and motivational when it came to money). Admittedly, the job placed huge demands on Jon's time, and Becky would have liked him to have been at home more, but given his success at AMOLAD she'd at last been able to give up her part-time nursing job, and their new stucco terrace in Bayswater was a dream come true for her and their two children, Samantha and Ben. No, Jon was working hard for all of them, and the sacrifice of rarely seeing him could be endured while he was establishing himself.

And establish himself he did, becoming, in Farren's own words, 'the man who made the trains run on time at AMOLAD.'

And now that Farren had discovered a trusted right-hand man, it meant that he could concentrate on what really kept AMOLAD in the public eye – being the PR figurehead, the self-made entrepreneurial genius who was changing people's lives, and deaths, for ever.

Farren and Jon evolved a distinctive working style – the Lennon and McCartney of commerce, working in partnership to trump their last composition. Recently, however, as in the case of the Scouse songsmiths, cracks had begun to appear in Farren and Jon's unity. Hairline at first, then perceptible but not, at this point, hugely noticeable to outsiders. The white heat of creation that their first five years together had generated had now begun to cool – no longer did they share everything and bask in an aura of invincibility and progress.

Jon didn't mention this to anyone, certainly not his wife, but the first seeds of disgruntlement had been sown. Now, as Farren became more and more involved in 'corporate' projects like PRD that saw him sashaying with politicians and the like, Jon felt that he was having to shoulder more and more responsibility. In fact he was beginning to think his wife might be right – without him AMOLAD would be nothing.

'Sod it, Becky, you're right. Let's push the boat out and have champagne,' he said. 'I think I'm allowed to have lunch with my wife once in a while.'

Becky squealed in delight. 'That's the spirit. New Year's resolution. No more Mr Nice Guy.'

And with that, Jon and Becky enjoyed an unusually convivial blowout, courtesy of AMOLAD, with Jon only checking his emails twice before letting the office know he wouldn't be back for the day.

Michael Morrison's lunch was an altogether different affair. Sat in the back of the black XJ40 Daimler parked outside Southern Cemetery he munched on the cheese and tomato sandwich he'd made that morning and poured a cup of hot coffee from his Thermos. The weather was atrocious, but as he ruefully noted to himself, as he had every January for the past 40 years, it was good weather for business, God forgive him.

That morning he'd had two funerals, and he awaited a third pickup in an hour. All the deceased were in their seventies and eighties – another three oldies who hadn't lasted the winter. The rest of his bearers had taken the hearse off in advance leaving him to his midday repast, and he would join them in the Daimler shortly to pick up the mourners, just the one car load unfortunately.

As he cleaned up the crumbs, squirted air freshener and turned on the demister to full blast to make the car fully presentable for the next three passengers, a phrase one of his professional colleagues had made to him about the state of the funeral business came back to him, not for the first time lately: 'Running a successful independent funeral business these days is like pushing water uphill with a fork.' If he didn't do something about it soon, matters may well be taken out of his hands.

PRD minus 285.

CHAPTER SIX

Here Comes The Knight

That weekend, in his Victorian town house in Highbury Grove, Mr Eulogy, the nation's bereavement czar, lay on his settee and blanked off. He stared into space, seeing and hearing nothing, and feeling only a rushing sensation in the blackness. Riding the roller coaster, he unresistingly submitted to its force knowing, from experience, that it would pass as quickly as it had arrived.

Farren had suffered from such blackouts all of his life, normally triggered when he was stressed in some way. As a child, Mum and Dad had taken him to the doctors when the stupors had first manifested themselves, but no plausible explanation could be found, and in all other respects Farren was exceptionally healthy and robust, so in time they all learned to live with it. As Farren got older, he began to recognise when an attack was imminent and would excuse himself before secreting himself in the toilet or his bedroom while the moment came and went. He also played it down with his mother and father telling them that the attacks hardly ever happened these days. To be truthful, for a while they hadn't happened with any regularity as Farren built his business into a success.

Recently however, the attacks had started to return. Farren guessed that the return of the disorder was a manifestation of a deep-seated anxiety, but what anxiety?

Relieved that the moment had passed, he turned the lights down low, opened a bottle of Birra Moratti, and poured a cognac chaser before reclining on the settee. Reaching for the remote control of his Linksys wireless home audio system he searched for some soothing music to suit his mood. Music had always been significant in Farren's life – since coming up with the Funerals Top Ten all those years before, he found that he couldn't listen to his music collection without spotting appropriate songs that could be played at his own service. Should his choice be poetic, poignant, upbeat or comedic in order to send one last message from beyond the grave to the assembled mourners? Perhaps, more disquietingly, in rather the same way an undertaker looks someone up and down for size on the first introduction, he began to conjecture what songs would best suit his friends at their funerals.

After a minute of scrolling through his music library, Farren settled on his home made Neil Young 'mellow compilation', his 'go to' preference after a blackout due to the melancholic and soothing effect the godfather of grunge unfailingly conjured.

Neil had a question for Farren as *Tell Me Why* kicked off the random selection. Farren ruminated that rather than expanding, his horizons were narrowing. Farren's whole life now was AMOLAD and therein lay a problem. Highly successful, yes, but to what end? Because of work, or so he told himself, he'd not yet forged a permanent relationship with any of the women he'd dated. While he cheesily told Mum and Dad he'd 'not found the one yet', the thought of spending his life with the same woman hadn't remotely interested him in the past. While he liked sex and female company, he preferred nothing better than returning home by himself, and waking up by himself. Farren rarely invited any girlfriends back to his place – he always went to their homes, or to a hotel, for liaisons. The longer this pattern went on, Farren's desire to change it lessened – he didn't even acknowledge that it may be odd, strange, or a problem. Besides, now that he was well-known and prosperous, he was exceptionally wary of gold diggers who threw themselves at him with scant regard to decorum. Such women made him recoil. Who, in these days of crazy divorce laws, would ever get married anyway?

Despite this, Farren knew that it wasn't women, or the lack of a permanent partner, that was troubling him. Could it be his father's illness that was making him so maudlin? Ernest's poor health had knocked them all sideways, of course, and he knew, as his parents knew, that the end was in sight. It saddened him as he loved and cared for Ernest and Agnes deeply, but he'd had long enough to get used to the idea and felt when the inevitable happened he'd somehow be prepared.

No, what was stirring Farren's soul and beginning to release the dark terrors again was an incipient feeling that his business, AMOLAD, was getting out of hand. On the face of it, AMOLAD, and Farren Mortimer, were unremitting success stories, but as the operation got bigger and bigger the whole enterprise was beset with fresh challenges as well as external opposition.

At first, with his adman 'not a problem' Pavlovian reflexes, he'd enjoyed the cut and thrust of business, and the opportunity it accorded him to consistently innovate. He relished any attacks or criticism, knowing that all antagonism served to stimulate the media and allow him to promote his ideas to a wider audience. He relished the growth of the enterprise and the closeness of his handpicked, talented and dedicated team. He revelled in the unfettered creativity he was able to apply to all aspects of the business. He was making a considerable amount of money as well, so what was the problem?

A succession of recent incidents had started to chip away at his certainty, sparking a sense of mounting unease within his inner consciousness. At a board meeting last year Jon had tabled a recommendation for AMOLAD to get involved in the right to die market. Jon's outline paper, entitled 'Route One', explored how AMOLAD could benefit from the growth in assisted suicides and the debate surrounding it. Farren had been appalled, not only at the suggestion, made quite seriously by Jon, but also by the complete lack of empathy Jon was displaying for AMOLAD's ideals. Is this what Jon really thought they were about? Up to that point, he and Jon had thought almost in unison, sharing a joined up understanding of the business and its goals, so where the hell had that come from?

Farren angrily quashed the suggestion and firmly stated he didn't want to see it tabled again – much to Jon's disappointment who tried to argue his case before Farren told him: 'Jon, when I say I don't want to hear it again, I mean it.'

Now there was People's Remembrance Day. PRD was, of course, the crowning glory in AMOLAD's rise. It had put the company on the map and opened up doors. AMOLAD, even now, was drawing up an international expansion blueprint, investing considerable amounts to research the religious and social impact their techniques could have on different cultures and national customs.

PRD had been Farren's concept – he'd come up with it,

and he'd sold the proposal to the government; in reality it was a retread from his agency Fond Farewell account days, but an adman like Farren never wasted an idea.

They were only months off the inaugural event, but instinctively Farren knew that the best part had been presenting the concept and winning the pitch. It always was the best part. In his ad agency days he used to say that the best ideas often didn't make it past clients who were too dozy to spot genius. Farren would muse on whether it was his selling skills or the clients' intellect at fault when ideas couldn't be green lighted. 'More pearls before swine' was the expression he used when he failed to win a pitch. In fact, that had been the beauty of setting up his own business – now he was his own client.

Even when you did a great pitch and sold in an idea, in most cases, and particularly that of PRD, the elation of winning was soon replaced by a struggle with the client who would inevitably water the original concept down to a point where it was almost unrecognisable. He was certainly having this issue now as the government team AMOLAD was working with reacted to any comment, criticism or question in a blind panic by making demands for 'modifications' – it was happening on an almost daily basis.

Well, he was used to that too, so why did this perturb him as much as it did? Farren's colour rose at the thought of the politicians and government staff AMOLAD was having to deal with over PRD – they were, to a man and a woman, vacuous, vain, self-seeking, greedy and duplicitous cretins, who wouldn't have held a job down for five minutes in any other 'profession'.

Take Nigel Adlington, for example. Now there was a man

who loved the sound of his own voice and entertained a profound appreciation of his own insight and abilities. Farren knew that the success of the AMOLAD pitch came down to Adlington's championing of the plan as much as his own presentation, and while that hadn't caused any concern to Farren at the time, it was now beginning to eat at him. He was beginning to recognise the true sense of 'one hand washing the other.'

Farren had first met Adlington in Manchester some years before, when he was first getting Forever in our Minds off the ground. Farren had been worried about payments for musical performance rights – he'd not wanted to be legally liable for fees if subscribers were uploading popular songs on to their entries – and someone had recommended that he speak to Adlington's law firm for advice. They sorted that issue out for him, and sensing a larger client in the making Adlington had gone out of his way to maintain a relationship with Farren thereafter.

Knowing Farren to be a marketeer, when Adlington was selected as a prospective parliamentary candidate, he invited Farren out for lunch so he could 'pick his brains' on how to get himself across to the electorate. An ever-obliging Farren not only gave him substantial helpful, and free, advice, he hit upon the idea of launching a personal profile campaign for Adlington in his constituency. Not only that, Farren offered to fund the campaign as in reality the local press ads and door drop leaflets wouldn't amount to much more than £20,000 which could well prove to be a good investment if Adlington got elected.

Farren's campaign centred on a series of half page ads and a mailshot championing 'Adlington Cares About Crime',

'Adlington Cares About Health', 'Adlington Cares About Education' and 'Adlington Cares About Welfare'. These stressed Nigel's local roots, his family and professional life, and his own common sense values. The best part of Farren's campaign though was that he ran it shortly before the next election was called, therefore ensuring Adlington didn't fall foul of general election funding rules. The campaign meant that not only was Adlington well known to potential voters when the election was called, he still had his official electoral war chest to spend in the immediate pre-election period. Adlington, a favourite with the bookies in any case, romped home with an increased majority, but equally importantly he brought himself to the attention of his parliamentary party as a smart operator (so smart in fact that he 'accidentally' overlooked declaring AMOLAD's contribution).

Farren's ultimate appointment as the bereavement czar was the MP's quid pro quo for Farren's help, and the eventual key to PRD. They were now quits, but Farren couldn't quite shake off his sense of discomfiture over the pair's history; he felt the unspoken collusion, no big deal at the time particularly, now somehow despoiled the point of AMOLAD and the aims of the PRD.

The next intruder into Farren's reverie was the noisome, self-proclaimed street artist Smudger. Farren still didn't understand Smudger's motivation. Sure, AMOLAD was an easy target, but so too were hundreds of other businesses. From a purely creative point of view, Farren considered Smudger to be rather unadventurous in continuing to plough the same furrow with AMOLAD.

Farren would tell the team after each stunt: 'maybe this one will be the last one. He's going to get bored with us soon and move on to somebody else.' This was just wishful thinking on Farren's behalf, because Smudger hadn't moved on yet. Who was Smudger, and what had Farren done, if anything, to wind him up so? Did he have psychiatric problems? Was it just bad luck? Surely he would find somebody else to terrorise soon?

Everything AMOLAD did these days now had to be as Smudger-proof as possible, which seemed crazy when Farren thought about it. His whole business being undermined by a little shit who was clearly socially maladjusted? It had been humiliating for Farren to have to introduce the 'Smudger factor' into the PRD planning sessions with the government. They seemed to think it wasn't a major concern, saying that there would be considerably more nut jobs than Smudger to deal with on the day, but nevertheless, Farren considered Smudger to be AMOLAD's own resident saboteur; ridiculously, Farren felt responsible for him.

But worse, with each new Smudger prank, Farren found himself shifting uneasily, his inner confidence under attack. Did Smudger have a point? Was AMOLAD an exploitative, grossly offensive, trivial stunt in itself? Did AMOLAD's ideas really celebrate life, or as other detractors said, did they cheapen rather than venerate the memory of the deceased?

'Jesus,' thought Farren, pulling himself together. '*I always get like this when I drink cognac. Get a grip. I'll be getting hauled off to the funny farm thinking like this.*' And with that, the captain of industry fell into bed and into an XO Grand Cru assisted slumber.

PRD minus 281.

CHAPTER SEVEN

Movin' On Up

Propped up in bed, Nigel Adlington watched Annie Brooks' perfectly formed posterior as she headed for his ensuite bathroom. He adored the way Annie was so assured and confident in her magnificent body, her unashamed adventurousness and the way she took the lead in their lovemaking (or 'shagging' as she preferred to call it). Nigel really had died and gone to heaven – he was utterly and totally besotted with this brazen, lustful and totally uninhibited creature.

Adlington and Annie had been 'at it' for two months now, ever since mid January when Nigel had, over dinner, invited Annie to speak at the Party's Spring Forum. Annie knew how to express gratitude and so it was no surprise that they ended up in bed that evening. Well, no surprise for Annie as to her this was just common courtesy. Nigel, on the other hand, was only too eager to take advantage of this unexpected bonus. He had anticipated he might have got there after maybe three dinners, but obviously his charms were growing.

The relationship had continued almost without thought as the two of them took every opportunity to 'discuss the presentation', normally at Nigel's apartment. Curiously, because there was the slimmest of a plausible pretext to their trysts, neither worried unduly over being discovered. Of course they were discreet, but not paranoically so, as this was business. For the same reason, neither felt a scintilla of concern over their respective partners at home.

Nigel was enjoying himself tremendously; couldn't believe his luck that this siren was calling in his direction. No Ulysses lashed to the mast he, Nigel set course straight for the source of the seductive melody, perhaps reasoning that parliamentary privilege would somehow provide protection against foundering on the rocks.

In the ensuite Annie sat washing herself, trying to eradicate any obvious olfactory indications of illicit sex before she returned home. She felt happy and excited. Christ, she'd bagged an MP, and he was now helping her to prepare for the biggest day of her life speaking to God knows how many MPs. She'd be all over the media, and who knows what else this might open up for her? Nigel was a catch, and she knew it.

Mutually beneficial arrangements were not new to Annie but this time, things were a bit different. Yes, she was married, but that wasn't the main problem. Stuart had thrown a couple of sulks over the amount of time she was spending on HASTE and related activities, but she knew instinctively that the help she could get, was getting, from this smitten representative of the people was likely to be the most important leg up that she had ever had – and she'd had quite a few of those already. This was the biggest door that had ever opened up for her and she wasn't going to risk it slamming back in her face. As for Stuart, well, she knew what he and the lads got up to on their pre-season tours and bonding weekends.

Annie – or Tiffany Wilkes as she was known at school – didn't have the easiest of childhoods. Growing up in Stockton – on – Tees didn't hold many fond memories for her, and her parents could hardly be considered positive role models. Her father worked on the shipyards, and was no stranger to a drink. Or two. Or three. He best communicated using his fist or his belt, and the young Tiffany and her mother, Margaret, learned that the best way to deal with him was to avoid him as much as possible. Margaret worked as a waitress; driven down by abuse, hard work and the continual struggle to make ends meet she found solace in drink and the occasional 'man-friend' to help dull the pain of existence away.

Tiffany – or 'Any' as she was called by her school friends who dispensed with the 'Tiff' – determined, very early on, to get away from the hellhole of home. Being blessed with a curvaceous and well endowed figure and a surprisingly attractive face given her own parents' looks, salvation for Tiffany arrived in the form of an invitation to do some glamour test shots for the local modelling agency when she was just fifteen years old – or seventeen years old as she told the photographer. Tiffany learned at this session that she was a natural in front of the camera; she also discovered that liberality with sexual favours could also help to speed up career progression, so much so that Tiffany threw herself into this aspect of her job as enthusiastically as she did into her diet and skin regimes. It worked, because within the year she moved to London and, chaperoned by her agent's best friend, began to live a life quite unlike that of anyone she'd ever met in Stockton.

Tiffany was committed, of that there was no doubt, and had some modest early success as a model, even appearing within the pages of *In The Saddle* lads' mag on one or two occasions. Men enjoyed her company so much she was never short of friends, parties, booze or cocaine.

When the modelling jobs began to slow, Tiffany had to widen her portfolio and started to accept jobs in the soft-porn industry to 'tide her over'. As this work was demanding and not very well paid, before long Tiffany joined the books of an escort agency to further supplement her income, and here she began to thrive in the free market economy surrounding non – contractual extras.

Tiffany knew this wasn't a lifestyle she could maintain for long – she'd seen enough of older peers to convince her of that – so she always had an eye out for the right sort of catch. A rich, generous, besotted sort of catch. After three or four years of playing the field she struck gold in the form of Championship footballer Stuart Brooks, who sweetly took her at face value when she described herself as a model.

After Tiffany became pregnant a few months into their relationship, Stuart gallantly proposed, and because it was the close season they quickly took advantage of a cancellation at Luton Register Office to tie the knot. So it was that Annie Brooks (not taking any chances over her recent past being discovered, she'd gone the whole hog and changed her Christian name as well as her surname) gave birth to a bouncing baby boy, Donny, in between Stuart's critical festive fixtures.

And in the unpredictable chain of events that is life, it was Donny's near death experience that led her to the bedroom of the Under Secretary of State for Social Responsibility, a man who even now was working on how he could please Annie even more.

Annie was totally clear in her own mind – for now, she was focused on the conference platform five weeks away, and the need to impress. In addition to her PR team, scriptwriter and presentation coach, she now had the guiding hand of a master who would ensure that the audience would rise up in applause as she connected with them. She was going to be a star.

Nothing was to get in the way of her forthcoming triumph. For example, she'd thought of enlivening her and Nigel's sex sessions with cocaine, which she'd always found most invigorating, but had decided against it. Nigel was really rather straight and it might scare him off – best leave that in reserve; nothing should endanger her mission, well not before the conference anyway. 'Keep this up, Annie,' she said to herself as she reached for the towel, 'and you'll be in the New Year's Honours list yet.'

Half an hour later, with Annie despatched into the night, Nigel called Emma at home in Cheshire. He felt no shame or remorse as he put on an especially weary voice to signify the gruelling day he'd just endured on behalf of the nation.

Nigel loved spending time in London, and being away from Emma. As his own personal priorities had changed he had begun to think of Emma as a stuck up, boring, lazy, child obsessed partner who had lost all sense of proportion. As for sex with Emma, this particular delight had been off the menu for some time – hardly a dozen occasions since the birth of their second son Teddy five years before. Nigel often thought that if he'd not made it to Parliament, with its many diversions and opportunities, and been able to comfort himself with a random conquest or two he'd have ended up wringing his wife's neck – metaphorically speaking of course.

The prospect of public interest in his private life, or worse still a Cheshire divorce, ensured he stayed his hand so he suffered in silence. Now, as an MP, he could tolerate playing the earnest husband and family man knowing that spending two days per weekend at the family home, topped up with five brief telephone calls to Emma per week, was a price worth paying to maintain the status quo. It never occurred to him to ask what Emma thought of the situation, but her lack of protest was probably eloquent enough a response.

Having determined that office would not only gain him profile and 'respect' (politicians seeing things rather differently from the rank and file), but also give him access to lucrative contacts and clients for the Manchester and Liverpool based law practice he'd made partner with in his early thirties, Nigel manoeuvred his way through the party hierarchy. Exuding a slick, boyish and modern persona so beloved of an electorate who had long ago given up on worrying about policies, Nigel, without ever having to overstate his case, was deemed a good candidate for a safe seat by the men in grey suits.

Propelled by his clever 'Adlington Cares' campaign, Nigel entered Parliament as MP for his largely rural and affluent Cheshire constituency with a clear 'one to watch' tag hanging from his handmade Gieves and Hawkes suit. Once at Westminster, he eagerly put himself forward for all manner of roles and tasks befitting an enterprising backbencher, and got further noticed.

Now his career was really looking up, and not only that he was getting the best sex of his life. As he drained the last dregs of the champagne glass by his bedside he smiled to himself and thought, 'Yes, young Nigel is very happy indeed in this world.'

PRD minus 253

CHAPTER EIGHT

This Woman's Work

Back home after a week in hospital, Ernest's life was nearly run. In recent months, other than Farren and Father Wilcox, Agnes had deterred visitors to the house as they weakened Ernest so, but since her husband had returned home this latest time she had determined to relent on her hard line. She knew, Ernest knew and their friends and relatives knew that any courtesy call made now fell into the category of an unstated farewell.

Carefully supporting Ernest's back, Agnes helped him ingest his night-time dose of painkillers before gently easing him back into an almost supine position. In the background, Radio 3 played classical music at an almost imperceptible volume. Agnes had decided the mellow melodies would be soothing for Ernest, but in reality she couldn't abide the still, sepulchral silence of the bedroom and habitually switched on the radio to combat the stillness without disturbing Ernest.

Ernest turned to Agnes and whispered, 'I don't want to go before saying goodbye, Agnes.'

'Get away with you,' replied Agnes. 'You're not going anywhere just yet. I think those drugs are making you all soppy.'

Ernest squeezed out a grin as she put him in his place and told him what's what. As she always had done.

'We've had a good life together, Agnes. You know that.'

'And we've still got some of it left, so don't get all maudlin on me,' said Agnes in response.

'What are you going to do about Farren?' murmured Ernest. This was a question that Agnes had anticipated, but the enquiry was no more welcome for that presentiment.

'You know what I mean,' sighed Ernest.

Agnes did know exactly what Ernest meant. They had discussed 'what to do about Farren' for some eight years now, ever since they had discovered the startling truth, or what purported to be the truth, about Farren's real background. For, thanks to Father Culshaw, yet again a central figure in their lives' unfolding drama, they had discovered the identity of not only Farren's birth mother, but also that of his blood father too.

Ernest had been vehemently opposed to sharing with Farren the knowledge that had been thrust upon them around the time their son had begun thinking about leaving advertising and setting up his own venture. 'Nothing good will come of it,' argued Ernest. 'He's got this far without knowing, and so have we. No point in raking all of this up – you don't know what it will do to the lad.'

Agnes, unsure, had struggled over whether disclosure was in order or not. She felt in her heart that Farren should be told, but as the details were so fantastical and barely credible, told what?

Father Culshaw, 75 years old at the time and still a force to be reckoned with, had himself struggled with what to do about the discovery. He rued the day he'd been handed a letter from Farren's birth mother by a nun at St Teresa's – some things were better off being left alone.

The letter read:

To the sisters of St Teresa's, Salford.

I was a mother at St Teresa's in September 1973 when my little boy, Fred, was taken from me. To this day, I have never forgotten him, and have shed many tears over losing him. I couldn't cope. I did some things I'll always regret, but I'll never regret anything as much as letting him go when he should have stayed with me.

I've not led a happy life, have never married or had another child, and life has been one long struggle. I've been in and out of psychiatric care all of my life, and hate myself for the things I've done. It's no-one's fault but my own, I know that and I am not looking for sympathy.

But Fred is approaching 30 by now, and I want him to know, if this can be passed on to him, that I've loved him every day, and thought of him every day, and hope he's had a good life. A better life than me.

If he ever wanted to see me, it would make me very happy, but I don't know where to start to look for him.

There's his real father too. He never knew about Fred, as it was a one-night stand before Christmas 1972 and I never saw him again. We met at a student party in Withington. His name was Michael and he said he was an undertaker, but I think he may have been joking about that. I can't believe I'm telling you this, but I feel better for putting it down on paper.

Can you help?
Thank you.
Linda Wilson

On first reading the letter Father Culshaw had been shocked. Not so much at the sorry tale of the unfortunate Linda, whose plight so sadly echoed that of many other young girls. Yes, that was tragic, but what drew his attention was the meagre description of the would-be father. An undertaker? Michael? 1972? Surely that couldn't be Michael Morrison? The Michael Morrison who was still despatching Father Culshaw's flock on a regular basis? There weren't many undertakers called Michael knocking around Withington in 1972, and surely no one would *claim* to be one? But what would he be doing with a student? And Michael surely wasn't the sort of man who would ever have indulged in a one-night stand? He'd known Michael and his wife almost all of their lives. Surely it couldn't be him?

Even if it was true, where did this leave him with the Mortimers? Should he even tell them? He'd never told them about the attempted smothering of the young baby by his distressed mother, but this? And what about Farren himself? What would this news, if revealed, do to him?

In truth Father Culshaw had a very disturbed evening contemplating his next move. The next morning, he called Sister Immaculata who had passed on the letter following its redirection from the long closed convent. Sister Immaculata couldn't furnish any further information, other than an almost perfect recall of the evening's events some thirty years previously. Consequently, Father Culshaw decided direct action was required. Looking up the phone number of the psychiatric hospital cited as the address the letter was sent from, he called and asked for the records department.

Eventually he was passed through to a ward manager who confirmed that she knew Linda. But all was not well. After years in and out of psychiatric care, a harrowing descent into a drug dependency – both legal and non-legal varieties – and an indelible despondency over the life that she had, or hadn't, led, Linda had committed suicide some three months earlier following her last release into society. An overdose of barbiturates swilled down by a half bottle of gin had been her final act. The time the letter had taken to find its way into Father Culshaw's hands could even have contributed to this distressing conclusion to her sad life.

Reeling still further from this additional unwelcome news, Father Culshaw was in a quandary. What should he do? Father Culshaw wrestled with his conscience as to whether this news had to be imparted further, and to whom exactly, before finally determining that this time, as well as being God's messenger, he should be Linda's too. And so, one November afternoon, Father Culshaw took himself off to the Mortimers with his grim tidings.

The news, as could be expected, was a shock, but Ernest immediately decided that the news should go no further. After all, Farren appeared to have moved on from any inquisitiveness he'd ever shown about his birth mother's identity, and the poor woman's memory should be left in peace. In addition, hadn't they told Farren she was dead already and his father unknown and untraceable? Despite Father Culshaw's educated guess, they couldn't be 100% sure that Michael Morrison was Farren's real father anyway. That was a crazy theory. No, that couldn't be right at all. They, too, knew Michael Morrison, and the very idea of him being Farren's real father was utterly absurd.

Agnes wasn't sure that a code of silence was the answer to this startling news, but as Ernest, backed up by Father Culshaw, felt so strongly they should say nothing the decision was taken – nothing more would be said.

Father Culshaw passed away some three years later leaving Agnes and Ernest to bear the secret alone, and naturally enough Ernest and Agnes did address the subject from time to time. Ernest, despite his own misfortunes, never waivered in his conviction that the omerta should prevail. Thus, as he approached the end, he was keen to receive some sign from his wife that after him, she would take the secret to her grave.

'What am I going to do about Farren?' Agnes softly chided. 'Don't let's start that again. Get some sleep, now, Ernest, and don't wear yourself out.'

And with that, she pulled up the coverlet to his chin, kissed him gently on the forehead, and switched off the bedroom light before making her way downstairs.

Michael Morrison yawned, stretched and flicked aimlessly through the limited entertainment panacea his freeview TV box provided. It was Friday night. Another boring Friday night spent in his own company. He considered trying a DVD, but decided against it as a film would probably be at least two hours long and he didn't want to stay up that late. Besides, there was nothing new that he wanted to see in the stack piled haphazardly under the television. Maybe a few chapters in bed?

Michael couldn't even summon up the energy to stir from his armchair. The remains of his evening meal, a Co-op Chicken Jalfrezi with Basmati Rice and two plain nans, lay on the coffee table in front of him together with three empty cans of Boddingtons. He gently cupped his waistline and grimaced at the realisation that he would soon have to get his trousers let out again unless he made a serious effort to control his weight. It was hard to get motivated about exercise and a calorie controlled diet when there was no compelling reason to do so, no goal to achieve. A beach holiday? An evening out with a female admirer? A day spent playing in the park with the grandchildren? Not very likely.

Michael had never really re-adjusted following his wife Carmel's death from breast cancer some four years before. Childless, he'd just plodded on with the family business, and subsequently narrowed his already rather limited expectations of life. His circle of friends was small, and mostly professional. Now the only thing in Michael's life was work, and the only thing work brought him was more and more worry.

Nothing exciting had ever happened in Michael's life, with the exception of his 'mad night' all those years ago. Even now he couldn't be sure it had actually happened, or if he'd merely dreamt it.

At the age of 60 Michael's life consisted of the emptiness of bereavement, to which his own experience of helping others through was of no avail, and a tottering family business. Could fate have dealt a better hand in respect of Michael Morrison's life? Possibly, but as Michael was about to discover, fate hadn't finished with him yet.

PRD minus 250.

CHAPTER NINE

I Am The Resurrection

'Right. Shall we start?' Farren kicked off the monthly board meeting with, unusually for him, a less than enthusiastic spring in his step.

Jon took his cue. 'Well, I think we should race through the figures, as we really need to focus on PRD today as it's only a few months away now. Plus, we have a fly in the ointment on the roadshow which I think we need to dedicate a bit of time to today.'

Farren couldn't help but imagine that Jon's tone seemed to be relishing the 'fly in the ointment' rather more than he would like to see from his director of operations. Maybe Farren was just being over sensitive. 'OK,' said Farren. 'Perhaps you can give us the top line figures first though, Graeme?'

Graeme, irked that his main contribution to the board meeting had been cursorily curtailed by Jon, handed out the latest figures while stressing that it was important for the whole board to give them their undivided attention.

Jon, however, was not to be sidetracked from the main purpose of the meeting as far as he was concerned – his planning update and critical path analysis counting down the six months to the inaugural People's Remembrance Day. 'Yes, Graeme, totally agree. We can always reconvene on these if we need to?' added Jon by way of consolation.

'Well, you'd better kick off then, Jon,' said Farren.

'OK. Everything's in the report which I've prepared, but the key areas I want to draw everybody's attention to today are the plans for the Royal Family, our celebrity ambassador scheme, the unveiling of the new People's Remembrance Memorial in Green Park on the day itself, plus the merchandise range.'

'We're going to be here all day,' said Peter the IT director.

Jon ignored the comment. 'First, the royals aren't playing ball according to the department. Apparently, they haven't forgotten the Diana debacle. The feeling we're getting is that they seem reluctant to let public grief upstage royal funereal traditions, particularly given the Queen's age. In other words, if everyone is remembering their own family and friends, will this replace the wave of sympathy the royal family receives every time they see one off, such as the spike in approval they got when the Queen Mother went?'

'I don't know why we're bothering with the royals anyway,' interjected Farren. 'It's the people's remembrance day, not the bloody royals remembrance day. They have plenty enough – they'll just detract from it in my view.'

'I agree, Farren, but this was one the department was very keen to push, so we've had to go along with it for now.'

'Well, what about boxing clever and just getting one of the junior royals to unveil the public remembrance memorial statue?' asked Farren.

'Well, we've already lined up Amber Diamond's mother for that. Amber's funeral was the biggest since Diana's, and you can't get more "of the people" than her.'

'Isn't she a bit downmarket?' ventured Peter. 'I mean all that Amber Diamond ever did was win a cheap reality TV programme, open supermarkets and carry on appallingly.'

'Exactly, Pete. Which is why she's perfect. Everybody has been touched by Amber's untimely death and her mother's tragic loss. The media will love it. Plus, the department are all one hundred per cent behind the idea, so best leave it well alone,' added Jon.

'It's good if the royals won't play ball. We don't want them anyway, so it will suit us down to the ground,' said Farren. 'Leave it at that. What about the celebrity ambassador scheme, Jon?'

'Better news on that. The PR company has now signed up fifty of the planned one hundred People's Remembrance ambassadors who are going to cite the names of the loved ones they're going to remember specifically on the day. It's a bit like a desert island discs approach – they all list ten names they want to remember, and why, and get to say how they're going to cherish their memories on the day. It's the biggest thrust of the advance PR phase.'

'Sounds good,' agreed Farren. 'Presume they're carefully selected on age, demography, ethnicity and religion grounds?'

'Absolutely. The PR team are working hard on that. Some of the celebs are asking for money, as they're not too keen on the donation to the Armed Forces welfare charity we've offered in lieu, but what we're doing there is, if they're sticking out for cash, and we really want them, we're getting them to endorse the merchandise range so it's worth the trade off.'

'OK. So, where are we on merchandise?'

'Making good progress. All will be ready for a mid-September launch so people can buy in good time for their own celebrations. We've commissioned Sir Gideon Blackstock, the 1960s artist, to do some fantastic simpatico designs around the theme of "There is a light which never goes out". Double-checking the copyright on that, but we can always tweak it to say the same thing if we hit a problem. We've got a range of picture frames lined up, plus a collection of tasteful, reusable, armbands, and we're doing a tie-in version of the Memory Archive plus a special offer on retrospective biovids. The one we're pinning our biggest hope on though is the memorial candle for the home, an eternal flame reminder of a loved one. Electric with battery back up, and space for a photo. They look fantastic and the mark up on them has got to be seen to be believed.'

'All sounds positive stuff,' opined Farren. 'And what about the lapel ribbons?'

'Going great too,' replied Jon. 'Narrowed it down now to a green and grey striped one, the same colours as rosemary. You wouldn't believe how many colours are registered now, but this is unique and it's ours. We're expecting those to fly out.'

'Right. So, what's the problem with the roadshow you mentioned?'

'Well, as you know, we've got a twenty-city roadshow going to shopping centres around the country at the moment under the heading of "Wouldn't be Seen Dead in That". We're promoting pre-need planning and pushing items like biovids, memories archives, departure lounge, bliogs et cetera, et cetera. We're just over halfway through at the moment, but Waverley Mallender, the fashion guru the PR company thought would be a great front man for the shows, is apparently being difficult. @wappinglie took the piss out of him saying he's the right man to push our services 'cos his career died years and he's suddenly threatening to walk out, the wuss, and we still have eight shows to go.'

'He can't walk out. He's under contract surely?' asked Farren.

'What's @wappinglie when it's at home?' asked Graeme.

Peter woke up. 'Basically a big mouthed journalist who comments on all and sundry. No one knows who she is or even who she works for, but she carries a lot of clout, and has thousands of followers.'

'Followers?' said Graeme, somewhat baffled.

'On Twitter. @wappinglie is a Twitter handle,' explained Jon helpfully.

'Can we get back to Mallender's contract, please?' Farren asked.

'Well, obviously he is under contract, but it only means he doesn't get paid if he doesn't do the shows. If he decides he can afford to jump, the negative publicity we'll get will be a killer. He may even be calculating it would give his image a boost to shaft us. Drafting a replacement in won't help us as the media will want to know why Mallender has bailed and it's unlikely he'll let us say he's been taken ill. He's got us by the balls.'

'But the shows have been going down well according to the daily reports – what's his problem?'

'His agent is giving us a line that he's been upset by comments from some older members of the public who've questioned the appropriateness of the roadshow, causing him "to reconsider his desire to complete the tour." I reckon it's more to do with @wappinglie – she's taken the piss out of him before and she's obviously got to him. That's where we are. The question is what do we do about it?'

Farren thought he could do without all of this – now they were being held to ransom by an oversensitive prima donna fashion presenter. He considered for a moment, and then spoke. 'I'm not going to spend hours on this. I'm really not. Contact the agent, and offer Waverley a 20% bonus to *complete* the tour. He'll have to sign a further trust agreement not to denigrate AMOLAD at any point in the future. He'll go for that – he's set us up is all.'

Jon was somewhat surprised to hear this solution. 'Surely you don't want to roll over to a little shit like Waverley Mallender?' said Jon. 'If he's trying to call our bluff, we should make sure we blink last?'

'Honestly, just do it – it's not worth the hassle,' was Farren's final word on the matter.

Jon said nothing further on the subject and switched the topic. 'I'm presuming I don't need to go over Smudger's latest on Little Mo do I? Think we've already spent quite enough time on that one.'

Farren ignored Jon's last comment and continued. 'I do have one last item to cover. I've been approached by Baccarat Productions over a new TV series on entrepreneurs they've been commissioned to do by the BBC. It's going to be called *Made Men* and they want me to be one of the subjects. I've checked out the editorial platform, and each programme is going to be a positive one-hour long championing of British enterprise, not some sort of cynical hatchet job. They've got Kieran McDonaghy who does *Feet Up* to present. I've met him so it's going to be a gentle treatment. I'm up for it, unless anyone has any objections?'

Farren's question was met by silence. Who knew if it was a good idea or not? Certainly not Graeme or Peter. On the other hand, the thought that struck Jon was that maybe it was about time the media took an interest in the people who made the trains run on time in successful British businesses rather than the media tarts who were always craning their necks to catch the limelight.

'Suppose it won't do any harm,' Jon eventually conceded. 'Mind you, it's a bloody daft title. Do they think there's no "made women" out there?'

Jon arrived home at 7.45pm just in time to kiss Samantha and Ben goodnight. He was in a tetchy mood, which he couldn't, didn't, try to hide from Becky.

'You look like you've had a hard day,' consoled Becky. 'Have a glass of wine and sit down. I've got your favourite fish pie and colcannon from Waitrose for tea – it's nearly ready.'

Jon did as he was told and glumly sat down at the live-in kitchen table. 'You'll never guess what he's done now,' essayed Jon.

'You mean Farren? No. What?'

'Only lined himself up to do a TV special on how bloody wonderful he is, while the rest of us get on with all of the work. You should have seen him today at the board meeting. Not a care in the world while we're all running round like blue-arsed flies.'

'It doesn't surprise me in the least. You're going to have to widen the doorways at The Steeple so he can get his head through at this rate.'

'Yes, but what gets me is that while we're all working harder than ever he seems to be losing interest. Today we had a problem over that horrible Waverley Mallender holding us to ransom, and he just gave in – "pay him more" was his solution. We'd have seen the little creep off in the old days. I don't know what Farren's game is, but he'd never have keeled over like that in the past.'

'Maybe he's in love or something – you never know.'

'I doubt that. Farren's only in love with himself and that's not likely to change anytime soon. If he were a cream puff, he'd eat himself. No, he's forgotten about how this business has become successful – down to the likes of me. It's just not the same as when I joined.'

'Well, maybe you should look at moving?'

'I can't do that. I've put too much into it. No, I want to get my due reward. I want to get shares in the business, which I deserve.'

'But I thought you had shares already?'

'They're only share options. And it's only 5%. I want some real shares that reflect my true value, say 25%. I'm the one running PRD and I'm going to hit him with it when we reach fever pitch. See how he reacts to that.'

'Are you sure? 25% sounds like a lot to me in one go. What if he says "no"?'

'If he does, I'm off. See how he likes that.'

'Don't do anything reckless, will you? You know you like it there most of the time, and the money is good. I know you work hard for it, but the salary is very good when you think about it.'

'I can get that somewhere else now, I reckon. No, I've got a plan, and it'll work, believe me. Just watch this space.'

'Well, as long as you know what you're doing.'

And with that the timer on the oven pinged to communicate that everything was well and truly cooked.

Farren sat contemplating a toasted ham, mayonnaise and tomato sandwich for his evening meal. He'd forgotten to get any shopping in, and the only bread he had left in the bread bin was stale, hence the need for the toaster and the enlivening accompaniments for the two slices of Wiltshire Ham remaining in their plastic wrapper. The sell by date was yesterday – it would do. He made a cup of tea to help wash his modest repast down and slumped on the settee to eat.

The board meeting had been moody today. Farren knew that he'd not been in the best of humours himself, but what the hell was Jon on? For some time now Farren had noticed that Jon was getting prickly over certain aspects of the business. They'd formerly got on really well, and still did superficially, but something had happened to him. Now Jon was clearly a bit too full of his own importance, and trying to exercise his will too much. He kept coming up with stupid ideas as a way to make his mark on the business. Well he would make a mark, a bloody bad one, if he let him loose. And he was getting secretive. In the early days they'd shared everything, but now Jon was turning up to board meetings with information that he'd kept back from him, putting him on the spot, challenging him to make immediate decisions, subtly trying to test him in front of Graeme and Peter. Plus, he seemed to take a delight in things when they went wrong, almost as if he was glad Farren had another problem being dumped in his lap to sort out.

It was also quite obvious to Farren that Jon eyed dividend payments to Farren with avaricious eyes. Jon was a super efficient employee, but how much more did Farren have to reward him? Jon hadn't set the business up, wasn't creative and he couldn't get anywhere near what he was being paid anywhere else, surely, so why was he rocking the boat?

Was Farren being unreasonable? No, he recognised naked ambition when he saw it. He didn't know Jon's endgame yet, but he knew he'd have to keep an eye on him.

As Farren brushed the crumbs from his lap on to the floor, he reflected, not for the first time, that running a business was bloody harder than people reckoned. It wasn't the work; it was the people you had to deal with.

PRD minus 239.

CHAPTER TEN

Box Of Rain

Nigel Adlington was on familiar territory. As he strode across the lobby of the Midland Hotel in Manchester he was assailed with greetings from sundry delegates, both high and low. The Spring Forum was underway, and as one of the prime architects of this landmark event in the party's calendar he was basking in the glow of a job well done. For he knew that whatever happened now, he had made his mark; a success was assured.

Nigel smiled as, en route to the conference centre one hundred yards away from the rear doors of the hotel, he encountered the camera crews on alert for VIPs. Like the rest of the Forum delegates he strode casually, but with studied purpose, the few short steps to the day's deliberations.

Uppermost on Nigel's mind was Annie Brooks who had been given a late morning slot in order to hit the lunchtime news and to give the media time to work up background on her sterling work. Normally a guest speaker such as Annie would have been diverted to a fringe meeting but Nigel had been most adamant at planning stage that a serious sea change in UK motorists' attitudes to speed was an essential plank in his agenda for a more socially responsible society. And so Annie was primed, prepped and plumed to within an inch of her life for her 15-minute address.

Annie, naturally, was nervous but Nigel had coaxed and reassured her that nothing could go wrong.

He settled into his seat, fingers and toes metaphorically crossed.

Annie was having a hell of a morning. She'd run through her speech three times with her presentation coach, and was still having a problem in eliminating the more extreme traces of her Teesside timbre from the delivery. Finally Annie had flipped and told the coach that her services were no longer needed. Her PR team had shuffled around looking uncomfortable, but as Annie was the client all they could really do was nod in silent assent as Annie declared: 'This is what I bloody well sound like, so that's what they'll have to have. If it's good enough for call centres it's good enough for this lot.'

The coach, understanding that the prospect of public speaking invoked different reactions in different individuals, had gallantly departed the scene figuring that to debate the point further would only increase the tension. Now the PR team got to work on the more important aspects of the speech, such as wardrobe, hair and make-up. Annie had brought eight outfits and twelve pairs of shoes along as 'possibles' for the address, and with the aid of her PR assistant had tried on most of them.

'This makes me look too dowdy,' she said of the dark two-piece suit from M&S that her PR assistant had advised her to buy so it wouldn't look as if she was trying too hard. Next up was a sky blue silk Sonia Rykiel Bow Dress. 'No, this makes me look too fat'. On to a black pencil skirt and slashed white silk blouse. 'No, this makes me look too tarty,' (overlooking the fact that it was the same blouse she'd worn when she first met Nigel).

In the end, all agreed an elegant YSL trouser suit in dark blue set exactly the right tone, serious yet classic looking. A similar debate over shoes was curtailed when Annie was given an urgent thirty minute call. Annie made a decisive choice – killer dress shoes in cochineal coloured velvet, topped off with a broad black leather strap and fastened with a brass buckle. 'Well, I can't look too frumpish, can I?' she said as they rushed to the lift.

Exactly sixty minutes later, Annie found herself stood outside the hall alongside Nigel as they were interviewed on live TV. They were positioned under the giant clock atop the conference centre, a former Victorian railway station that had long since been converted to alternative use.

Nigel was delivering his sound bite: 'Mrs Brooks has outlined the human cost speeding represents to our society each and every day. Let us not forget that speeding is socially irresponsible, and the next victim might be your son, daughter, sister, wife, husband or brother. That is the key message to motorists from today's forum. Think about it, and as the slogan says, "Brake the habit".'

Cue Annie: 'I'd just like to add, speaking as a Mother who nearly lost her little boy to a speeding motorist, that nothing, nothing in this world, is worth arriving ten seconds early for if the price is a life.'

Cut.

Farren Mortimer was also on familiar territory as he exited the ring of steel surrounding the Manchester Conference Centre to head down Peter Street. Turning right on to

Deansgate and up to Spinningfields he descended to the subterranean surroundings of the Australasia restaurant where he was meeting Kieran McDonaghy to discuss *Made Men* over lunch.

There, at the bar, he spotted Kieran and the assistant producer on the *Made Men* series, Anna Vernon, nursing two rather ostentatious cocktails. Before long they were ensconced in a booth and getting down to business.

Anna set the ball rolling. 'The thing is, Farren, this is the lynchpin programme in the entire series. We want to kick the run off with you just before People's Remembrance Day, get viewer interest high, which we can then hold, hopefully build, until we finish just before Christmas.'

'If you're sure, that's fine by me. Maxing PRD would obviously work for us,' replied Farren.

'I've got a draft shooting schedule together,' continued Anna, 'and it's mainly going to be shot in July and September. We've left space to do some post-edit additions if required, but hopefully that won't be necessary. We want to get this one in the can early and build the overall PR for the series around it.'

'Which, again, works for PRD,' added Kieran, who'd been looking at the menu up to this point.

'So, what and where do you want to shoot?' asked Farren.

'Well, we'd like to bounce a few ideas off you that we've had for the format,' said Anna.

Kieran, who'd been most assiduous in pre-production meetings in coming up with angles and ideas for enlivening the series, took over. 'Well, we know that AMOLAD stands for A Matter Of life and Death, so we were thinking the David Niven film, you know, where he appears to die, and then goes off to heaven to argue his time hasn't come, and then gets to go back to earth to finish off his life with the girl of his dreams.'

'I know the film, but I'm not immediately struck with how relevant that imagery could be to our story,' replied Farren.

'Exactly what we thought when we'd given it a bit more thought,' shot back Kieran who knew that to sell an idea it was always best to let the mark exercise a power of veto, thus creating buy-in to the next idea. 'Well, are you familiar with the film *Billy Liar*? Yes? There's a scene in that we liked, where Tom Courtenay's Billy dreams he's a government minister. He's sat in the back of an official car leaving the Houses Of Parliament with Shadrack, the undertaker he actually works for as a clerk. "Sir William" tells Shadrack that they intend to nationalise the undertaking business, and asks if he remembers showing a certain clerk a revolutionary plastic coffin? They laugh at how such ideas had appeared preposterous in the past, but now here they were doing them. We think it would be a great intro to the programme and how you've revolutionised bereavement. It also ties in nicely with your czar status.'

'I know the film well. I watched it many times with my dad when I was younger,' said Farren. 'I must say, yes, I quite like the sound of that – I can see what you're getting at there. Last thing we want is for it to be boring.'

Sensing a green light, Anna suggested that perhaps they'd better order. The main business having been dispensed with as far as Anna and Kieran were concerned, they settled down for a relaxing 'getting to know you' lunch.

'I believe you're speaking at the Forum tomorrow?' said Kieran.

'Yes, it's just a fringe meeting, but it all helps, especially this year. Will you be coming along?'

'Unfortunately not,' replied Anna. 'Back to London this afternoon, and our production budget doesn't extend to conference passes in any case.'

'Well, my press office will let you have the transcript, in fact everything we put out from this point on. I think going back to London is a good call. It's going to be a dreary evening based on my previous conference experiences.'

Lunch concluded on a positive, constructive note a happy Kieran and Anna jumped a black cab for Piccadilly Station and the 15.35 train back to Euston.

Farren took a second taxi to Didsbury to see his parents. He couldn't wait to tell Ernest about the *Billy Liar* angle. He'd be tickled pink.

As Farren's taxi sped down Kingsway in the spring sunshine, Smudger was having an uncontrollable laughing fit in his London lair. He'd just put the finishing touches to his latest opus, and was finding it difficult to contain his glee. On his Tweetdeck was a draft message, attributed to @last, that read: *'unconfirmed news coming in that ex PM Lady Thatcher has passed away after long illness bit.ly/memoriamplsbj7q'.* All Smudger had to do was hit the 'Tweet' button and he knew that there would be a massive multiplier surge pushing the news worldwide. He'd be seeing 'Lady Thatcher dead' trending within minutes. Counting to three, he sent the message on its way, and simultaneously launched the online link embedded in the tweet that would lead the twitterati to a memoriam page he'd just designed.

Smudger knew that his hoax would be outed within half

an hour, but he also knew that outrage at the spoof would dominate the news for days. He couldn't wait to hear Farren Mortimer's address to the Spring Conference tomorrow – that is if Mr Eulogy dared to show up.

Safely ensconced in his reserved seat on the 15.35 Pendolino from Manchester Piccadilly to Euston @kieranmcdonaghy spent the five minutes before departure checking his Twitter feed. 'Jesus Christ!' he exclaimed to Anna. 'Maggie Thatcher has kicked the bucket, it says here.'

Clicking on the link, he waited three seconds as the page loaded up – an online memoriam, looking exactly like a Forever in our Minds listing with a photograph of Margaret Thatcher at its head. Underneath there was a panel for 'tributes' to the former PM. As Kieran watched, postings started to appear, several of them not particularly sympathetic. One read: *'If this is true, we'll be dancing on her grave tonight. Good riddance. Yorkshire Miner, 1968 – 1984.'* Kieran quickly switched to the Press Association and BBC sites. Nothing. Straightaway, Kieran was suspicious. Although the main news sites were nearly always slower than Twitter, this was obviously a spoof, no doubt timed to set the cat among the pigeons at the Spring Forum. Using a Forever in our Minds lookalike page was cruel indeed but it could come in useful in respect of presenting another dimension to their story on Farren? Maybe. Kieran thought for a second, then he set up a re-tweet to allow @kieranmcdonaghy to share the 'rumour' with his current 57,458 followers. Before hitting send he added a message to the re-tweet reading: *'Spoof – don't think the lady's for burning just yet.'*

Farren stood on the front doorstep of his parents' home, and turned his mobile off. The last thing he wanted was to have his phone buzzing away when he was seeing Ernest. Agnes beamed on seeing Farren, whom she commented was looking very handsome and smart indeed. Farren laughed self-effacingly at his stylish grey marl Armani Collezioni 2 button metropolitan suit and white open-necked shirt: 'I'm dressed for work, Mum, that's all.'

Farren, as all visitors to the Mortimer household now did, lowered his voice. 'How's he doing?' was the standard whispered enquiry and Farren didn't deviate from the incantation.

'As well as can be expected. He's holding on. Always was a fighter your Dad, but he's in a lot of pain,' said Agnes. Then, brightening up, 'Go on, you go up; he's been looking forward to you coming all day. I'll bring some tea up.'

Farren climbed the stairs to his parents' bedroom. Despite visiting virtually every week Farren was never quite prepared to see his once robust father shrinking further and further into the embrace of the surrounding mattress. He composed himself, knocked and entered the room. Ernest smiled to see his son's head peer round the door.

'You not up for your jog yet, Dad?' joked Farren.

'Get away with you!' replied Ernest weakly.

Farren sat on the chair, by now almost permanently positioned at 45% to the bed for the benefit of visitors, and engaged Ernest in conversation. Naturally enough, given Ernest's fragile state, it was a pretty one sided conversation. When, after a respectful period to allow them time together, Agnes joined them with tea for her and Farren the game changed to a form of verbal tennis over the duvet with Ernest an interested bystander.

It wasn't sad. They recalled occasions spent together, laughed aloud at incidents from earlier in their lives, and took the mickey out of people they'd known in the past. The past that was now about to catch up with all of them. Agnes teased Farren about appearing at the party conference, and Ernest summoned up enough strength to say, 'thought you may have waited till I'd popped my clogs before agreeing to that one.'

Nothing was said about Ernest's deteriorating condition, the prognosis, the time left, the arrangements or anything of that ilk. They all understood each other, and felt comfortable in each other's company, despite the circumstances.

Eventually, as Farren got ready to leave to head back to Manchester, Ernest squeezed his hand and said, 'Look after your Mum, won't you? I know you will. Everything's taken care of.'

Farren knew that there wasn't much to take care of, but recognised that this was his father's way of saying you may not see me again. Farren smiled at him. 'See you next week, Dad. Make sure you're not down at the pub when I get here.'

He stooped and squeezed Ernest's hand, before backing out of the room, his arm raised in a gesture of farewell. Would this be his last visit to his dying father? Who could tell? It was enough that he could still share these moments with him.

As they waited downstairs for a taxi to pick Farren up, he checked on how Agnes was coping. The usual enquiries. 'Have you got everything you need? Are you sleeping? Are you getting help with the shopping? Are you getting cover for when you need to go out? You'll let me know the minute anything changes?'

Agnes brushed his questions away. They all knew their parts at this point.

As Farren sat in the back of the cab on the way back to Manchester, for the first time in a long while he allowed his feelings to overwhelm him. A tear fell down his cheek as he contemplated how one of the two most permanent fixtures in his entire life was about to be stripped away. He knew he would need all of his strength to endure what was to come.

Pulling himself together as the taxi negotiated the traffic on Plymouth Grove, Farren switched his mobile back on. Within thirty seconds, the number of calls, messages and texts that he'd missed flashed on the screen. Seventy-two missed calls, forty-four texts and thirty-six messages waiting to be picked up. An avalanche of entreaties from Jon, his head of PR, Nigel Adlington, and various journalists. What the hell had happened? Farren accessed the texts first for speed, and soon began to piece together the events that had bypassed his parents' Didsbury home that afternoon. The sense of what had happened very clearly reflected in the unfolding texts, especially those from his own team:

'Lady Thatcher death rumour.'
'Spoof Forever in our Minds page with miners putting the boot in.'
'Media want statement/comment.'
'Spoof page now down.'
'Hoax now been confirmed by BBC.'
'Urgently need to issue a statement.'
'Re-write for tomorrow's fringe essential?'
'Have now issued statement.'
'Where are you?'
'Can we/should we pull tomorrow?'

'Adlington on the war path – be warned.'
'Smudger, surely?'

Ignoring the telephone messages, Farren accessed the Internet and the BBC news page. There it was, a summary of the scandalous and offensive stunt pulled by anonymous perpetrators that afternoon, no doubt intended to besmirch the reputation of the former PM and to cause maximum damage to the party forum in Manchester. No mention of AMOLAD though, just a reference to a hoax in memoriam page which had now been taken down.

Farren asked the taxi driver to pull in at All Saints near the university, checked the cab audio light was extinguished, and called Jon.

'Where have you been, we've been trying to get hold of you all afternoon,' gasped Jon.

'So I see. I've been at Mum and Dad's – just picked all of this stuff up. What's the latest?'

'Well, it's calming down now, thank God. We put out a statement, the usual stuff, but we've still got a few journos clamouring for more.'

'Was our site hacked again, I mean with this spoof page?'

'No. It was just a link. Nothing to do with our site, it just looked like one of our pages.'

'Smudger again, you reckon?'

'It has all of his hallmarks, but it's hard to be sure.'

'The BBC story doesn't mention us. Does anyone else?'

'Some of the red tops are making the connection with the spoof page and us, and one journo has dragged up previous attacks on the business.'

'We've got to insulate ourselves. It's an attack on the party, not us. It's not part of an ongoing campaign; it's a one off. It's offensive and in considerable bad taste and our sympathies go out to Lady Thatcher, etcetera.'

'What about tomorrow?'

'No need to prepare anything, I'll play it by ear. I'm more worried about Adlington and how he's going to react at the moment– I get the impression he's not a happy bunny?'

'That's the impression I get as well.'

'I'll make him my next port of call.'

'Yes, well good luck with that, Farren.'

'Will do. I'll be contactable for the rest of the night now.'

Farren decided to pay the taxi driver at the point he'd pulled in so he could walk the last three-quarters of a mile to the Midland Hotel, allowing him time to think. Smudger's hand was all over this. Why was he doing it? No, this wasn't aimed at AMOLAD specifically; it was aimed at the party. He couldn't skip tomorrow, no – he'd put on a brave face, condemn it, and move on. PRD was the priority. The attack was akin to defacing a graveyard, and vandalism is vandalism whether on a brick wall or a cyber one. An attack on us all.

On gaining access to the hotel, Farren went up to Adlington's room. Face the music time. Hope he was in and get it out of the way. As Farren had suspected, Nigel had not been in the best of humours, but at least his anger had subsided somewhat in the intervening hours once the fuss had started to die down.

Nigel had been annoyed on a number of accounts. The attack on the former leader had of course been outrageous. More pertinently, the spoof Forever in our Minds page and perceptible association with his bereavement czar had cast a shadow on PRD in his view. In addition, Nigel's triumph at the Forum had been somewhat undermined with this scandal which was now the only topic on everyone's lips. And to add insult to injury, it had meant that the mid-afternoon liaison with Annie Brooks he had so carefully engineered had been overtaken by events.

By the time Farren knocked on Adlington's door Annie had done the decent thing and postponed her return home so she could spend most of the night with Nigel after the evening's reception, restoring in part his earlier good cheer.

'Good of you to show up, Farren. Where were you hiding all afternoon?'

'Sorry about that, Nigel. Was visiting my parents. Completely out of the loop. What's the latest?'

'Well, as you can imagine, very distressing for everybody. We don't know who's behind this attack, and it's no doubt just a leftie prank, but it's detracted from the Forum. Upset people.'

'Best then to move on, surely? Don't draw any more attention to it?'

'Absolutely, Farren. We can't let these people win. As far as I'm concerned we won't benefit this atrocity with the oxygen of publicity. We're made of stronger stuff than that.'

Farren was suitably impressed at Adlington's stoicism, being unaware that Nigel was merely echoing the sentiments of the PM who'd put the issue to bed in a similar vein an hour before. Farren was also unaware that, having been blown off course in his afternoon plans, Nigel was once more on a promise as far as his secret tryst was concerned.

'So that's the party line, Farren, and all we have to do is maintain it. Now, I'm going down to the reception, so I suggest you accompany me as a show of solidarity and to emphasise it's business as usual? You ready?'

Farren nodded. Adlington wasn't as big a flapper as he'd expected. Panic over. Time to go and perform.

Downstairs in the Trafford Suite the reception was in full swing. Farren stuck attentively to Nigel's side, meeting and greeting a succession of the great and the good, smiling charmingly when the need arose, and wearing an aspect somewhere between indignation and dismay whenever the topic of the afternoon's outrage was raised.

Mentally calculating how long to give himself before he could slip off unnoticed, Farren's attention was captured by a stunning blonde, dressed in a dazzling scarlet velvet evening gown with a precipitous plunge neck, who had suddenly come into their eye line. Nigel closed the gap swiftly and effected an introduction. 'Ah, Mrs Brooks, how nice to see you. Please, let me introduce you to Farren Mortimer, our bereavement czar. Farren, Annie Brooks of HASTE who spoke, I must say, very persuasively on the perils of reckless speeding earlier today. I think her address is going to play very well with the media if truth be told.'

'But not as well as it might have if we hadn't had the Lady Thatcher scare,' replied Annie, who by now had had her media coverage expectations well and truly managed by her PR team.

'Mrs Brooks, how nice to meet you,' said Farren, trying to tear his gaze away from her rather impressive breasts. 'I've heard very good accounts of your work. Did you find today's audience sympathetic?'

'Delighted to meet you too, Farren. Oh, yes, they were very supportive. I've had lots of them coming up to me all day telling me to carry on the good work. I believe that you're speaking tomorrow as well, aren't you?'

'Yes, on the fringe. Not as impressive as the main platform like you!'

Nigel, also taking in Annie's stunning dress and contours and anticipating the delights to follow later that evening, then boldly teed up the dauntless road safety campaigner. 'Mrs Brooks, you really should talk to Farren here about your campaign strategy. I'm sure your organisations both have a lot in common, and after all, you won't find a better marketing guru; I'm sure you don't mind me saying so, do you Farren?'

'You flatter me, Nigel, but yes, I'd be delighted to assist in any way I can,' ventured Farren.

Annie wasn't slow in nipping through this unexpected window of opportunity. 'Really? That would be fantastic. In that case, Farren, would you mind if I call you to arrange a meeting in the near future? I have so many plans that I'd like to share with you.'

Farren knew exactly what was coming, namely a request for funding and a HASTE charity donation scheme built in to road victim death pages – they'd had one of her lackeys punting this to them a few months ago.

'Of course, Mrs Brooks, just get your people to get in touch with my PA and she'll arrange it.'

The evening could now take a different direction for all three of them. Farren, having conceded ground to Nigel and Annie Brooks, could justifiably do a bunk and go upstairs to his room for a cold beer and *Match of the Day*. Meeting Annie one to one wouldn't be too much of a hardship anyway as she was certainly a bit of a looker.

Annie could mentally tick Farren off her hit list. He was in her sights and she would hunt him down. The power of networking was truly amazing – it really was the only way to cut through and get things done.

Nigel, on the other hand, could console himself that his day of triumph was now back on track after its temporary diversion. He could also hope that his brazen intercession with Farren on HASTE's behalf would earn him extra privileges when he and Annie finally made it to bed after this dreary and interminable reception.

PRD minus 208.

CHAPTER ELEVEN

I Shall Be Released

It was a beautiful May morning, and the Mortimers' garden was in full bloom, an explosion of azaleas, tulips, lilac and peonies competing in colour and scent to seduce the senses. Michael Morrison rapped gently on his latest client's front door. Ernest had finally succumbed to his long illness at Withington Community Hospital the previous evening and Michael had been summoned to finalise funeral arrangements with Mrs Mortimer and her son.

Farren answered the door, and shaking Michael's hand ushered him into the living room where Agnes was already sat in front of a tray replete with tea pot, milk jug, sugar bowl, a plate of Rich Tea biscuits and cups and saucers for three people.

'Mrs Mortimer, I'm deeply sorry for your loss. Ernest was a fine man.'

'Thank you, Mr Morrison. He was. At least he's at peace now. Goodness knows he suffered, but it's over now.'

'I believe he slipped away peacefully in the end, which is a mercy?'

'Yes. It was as good a death as we could have hoped for. We were both there for him at the end, and the hospital staff were very good helping Ernest through his final hours.'

'That's a blessing. And are you feeling up to discussing arrangements at this point?'

'Yes, of course. It's best to get things organised.'

As Michael and Agnes went through requirements for plots, caskets, cars, flowers, notices and likely time slots, Farren poured the tea, and remained largely silent. It struck him that the mundane nature of the exchange, the process, was stark and sobering in its practicality and rather a long way from his own, some would say, extravagant and upbeat interpretation of a send-off.

The key decisions having been solidly recorded in blue biro on Michael's planning sheet, the undertaker ventured his supplementary set of questions.

'Will there be any music requirements, any particular favourite songs or hymns that Ernest would like?'

'Oh yes, Ernest loved music, and he did pick some songs to be played. Farren, can you get that piece of paper from the top drawer of the sideboard?'

This was news to Farren who had been unaware of any such decision on his late father's behalf. He reached across and pulled open the drawer, and there, scribbled on a spiral-bound typist's notepad, he recognised his mother's spidery scribble:

'*Memories Are Made Of This*, Dean Martin.'

'*Ernie*, Benny Hill.'

Farren hesitated briefly. 'This one, Mum? With *Ernie* on it?'

'Yes, that's the one.'

'Are you sure? I mean, did he really mean to play it, or was he just joking with you?' said Farren.

'No, he meant it to be played. Why, what's wrong with it?' said Agnes.

'Nothing. I'm just a bit surprised, that's all. I didn't think he'd choose a comedy song like that for his own funeral.'

'He always had a good sense of humour. You know that, Farren. No, Mr Morrison, these are the two.'

'Very good, Mrs Mortimer. Perhaps if you could have these songs transferred to a single CD that would be most helpful for the service?'

'Yes, of course,' replied a still somewhat perplexed Farren.

'And will there be anything else? Perhaps a stone?'

'Well, yes, we'd like one, and I'd like to leave room on it for me when it's my time to go, but can we leave that for now as it can't be done in time for the funeral in any case if I understand right?'

'Quite right, Mrs Mortimer. It's best not to rush such an item. I can discuss that with you after the funeral if that's preferable?'

'Yes, that would be fine, Mr Morrison.'

'In that case, I'll leave you now and get on with the arrangements as discussed. Thank you for your time, and again, my deepest condolences.'

Following Mr Morrison's departure, Farren decided to take a walk to clear his head. He and Agnes had hardly slept over the past three days as they'd maintained a vigil at Ernest's bedside, but they had at least been with him at the last. His father had been too weak and sedated by painkillers to acknowledge their presence beyond an occasional nod and squeeze of the hand. But it had been peaceful, and it had been some sort of conclusion. Or had it?

Farren considered how he felt. He was upset, but was this grief? He felt numbed, but he didn't feel crushed or desolate; he could still function. He'd shed a tear at the bedside, but in reality he had been more concerned for his mum, who had been, it must be said, magnificent in her composure throughout. Dignity, that's what she'd displayed, and again today with the undertaker, who had conducted himself with equal propriety.

Farren grimaced as he thought about the choice of music Dad had made for his own funeral. *Ernie*? What was all that about? Farren just didn't get it and felt he should have known about the choice – it was his dad after all. How come something as small and insignificant in the scheme of things as that had come as such as a surprise to him? To the man who had invented the Funerals Top Ten of all people?

Farren knew he'd been nothing more than a bystander at the funeral planning meeting which had largely been a private conversation between Mum and Mr Morrison. He felt hollow at his lack of contribution, and could only reflect that they knew what they were talking about while it was a new experience for him. He grasped how utterly and incredibly ironic it was that the so-called Mr Eulogy was so out of his depth. Farren may have been a creative genius, singlehandedly revolutionising modern bereavement, but that hadn't helped him to contribute to this morning's discussion. He may have studied, and commissioned, extensive research into the funerals market and been acknowledged as an expert on such matters, but that knowledge counted for nothing in dealing with the practicalities of burying his own father.

He felt a surge of shame as he recalled the joking and the self-congratulatory glee he and his team had engaged in as they came up with new initiatives. The language they'd used in describing the deceased as 'punters', 'stiffs' or 'units'. The sham lexicon that populated their websites and literature speaking of 'legacy', 'celebration', 'cherished memories' and a hundred euphemisms for death.

His father was dead, and the last thing on his mind was a biovid or an online memorial. Christ, what must Agnes think of his business? And Ernest too when he was alive? They'd always seemed so proud of his achievements, and had never questioned him or taken him to task about his activities, but all along had they secretly been appalled? Farren now couldn't help but imagine that maybe they'd been humouring him while in private they'd condemned his antics, possibly in the hope of, what, he'd grow out of it and get a proper job?

Farren groaned inwardly at the implication of all these questions. He was tired, he was upset and he had his dad's funeral to help arrange. Agnes would be receiving a succession of well-wishers around now, and he should go back and support her. Turning across the football pitches on Fog Lane he headed back to be with Mum.

Agnes in the meantime was stripping the double bed that Ernest had last slept in some five nights ago – she'd not had time to change the sheets in the interim. As she surveyed the room, all she could see were reminders of her dead husband – his glasses case, his comb, the clean pair of pyjamas on the chair, his slippers tucked under the bed. While she'd had ample time to rehearse this scene, nevertheless it didn't seem real. It felt that Ernest had maybe just gone to the hospital for treatment and would be returning anytime soon, as he had before.

As soon as she had changed the bed she tidied around before going back downstairs. She must occupy herself, keep herself busy – she knew it was the right thing to do. She'd get round to this room properly after the funeral. As she went into the kitchen, she was aware of a deafening silence. It was the first time she'd been alone since she and Farren had come back from the hospital. She had been in the house by herself many times before when Ernest was in hospital, but this felt different – it was profoundly, eerily, savagely still. She turned on the radio station to provide some diversion. It was tuned to classical, and she immediately turned it off again.

Agnes sat at the kitchen table and stared at the clock on the wall. She wasn't in a rush. For anything now. She held the image of Ernest in her mind, lying there on his deathbed, his pain and suffering mercifully about to be relieved. She didn't think about herself. The next task was the funeral, which Farren would help her through. Farren had been quiet this morning she thought. Poor lamb, not used to dealing with funerals, which when you think about it was a little odd considering what he did for a living. And why had Farren been so sensitive about *Ernie* being played at his dad's funeral? Isn't that the sort of thing Farren's business was all about in any case? She'd been a little taken aback at how he'd questioned that choice of song. Why not, if that's what Ernest had wanted?

Ernest had always said he had brains did Farren. In the beginning her husband had said Farren's business, while clever, was most likely a temporary creative fling for him before he moved on to something else. His gimmicks were all right for people who wanted that kind of thing, he'd said, but it was very likely a passing fad. He said less and less about that though as Farren's business prospered.

Agnes and Ernest were immensely proud of Farren, but they did occasionally worry about how happy he was. He was successful, yes, but he needed a young lady in his life was what they thought. Still, none of their business, and they were sure it would happen in good time. Shame Ernest wouldn't be around to see it now.

'What are you going to do about Farren?' Ernest's question came back to her. What was she going to do about Farren, and the unlikely story of his parentage? 'Nothing good will come of it,' Ernest had warned.

Agnes had maintained a diplomatic silence over the subject whenever Ernest raised it, because she knew that he knew she saw things slightly differently. No, she shouldn't be thinking of that on a day like today. But she couldn't help but notice, that very morning when she sat opposite the two of them in the living room, a remarkable similarity in features between Farren and Michael Morrison. Morrison may be going to seed, but there was a discernible coincidence of nose, mouth and eye features when the two were juxtaposed. No – don't go there.

At that moment, there was a knock on the door. The first of numerous well-wishers, probably her younger brother, Paddy, she guessed. She drew herself up from the table, smoothed her dress, checked her face in the hall mirror and went to admit the shades silhouetted against the opaque glass of the front door.

Michael Morrison had put all of the decisions made that morning at the Mortimer household in train, and stretched back in his chair for a moment's relaxation before heading for home. Everything was in hand, and the funeral was now scheduled at St Augustine's for the following Friday, with the interment to take place immediately afterwards at Southern Cemetery. So nothing out of the ordinary then, just like the thousands of funerals he'd organised before. No sign of any of this AMOLAD nonsense, despite the man behind it all being sat there this morning.

Michael had been intrigued discussing the funeral with Farren Mortimer. He had suspected that he may try to come up with some flashy ideas for the send-off, but no, not a whisper of anything that wasn't strictly traditional. In fact he'd said very little at all this morning.

Could this be in deference to his parents' wishes? Had he just decided to keep *schtum* knowing that the plans were laid? No, he didn't think so because Michael couldn't help but notice how Farren had appeared a little disconcerted at the choice of *Ernie* as one of the funeral songs. Well, that didn't even surprise Michael who by now had heard considerably odder songs than that played at funerals, and surely Farren Mortimer had been responsible for far more outlandish demonstrations of remembrance than that to be sat there looking so pained? At least he'd not kyboshed the idea of a headstone, so this would be a reasonably profitable funeral for Morrison Family Funeral Services, and he could do with as many of those as he could lay his hands on, thank you very much.

At one point that morning Michael had considered asking Farren if he'd wanted to suggest any further ideas for the funeral, perhaps something that he'd pioneered with his own business? But no, he'd not had the heart. If the truth was told, he felt sorry for the lad. For all of his fancy ideas, his success, his shaking up of the bereavement sector and his negative impact on Morrison Family Funeral Services, Michael had to conclude that Farren was simply a man suffering from his first real exposure to grief at the loss of a close loved one.

There was no cause for Michael to revel in Farren's obvious desolation. Here was a recognisable and good old-fashioned reaction to the reality of death and wasn't it exactly this that Michael was here to help people through?

PRD minus 166.

CHAPTER TWELVE

Enough To Be On Your Way

Jon was in a tetchy mood. Farren, including his father's last days and the funeral the previous week, had been away from the office now for nearly a fortnight, leaving even more for Jon to do. Yes, it was a shame his father had died, but Farren still had a duty of responsibility to the business – it wasn't going to run itself. Jon supposed, on one level, Farren's protracted absence on account of a family bereavement may actually send out a positive message. After all, they were in the business of bereavement so it would be wholly appropriate for the CEO to be seen to be taking his grieving seriously. At least that's what their press office was saying.

Ernest Mortimer's funeral could have been an opportunity for them, but Farren had been most uncooperative. They'd known since news of Farren's father's death had got out that certain sections of the media would try to capitalise – the story was just too inviting; how would the bereavement czar say farewell to his own father? What eulogy would Mr Eulogy summon up for the occasion?

Tipped off by the press office about this inevitable intrusion Jon had called Farren to warn him and also to suggest that they could put a team on preparing a biovid for Ernest in time for the funeral. Farren hadn't been interested at all. 'My mother doesn't want a circus when she's burying her husband, and neither do I; and no, we don't want a biovid.'

'Well,' Jon had suggested, 'can we at least state that an especial A Life Remembered celebration for Ernest is being planned?' Jon felt, but didn't say, that such a strategy would give them at least three months leeway and it would fall in nicely with the run up to PRD. Again, Farren was dismissive.

Jon, not for the first time, felt exasperated with Farren. He surveyed the coverage of the funeral sat in a ring binder on his desk. At least it may have helped if they'd tried to protect themselves instead of leaving themselves wide open. Fortunately, in the event, broadcast had skipped the story, as had the qualities, and the tabloids who covered it had been largely merciful sticking to non-controversial lines such as 'Mr Eulogy's emotional farewell to his father,' and 'Trad rules at bereavement czar's family funeral.'

No, the main problem was the bloggers and the accompanying Twitter chatter that for some inexplicable reason had chosen to treat the funeral as a golden opportunity to satirise AMOLAD. Reading some of the blogs it made one wonder who had phoned in their report from the pub – the bloggers or the reporters? – so wildly did their accounts differ. Jon picked out a random sample of this vituperation, a blog by @wappinglie. This was not what Jon would consider positive for the business:

> **'Mr Eulogy fails screen test at Dad's send-off**
> *The man accredited with putting the 'fun' into funerals demonstrated this week that he has a different set of rules when it comes to seeing off his own. Attending the funeral of his 84-year-old father, Ernest Mortimer,*

at St Augustine's RC church in Didsbury, Manchester, on Friday one could imagine AMOLAD and its ideas on 'celebrating life' had never swept Britain. Not for poor old Ernest an online memoriam site for friends and families to leave everlasting bon mots, like footprints on the moon, never to be removed. Not for Farren's dad a pop video treatment of his finest moments flash cut to his favourite tunes. What we did have in the music department was a bizarre rendition of Benny Hill's Ernie, a 'novelty' innuendo laden song that topped the charts back in 1971. As far as I know Farren Mortimer's father was never a milkman, and surely someone should have checked the lyrics of the song out to the end when 'Ernie' comes back from the dead to haunt his former lover and his love rival on their wedding night.

As if that wasn't bad enough, the nadir arrived when Mr Eulogy himself, Farren Mortimer, took to the pulpit to deliver a valediction to his father. It was apparent that Mortimer hadn't referenced his own company's "How to make the perfect Eulogy" guide as he struggled to make sense of the occasion, breaking down and being unable to finish. Or maybe we were all being conned and Mortimer was just demonstrating that he had a different class of grief to the one he was peddling to the masses. Look out for the updated version of the guide soon, complete with tips on how to shed tears at will.

Within a few short months the nation will be asked, on People's Remembrance Day, to cherish the memory of their dearly departed in a rather different manner to the above. One can't help but think that the only thing to remember on that day should be to stay in bed.'

First Smudger and now attacks like this, or could they be from one and the same person? It didn't matter – these were all reminders of the need for the strictest corporate discipline as AMOLAD faced its biggest challenge in mounting PRD. If Farren wanted to screw up the business he was going about it the right way through his prolonged absence and lack of proactivity thought Jon. It was clear to Jon that his role within AMOLAD was now even more vital than ever.

Kieran McDonaghy was studying the press cuttings on Ernest Mortimer's funeral as he sat in Baccarat's offices. Farren Mortimer's dad dying during the run up to *Made Men* and PRD was a stroke of luck as it would definitely give them an additional angle to play with. Baccarat had sent a junior researcher – incognito of course – to the funeral to gather anything useful and his summary of the proceedings had taken the production team aback slightly. Kieran in particular had been surprised at the account of the funeral as his impression of Farren to date led him to believe he would have performed with élan under such circumstances. Not only that, he was convinced Farren would have used a set-piece occasion like this to his own and his company's advantages – he was a marketeer at heart after all, and hardly a shrinking violet. But, no, the whole thing was very curious indeed – not a trace of AMOLAD embellishments, and a clearly distressed Farren Mortimer during the service. What had really stood out to Kieran was the song *Ernie* that was played. Surely Farren must have known people would jump on that; how could he have allowed it? Kieran shrugged and addressed himself to the photo of Farren on the cutting he held in his hand: 'Don't go cold on me now, Farren. I've got a BAFTA riding on you.'

Agnes Mortimer knelt at Ernest's grave transferring the numerous bouquets, now turning brown after a week in the open, into a large black bin bag. In their stead she placed simple posies of tulips and lilac, Ernest's favourites from their own garden, on to the raised earth. Later that day she was due to see Michael Morrison for the funeral bill and to look through the variety of memorial stones on offer.

The last week had passed in slow motion. Up until the funeral she'd kept busy; as there were so many callers it had been hard to get a minute to herself anyway. Farren had stayed until the day after the funeral, but since then she'd been drifting, meandering, along without any real purpose. Paddy's wife Patricia had suggested taking sleeping pills to help, or even going to the doctors to ask for something stronger. Agnes had dismissed the suggestion out of hand. It wasn't a prescription she needed to make her feel whole again. She had the sensation an amputee is supposed to feel, an itch in a phantom limb and no means to scratch it.

Agnes had witnessed sufficient bereavement to recognise the way she was feeling, and was resolute enough to weather the storm which she knew, deep down, would abate even if it would never cease entirely. Such was the purpose of faith.

The service for Ernest had been lovely; everybody had agreed it was a fitting send-off. The church had been packed with family, friends and fellow parishioners keen to pay their last respects. Father Wilcox had been wonderful too, talking about how, despite his suffering, Ernest had never lost heart or his commitment to the church. Poor Farren had struggled emotionally with the eulogy, poor lad, and all who were present had been deeply touched by his hesitant delivery, but he'd got there in the end and made the congregation smile with some of his anecdotes about his dad. Yes, they couldn't have asked for a better funeral.

She had to think forward now, she knew, but there was one thing that still required settling from the past. Every time she looked at Michael Morrison the day Father Culshaw had shared his suspicions with her and Ernest shot back into her mind. Since Ernest's death, every time she espied Michael Morrison and Farren in the same room together she had to suppress the inconceivable thought that they could be father and son. It was ridiculous, and Ernest was right that no good would come of giving the idea any credence or investigating it further. In any event, where would you start – she could hardly just come straight out with it and casually ask Michael Morrison if he knew of any offspring he'd not fully accounted for? Should she show Farren his mother's letter, and share the problem with him? Why rake up the past when she and Ernest were Farren's Mum and Dad and always had been?

'Ee, Ernest,' she said to the temporary wooden cross marking his final resting place, 'I know what you think, and you're right, but I can't help myself. You didn't see the two of them stood next to each other.'

Farren was sat in his living room, with the curtains drawn against the bright blue sky outside. He'd been back in London for six days now, but still couldn't face the prospect of going back to work. He spoke to Mum every day, and did his best to be upbeat and positive when on the phone to her, but as soon as he hung up, he relapsed into a melancholic and listless state of mind.

The night before the funeral he'd suffered from one of his blackouts, the second in a couple of months. He'd felt it coming on and had managed to lock himself in the toilet so Mum and the handful of people who were at the house after conveying Ernest's body into church had been none the wiser. He recognised that he must be stressed – who wouldn't be in such circumstances? – and worried about a repeat on the day of the funeral itself.

In any event, the funeral passed off smoothly, everybody had said so, and he had been touched by the atmosphere of serenity and the purpose of unity displayed at the ceremonies, both in the church and at the cemetery. The dignity, the empathy, the mutual support, the unquestioned love and affection displayed by all present had been a revelation to Farren who had only ever attended funerals before as an interested bystander rather than as a committed participant. The only sour note had come from Jon and his mithering him about press intrusion at the church and doing a biovid for Ernest. He'd hardly been able to contain his anger at him – who did he think he was coming on like that at such a moment? Jon had clearly lost all sense of perspective. Farren had also been less than impressed by Baccarat Productions who'd actually asked to bring cameras into the church as part of the *Made Men* programme. You just couldn't put anything past these people – nothing was sacred.

As Farren contemplated at length over the ensuing days, he began to think that maybe it was him that had it wrong.

Who was he kidding? Who was the one who had invented biovids and memory archives and come up with the People's Remembrance Day for goodness sake? He had. Who was the one chasing a headline all of the time? He was. Who had been treating bereavement like a new brand of breakfast cereal? Look no further.

Farren fingered a book he'd picked up off the bookshelf when he'd been back in Didsbury. *Edward II* by Christopher Marlowe. He'd studied it at school for his 'A' levels and his eventual 'A' grade in English had helped him on his way to Leeds University. Farren had delighted in telling Ernest, no aficionado of Elizabethan drama, the fate of Young Mortimer, the ambitious kingmaker who is eventually executed.

'A good lesson there,' Ernest had said after he'd heard the tale. 'Mind you don't end up the same.' Had he bitten off more than he could chew? And if he had, how could he yet avoid the fall?

Agnes had been looking at the book of headstones for half an hour, and had finally narrowed her choice down to two alternatives. The bill for the funeral had already been presented to her, and Agnes had put it straight in her handbag intending to read it in detail when she got home – it would have been impolite to pour over it in front of Michael Morrison. She had no reason to suspect it wouldn't be 100% accurate and reasonable, and anyway, the cost was going to be covered by their Co-op insurance policy.

Michael Morrison busied himself, going in and out of his office, checking Agnes had sufficient tea, enquiring if she had come across anything yet that appealed. Agnes was finding it difficult to concentrate on the task in hand as she made furtive sidelong glances at Michael Morrison every time he came back into the office. There was a definite resemblance to Farren if she stripped away nigh on twenty years of unhealthy living from the portly undertaker. Was it an uncanny likeness, a coincidental one, or was it more a case of her desperation to know playing tricks on her mind?

Michael Morrison, keen to get home by this point, sat down opposite Agnes in the hope of moving things on to a conclusion. 'Ah, I see you have your eye on the double upright in granite – a very good choice if I may say so, particularly for a family plot.'

Agnes looked down at the page. The photography depicted a 36 x 20 x 6 inch tablet mounted on a 10 x 24 x 10 inch base. On the tablet depicted there was room for up to four names, depending on the family requirements. 'Well, it's just for me and Ernest,' she replied. 'I'm not sure what Farren's plans are, but I doubt he'll want to be buried with us.'

'No, quite,' ventured Michael. 'Such plots are becoming rarer and rarer, mainly I think due to the increase in cremations.'

'Can I ask, Mr Morrison, do you have any family to consider in this way?'

'I'll be joining my poor wife Carmel when the time comes. Those arrangements have already been made.'

'And do you have children, to make sure your wishes are carried out?'

'Sadly, no children. Carmel and myself were never blessed in that way. I'm afraid to say that when I go that's the end of the Morrison line.'

Agnes couldn't help herself. She could almost feel the restraining hand of Ernest on her shoulder as she wound up to her next question, but to no avail. 'So you never had any children, Mr Morrison?'

'Er, no. As I mentioned, we were never blessed in that department.'

'It's just that, well, I don't really know how to say this. Did you ever know a young lady by the name of Linda Wilson?'

'Linda Wilson? No. I'm sorry; that name doesn't ring any bells, Mrs Mortimer. Why do you ask?'

'You slept with her by all accounts.'

Agnes was shocked. She'd come out with it, and immediately regretted it as she looked at the confusion and alarm on Michael's face as he was confronted with this crazy, grief stricken old woman.

'Mrs Mortimer. I'm a little taken aback. I do assure you that I don't know anybody of that name. I think perhaps you must be confusing me with someone else?'

Agnes, panicking as she contemplated where to go next with this, decided the whole nine yards was called for: 'Well, according to Father Culshaw, you put this Linda in the family way back in 1972. The baby was born in September 1973. That baby is Farren, who we adopted before he was two weeks old. You *apparently* didn't know, so does Linda Wilson ring any bells now?' There, it was out now, God forgive her. What if she'd just made the biggest fool of herself ever in her 83 years?

A cold sweat broke out on Michael's forehead. The colour drained from his face. His mind whirled as he tried to assimilate the barrage of information that had just been uploaded, unexpectedly and unprompted, from Mrs Mortimer. Linda Wilson? Looby! As if he could ever forget her. A baby? Farren? The Mortimers? Father Culshaw? Suddenly, it fell into place. He'd made Looby pregnant? Farren? Jesus, Mary and Joseph. What had he done? After a gap of nearly forty years, here was secondary confirmation that the night in question *had* actually taken place. For many years now he'd begun to fancy it must have been some sort of illusion, a fantastical concoction he'd somehow invented. Now here was a witness stepping forward to confirm that it hadn't been a mirage – it had actually happened.

PRD minus 155.

CHAPTER THIRTEEN

I Am Stretched On Your Grave

December 8, 1972 was a bitterly cold night. As usual for a Friday young Michael Morrison wound down after a busy week by sharing a few pints with Tom and Colin, two old friends from school, in The Friendship Inn in Fallowfield. Michael was doing well at work, having by now passed his National Association of Funeral Directors Foundation Certificate in Funeral Services – one of the youngest people ever to qualify. He was assuming greater responsibility in the family business, much to the approval of his father, and was enjoying serving the community with his specialist skills. He was courting young Carmel Kilpatrick with whom he was due to go Christmas shopping the following day; the festive spirit was in the air and his future lay mapped out before him – life was good.

At chucking out time, the three friends buttoned up against the cold and, seeking sustenance to soak up the six pints of Hydes Anvil Ale they'd each consumed, headed towards the Canadian Charcoal Pit, a popular burger bar located directly opposite the Owens Park and Oak House student halls of residence on Wilmslow Road. Tom, a newly qualified electrician, and Colin, a clerk of works at the Town Hall, each cradled under their arm a four pint Bodkan of Boddingtons

Bitter to keep the evening going over a marathon session of Pontoon back at Tom's parents' house just down the road in Ladybarn. Michael's shout was the three Double-Decker burgers that were guaranteed to satisfy most appetites, particularly those sharpened by the best part of a gallon of bitter.

The Charcoal Pit was busy, and there was plenty of banter going on as a combination of students and locals refuelled for the next part of their Friday evening revels. Then, just as Michael was adding extra onions, ketchup and American mustard to his heavy-duty double patty, in walked one of the most beautiful girls he had ever set eyes on. She was dressed in a bright red three-quarter coat replete with two rows of black buttons, a black skirt, thick woollen tights and knee-length boots of the same colour. A ten-foot yellow woollen scarf encircled her neck in banks, and the look was topped off with a dark green beret keeping her mid length dark hair in check. Michael's wasn't the only head to turn in her direction, her unadorned olive skin, hazel eyes and concupiscent pout setting her apart from the standard issue duffle coat wearing female undergraduate. Her exotic beauty and sensuous air clashed strongly with the mundane setting. Spanish or Italian perhaps? Sophia Loren's long lost daughter?

Michael would never have had the nerve, wit or confidence to address such a beautiful woman, but as he was about to discover, that wouldn't be necessary.

Surveying the length of the queue, the beguiling brunette turned in Michael's direction and in a broad cockney accent chirped: 'Tell you what mate, give me half of your burger and I'll take you to a Christmas party.'

Michael didn't quite register at first that she was talking to him. He met her enquiry with a dozy, uncomprehending facial expression that prompted a second attempt from the would-be queue jumper. 'How about it, then?'

Was this a wind-up? Surely she couldn't be serious? She was talking to him, of that he was now sure. Hesitatingly, Michael extended the burger in her direction. 'Go on, then.'

Giggling, she took the burger, placed it on the counter and tore it expertly in half before handing Michael's portion back to him. Michael didn't know what to say – he just stared at her like a village idiot and smiled goofily in her direction.

'Ta, that's a life saver,' she said, before taking an elaborate 'stage' bite of the contraband and rolling her eyes in a dumbshow of pleasure as the hot and greasy food hit her taste buds.

Tom and Colin shuffled over to see what was going on, both placing their Bodkans on the floor in front to them the better to attack their burgers. Tom broke the bubble first with a smooth and charming, 'I wouldn't if I were you, love; you don't know where he's been.'

Spotting the beer cans on the floor, their fellow dinner guest reinforced the earlier invitation. 'Bodkans? Brilliant. You can all come along then.' With that, she giggled again and, clutching the remnants of her burger, headed for the door as quickly as she'd arrived. Turning briefly before she exited into a freezing Wilmslow Road, she applied the gilt edge to the invitation: '8, Constantine Avenue. Ask for Looby. Bye!' And with that she was gone.

'Can't leave you alone for a minute, Michael,' Colin said, rather impressed at the exchanges that had just taken place.

'Blimey, she's invited us to a party,' said Michael, 'What shall we do?'

Tom rapped his knuckles on the top of Michael's head in mock incredulity. 'She's not serious you sap – she was just giving you a line to get half of your burger! And it worked, didn't it?'

Michael wasn't convinced. 'Yes, but she didn't have to tell us there was a party to do that.'

'Constantine Avenue is in Withington,' said Colin. 'We can hardly go traipsing all the way up there to some non-existent do. Even if there is a party it'll be full of poxy students. No, we should stick to Plan 'A' and get our card game on.'

Michael was generally deferential to his friends' needs, and would usually have meekly acquiesced to their demands without argument, but tonight, no, he was going to fight his corner. 'Come on, don't be boring all your lives,' he said. 'Let's give it a go. If it's crap, we can still come back and play cards.'

'But it's miles, and how are we going to get back?' protested Colin. 'There'll be no buses – it'll have to be a taxi job.'

'It's not *that* far. I'll pay for the taxi, if that's the only problem,' suggested Michael.

Tom pronounced the casting vote: 'Ah, he's in love! Poor old Michael has got the love bug for a studie! Looby, Looby Loo. Pay for a taxi? Well, I'm in, in that case. It might be a laugh.'

Michael blushed. He wouldn't normally be so bold and insistent on going to this party, a party that may not even exist. Was it Dutch courage from the beer he'd consumed that evening, or was it, as Tom averred, a case of him being smitten? 'Right. That's sorted then,' said Michael. 'Let's finish up these burgers, and get the bus up Palatine Road.'

'Thought you were standing a taxi?' protested Colin.

'I am – on the way back,' replied Michael.

Twenty-five minutes later they were knocking on the door of a large brick-built semi-detached house at the bottom of a well-appointed cul-de-sac, surprisingly smart for a student house. On the way, the spirit of gay abandon at the burger bar had somewhat diminished given the cold, the journey on the late bus, and the suspicion that they were on a wild goose chase. Michael wouldn't back down though – he was a man on a mission and drove the other two on in his quest.

The door was opened by a vague looking bearded youth who stood staring quizzically at them. Michael uttered the magic formula: 'We're with Looby,' while Tom and Colin stood clutching the real means of entry – the two Bodkans.

'Yeah,' came the reply, and the door swung open to admit them.

It wasn't as if the bearded youth actually lived there; he'd just dropped in too. Michael, Tom and Colin self-consciously headed for the back of the house where the music emanated from, taking their coats off as they went in order to look as if they belonged despite their garb being decidedly non-student like. It didn't matter, as no one seemed to be paying any particular attention to them. Five minutes later, as they tucked into the first of their Bodkans in the comfort of the kitchen, they began to relax somewhat. Various students came and went into the kitchen, saying 'hi' but otherwise ignoring them.

Tom was bemused that a couple of students seemed to be engrossed in hiding their booze in the unlit oven from where they might retrieve it later. 'But we know it's there now, so that's just bloody daft.'

After the first Bodkan was despatched they felt a little bit braver, so filling their pint pots afresh they decided to go exploring in the main living room where the music was

117

booming out. There were around forty people, obviously students, crammed in there, some sat around, some dancing. The overhead light fittings had been replaced by red bulbs, and the room was dominated by a twin turntable attached to an enormous amplifier. The music was pumping out of two giant speakers that someone had taken the precaution of covering with plastic sheeting to protect against drink spillages. To complete the tableau there was a heavy scent of incense hanging over the proceedings.

Surveying the scene, Michael spotted Looby sat down on the settee, trying to have a conversation above the sound of the music with a longhaired boy wearing a pair of pale blue jeans and a red Wrangler shirt.

Colin spotted them too. 'Looks like you've been beaten to it, Michael. I say let's neck these and head off. OK?'

Colin addressed the same question to Tom who nodded in assent – time to go. But Michael determined he was going nowhere until he had spoken to Looby properly; after all, she'd invited them. At that precise moment Looby looked across and, seeing the three stooges gawping in her direction, threw a quick wave of recognition at them before returning to her conversation.

'Game, set and match, Michael,' said Tom. 'She's pretending that we're nothing to do with her. We're sticking out like sore thumbs here. Come on, let's go.'

Michael didn't want to go though. 'Look, you two go – I'll walk home later. I'm enjoying it.'

'What about the taxi you were going to pay for? You can't welsh on that,' argued Tom.

'Bloody hell, OK, I'll square it with you next week. I'm staying. You go if you want to.'

As soon as his two friends had departed into the frost-bound night Michael began to feel a little less self-conscious. Could he be taken for a student? Why not? Some of them looked quite ordinary. Luckily he'd got changed after work, although his brown flares, beige tank top and mulberry flower pattern penny drop collar shirt were not, strictly speaking, regulation undergraduate issue. No matter – intoxicated by all of the sights and sounds around him Michael felt himself blend in to the environment.

Michael had never been to a party like this before and he felt wonderful; it was a different world. Michael's senses were further stimulated by the throb of the driving rock music performed by artists who, he had to admit, were largely unknown to him. He nodded amiably at fellow guests as they went to and from to the kitchen and he set himself a strict condition – he wasn't going to go anywhere until he'd at least spoken to her.

After twenty minutes, Looby suddenly appeared at his side. 'Where's your mates, then?'

'Oh, hi. They decided to go,' he shouted over the fade out from *Whole Lotta Love*.

'But you've stayed. Are you having a good time?'

'Yes – it's great. I'm Michael by the way.'

'The burger man. Hello Burger man. You saved my life tonight.'

The opening chords of the next song came crashing through the speakers. 'I love this one,' said Looby. 'Come on.'

Before Michael knew it he was in the middle of the floor, shuffling his feet and nodding his head in emulation of the dancers around him. As Steppenwolf pushed their heavy metal thunder, Michael couldn't take his eyes off Looby. Now she'd dispensed with the coat he could see close up the detail on her embroidered cream silk blouse. She clearly wasn't wearing a bra underneath and Michael felt his excitement mount another notch. He could also smell her distinctive scent. What was it? Musk, definitely, and something else? He recognised a faint whiff of raw onion from the burger.

As the strains of Steppenwolf died away, Neil Young's *When You Dance* caused Michael's senses to tingle even more. Looby threw herself around with a rhythm and passion worthy of Salome. Michael was transported – he could have danced all night, but that wasn't going to happen because as soon as his second dance with Looby finished she shouted at him, 'I'm off now. You staying?'

She was leaving? So soon? '*Not if you're not,*' he thought and trailed after her to where a pile of coats was heaped in the bedroom between the kitchen and the living room. At least it was easier to be heard there. 'Are you going home?' he asked her.

'Yeah, got to get off.'

'Have you far to go?'

'Hardy Lane in Chorlton.'

'I can walk you if you want?'

'Very gallant of you, Burger man, but I've got my bike.'

'I'll push it for you if you like. It's on my way too.' This last statement was a downright fabrication as Chorlton was nowhere near where Michael lived; in fact Michael could walk home in twenty minutes if he wanted to, but that was the last thing on his mind as he desperately sought to prolong the evening in the company of this enchantress.

Michael had no clear motive for his chivalry. He wasn't what was euphemistically called a ladies' man; in fact he was very inexperienced and shy around women. He just didn't want the night to end. He had become enthralled by Looby's sense of freedom, confidence, beauty and mystique, and all he knew was that he had to try to prolong his exposure to her for as long as he could. All thoughts of Carmel had by this stage disappeared in a cloud of Hydes, burger, onions, Player's No. 6, incense, musk and infatuation.

'Alright then,' she replied as she buttoned up her bright red coat and wound the yellow wool scarf around and around her neck. 'If you're going to push my bike, how can I refuse?'

As they ventured outside, the sharp, sub-zero temperature of the crystal clear night impacted on their faces and made their breath condense. Looby unchained her bike from the drainpipe she'd attached it to, and strode off at a brisk lick. Michael immediately made good his offer to push the bike, which amused Looby no end.

'What do you do then?' she asked him. 'You're not a student, are you?'

'Is it *that* obvious?' said Michael in feigned indignation. 'No, I'm not a student at the university. I've finished my academic studies now.' He thought that sounded intriguing enough to pardon his failure to matriculate.

'So what do you do, then?' asked Looby.

This was, of course a perfectly reasonable question, part of the standard conversational formula for all young people meeting for the first time, be it at uni, a pub, a night club or wherever. Often the rules of engagement in such a game entailed avoiding the truth like the plague and claiming an outlandish occupation such as painting the red Smarties or training to be an acrobat. Michael, totally lacking in artifice, couldn't think of anything to say other than the truth. He fancied, as had happened in the past, any conversation following his revelation may be rather curtailed; nevertheless he stuttered, 'I'm an undertaker, actually.'

'You're kidding! I don't believe you!' laughed Looby, who was half expecting him to tell her he worked in a bank.

'No, it's true,' said Michael. 'It's not that funny. It's the family business in Didsbury, and that's what I do.'

'Still don't believe you,' Looby replied. 'Mind you, it's not the sort of thing you'd make up, is it?'

'No, I don't suppose it is,' ventured Michael, now on the edge of despair for having blurted out the truth.

'So you handle dead bodies, like Burke and Hare?'

'Well, no, they were body snatchers, not undertakers. It's a very skilled profession really. Anyway, what are you studying?' asked Michael desperately trying to change the subject.

'English, in the middle of my second year.'

'Do you like it?'

'Yeah – it's OK. A lot of reading, but I don't have that many lectures or tutorials so it's great.'

As the pair traversed Burton Road before turning right on to Nell Lane, Looby didn't appear to be put off in the slightest at making her first acquaintance with a real life Manchester mortician (presumably any mortician at all). She kept asking questions about what he had to do. Was it true that hair and nails on dead bodies kept growing? How did they get bodies that had rigor mortis into the coffins?

She was teasing him, surely? Somehow, Michael was reassured that she was at least still walking with him. It was a good two-mile walk but it felt to Michael that they were devouring the ground at record speed. Michael wished it could have been further still.

As they approached Princess Road, with her destination of Hardy Lane seemingly within touching distance (it wasn't, but it felt like that to Michael), Looby suddenly spotted across the traffic lanes the foreboding and frost shrouded shape of Southern Cemetery looming out of the darkness. 'Look! It's the cemetery. Come on, you give me a personal tour!" and with that she sprinted across the dual carriageway and slipped thought the gate into the blackness beyond.

As Michael, still wheeling Looby's bike, frantically followed her a macabre game of hide and seek played itself out amongst the white encrusted headstones until Michael finally came upon Looby, gasping with laughter, laying flat out on a rather ornate stone tomb. Before Michael could catch his own breath, Looby pulled him down on to the cold slab, and their lips met in a passionate embrace.

As their tongues entwined it felt like an explosion of molten lava against the perishing temperature of the Arctic night. A kiss like Baked Alaska. Michael had never experienced anything as carnal and sensual in his entire life and never would again. Michael's limited sexual experience was of no avail in such an encounter – he was the pupil; she was the master.

As Michael's hand clumsily groped at Looby's breast through the thick layer of her topcoat, she athletically twisted upwards, pushed Michael down on the unyielding tombstone and straddled him. Oblivious to the freezing cold she quickly unbuttoned her coat and blouse, before bending forward to continue kissing Michael whose hands now reached up to meet the brown tipped breasts she had exposed. Then, reaching down, she unzipped Michael's flies, manoeuvred to slide her tights down, and guided him into her. Michael abandoned himself completely to the forces of nature as Looby writhed on top of him; all thoughts of Carmel, family, work, life, friends, the teachings of the church and last Saturday's football results were obliterated from his mind, seemingly forever. The only image to subliminally penetrate his consciousness was that of the angel watching over the grave he and Looby were now desecrating. The seraph was unable to divert his gaze as the hallelujah was drawn, somewhat precipitously, from Michael's lips. Looby, whether similarly in excelsis or just plain disappointed, collapsed in a heap on top of him.

As Michael recovered his senses, he didn't know what to say or do; it was Looby who took the lead in breaking the post-coital spell. 'A graveyard shag with an undertaker – that's a first!'

Michael, oblivious to the imprint on his backside that read *1881.b*, was immediately stung by the apparent mockery displayed by his lover at this moment of blissful union: '*Is she laughing at me?*'

'I can't believe we just did that,' continued Looby as she fastened up her clothes. 'I must be drunker than I thought.'

Michael, too, adjusted his garments as the enormity of their act hit him along with the cold. A wave of guilt replaced the elation he had just felt, not helped by Looby's flippant remarks. The thought went through his head: '*Did she do that just for a joke, or a dare of some sort?*'

He didn't get to find out, for in an instant Looby brought their evening to a close. 'I'm going to head off on the bike. It will be quicker and warmer.'

Michael, dazed and embarrassed in equal measure at this unexpected moment of intimacy with his new acquaintance, could only meekly enquire: 'Can I see you again?'

Her reply, 'Maybe you can buy me a burger sometime,' didn't strike him as being overly encouraging.

And with that she mounted her bicycle, switched on her front and rear lamps, and rode off the down the wide cemetery path of Plot I R/C. Michael collapsed backward, seating himself once more of the tomb of Mrs Violet Charlotte Byrom as he watched the small red light recede into the distance.

PRD minus 14,655.

CHAPTER FOURTEEN

Who Knows Where the Time Goes?

Agnes was waiting for an answer. 'Well, do you know her?'

Michael stared at her for what seemed like an age before finally whispering, 'It's Looby.'

'Looby? Looby is Linda?'

'I think so.'

'And you made her pregnant?'

'I didn't know that.'

'Well, you must have been a callous one, putting it about and not bothering if they might get pregnant.'

'No, Mrs Mortimer, hear me out. I'm as shocked as you to hear this. I must confess that I find it all rather hard to credit. Farren is supposed to be my son?'

'That's what Father Culshaw said. You didn't know apparently, but it strikes me as strange that you can put your girlfriend in the family way and not know about it.'

'But she wasn't my girlfriend, Mrs Mortimer. I only met her once, and, well, things happened, and I never saw her again after that.'

'Oh, I suppose she just jumped on you and you couldn't resist?'

'Well, strange as it may sound, it was a little like that.'

'Pull the other one – I can see you now, Jack the Lad,

like some sort of rutting stag with no concern over the consequences.'

'I implore you, Mrs Mortimer, that wasn't the case. Besides that one-off occasion, I was never unfaithful. It just happened out of the blue. She was, how shall I say, very forward.'

'So you're saying Farren could be someone else's son, not yours?'

'Yes. No. I don't know. I never thought that she could have become pregnant – I assumed she, well, had that in hand. But if Looby is Farren's mother, then there is a possibility that I am his father. But how have you discovered all of this?'

'Here,' said Mrs Mortimer and thrust the letter into Michael's hand. It's all in there. She's been dead now for eight years and can't speak up for herself beyond that.

'Dead?' Michael gasped. 'What happened to her?'

'She led a poor life did that one, no thanks to you it would seem. Killed herself with a drug overdose.'

Struggling to take in this cascade of data, Michael read the letter in silence and tried to force the pieces into place.

'Father Culshaw knew all of this? And never said anything?'

'We discussed it, and he guessed it was you. He wasn't far wrong, was he?'

'Does Farren know about this?'

'No, we couldn't bring ourselves to tell him and besides, we had no proof.'

'But we still have no proof.'

'Not at the moment, but you can have a test to see if you and Farren are related now you've owned up to it.'

'I don't think it's a question of owning up, Mrs Mortimer. This is a tremendous shock to me. I don't know what to say.'

127

'You'll do a test though, won't you?'

'Yes. I must.'

As Agnes left Morrison Family Funeral Services, the issue of the tombstone still unresolved, she was torn between conflicting emotions. Michael Morrison had conceded that Farren could be his son, but maintained he hadn't known about the possibility of this poor girl being pregnant. That's what Father Culshaw had said, but she still felt a flash of anger towards Michael that he'd managed to evade his responsibilities for all these years. As for his account of the one-night stand, he'd not added much detail and it all sounded a bit implausible. He appeared genuinely shocked at the news though – she couldn't deny that. She would also have to concede that Michael Morrison hardly came across as one of life's Lotharios, even allowing for the passage of almost four decades. He'd not denied the possibility of being Farren's father either, and seemed happy to do the DNA test to establish if he was or wasn't, so that must be a good sign.

But what if he was Farren's father? Where would that leave her after all of these years? Her maternal status, unchallenged since Farren was two weeks old, would be reduced at a stroke; she'd merely have been an unpaid babysitting service for an absentee father. How would Farren view her now if Michael Morrison did turn out to be his father? And how would she tell Farren? Should she tell Farren? He'd have to be party to the DNA test presumably? And if and when the truth was established, how would Farren react to discovering he had a real live blood father not to mention a real dead blood mother? Wouldn't he also question her over why she and Ernest had kept it a secret from him over eight years when it could have been addressed back then? Would Farren even believe that she'd only had an inkling for eight years? He may suspect she and Ernest had known all along.

Ernest! What would he think about the can of worms she'd just opened up? 'Nothing good will come of it,' he'd warned. 'No point in raking all of this up – you don't know what it will do to the lad,' he'd said. She decided to head to the church where she could sit in solitude, mull the numerous questions and outcomes over, and beseech some form of heavenly guidance.

As Michael Morrison gently bade farewell to Mrs Mortimer he was still in somewhat of a daze. Could he be the father of Farren Mortimer? He had long ago given up on the prospect of being a father, and Carmel would be spinning in her grave at the news. Could it actually be true though? Poor Looby – the memory of her had remained with him for two-thirds of his life. His 'mad night' had long since assumed the proportion of a dream, a fantasy, something he'd imagined couldn't really have taken place there being no tangible evidence to the contrary. Well there might be evidence now, that was for sure.

He'd never breathed a single word of the night's events to anyone. Certainly not to Carmel, although she did tease him when he suddenly bought Neil Young's *After The Gold Rush* LP – 'Michael, you'll be growing your hair long next – I don't think it will go down well with the mourners!' she'd said. He'd quickly reverted to type so as not to attract any more attention.

Colin and Tom had quizzed him to be sure, but he'd dead-batted their enquiries, merely saying Looby had continued to ignore him at the party, and he had given up without speaking to her, leaving half an hour after them. They certainly had no grounds for suspecting anything else, as that's exactly what they'd predicted when they had taken their early leave of the party. Michael pull a sexy bird? Ha! Never.

Over the Christmas of 1972 Michael had swung between a feeling of shame and guilt at the betrayal of his fiancée and a burning desire to see Looby again. He would replay the sexual encounter in his mind and longed to catch sight of her again. Then he would recall the speed at which she left him at the cemetery, her 'I must be drunker than I thought' reaction at the end of their lovemaking, and his deep-seated suspicion that she had only done it for a dare or out of mockery for him.

In the January of the following year, Michael was on alert to spot Looby. He knew the students would be back now and he lived in hope of bumping into her. He would rehearse the encounter in his mind so he wouldn't be caught flat-footed. Every time he insisted on going to the Canadian Charcoal Pit on a Friday night Tom and Colin would pathetically joke about Michael going 'studie hunting' or 'fancying a Looby bun'. After a while, with no sign of her, the encounter was forgotten and they moved on to other topics of varying degrees of banality.

Michael didn't forget though, and continued to keep his secret close to his chest. He knew Looby lived at Hardy Lane, presumably in a student residence, and that she studied English. Should he go and look for her? No, he'd get locked up for hanging around the university campus preying on a student, and if he did happen to see her, how could he cope with the inevitable rejection? As the months progressed, Michael had to concede that the affair, if he could even call it that, was over as soon as it began. It wasn't his lot to think about anything other than what was already destined for him.

Gradually he began to refocus on his wedding plans and future life with Carmel, pushing, as well as he could, all thoughts of Looby into the furthest recesses of his mind.

One thing he never gave a single consideration towards was the possibility that Looby may be pregnant following their graveyard grapple. If it had crossed his mind in the days after their liaison he had quickly dismissed it – she was a student, she would be on the pill, and she obviously knew what she was doing so wouldn't be taking any chances. No, that wasn't the problem – he just yearned to see her again.

Now he knew the truth – for in his mind there was no need for a DNA test – he was confronted with a number of ghosts and outcomes. Would his son want to know him? Mrs Mortimer had been a bit fiery when they'd discussed it, and seemed to blame him – would she make his life difficult? If the news got out, how would he be viewed in the community? What would Carmel's family think of him – it would make his entire marriage to Carmel look like a fraud, surely? He couldn't help but having the same thought as he tried to guess their reaction.

He and Mrs Mortimer had agreed to say nothing to anybody until they were sure what was what and could take it from there. Good, that was sensible. His thoughts returned to Farren. A son! After all those barren years. He had thought he was the end of the Morrison line. Had it been rescued at the eleventh hour? The family line *and* business upheld? No, that wasn't going to happen. His son was actually one of the reasons his business was on the skids. How many times had he joined in the condemnation of this gimmicky whizz kid who was helping apply the coup de grace to the traditional independent family funeral trade? The irony.

Michael's thoughts raged all night in this manner. Looby – what must she have gone through? Did her being pregnant contribute to her downward slide, which would make him a contributory cause? Or was her mental frailty part of the reason they had actually made love in the cemetery that cold frosty night so many years before?

Before he turned in for the night he logged on to his computer and ordered a DNA testing kit online. He couldn't risk going into Boots for one, even the branch in town. That was his side of the bargain fulfilled. Now he had to await news from Mrs Mortimer on how and when she was going to tackle Farren and how the test could and should be conducted. As he turned off his bedside lamp and lay in the darkness, he thought both of Looby and of Carmel.

'Goodnight, Looby. I won't let you down. Goodnight Carmel. I'm sorry.'

PRD minus 154.

CHAPTER FIFTEEN

The End

Farren started the board meeting in a businesslike manner: 'Right, what have we got?' After his absence from work following Ernest's death and funeral, extended by his soul-searching week in the wilderness, he had determined to get a firm grip back on his life. No more doubts. He had a business that was going places, and it needed him at the helm to succeed. That, at least, was what he was telling himself.

People in the office were apprehensive about seeing him on his return. What should they say to him? How would he react? Most were surprised to encounter a positive, almost bouncy Farren whose brio exuded a clear 'business as usual' message.

Despite everyone's guardedness about how Farren was feeling after his father's funeral, Jon waded straight in even before item one on the agenda. 'Can I just mention that we may have a slight challenge on our hands from NAFF?' (this was the name used by AMOLAD insiders for the National Association of Funeral Directors).

Graeme and Peter shot a glance at each other – wasn't it a bit insensitive of Jon to start talking funerals in Farren's first five minutes back? Plus, it was hardly a priority.

Farren, appearing to not even notice, merely enquired: 'What are they moaning about now?'

'It's not really one for us, to be honest, it's just the knock on effect we'll have to be careful about,' said Jon. 'Basically, they're protesting that the extra bank holiday is another day less in the calendar in which to conduct funerals, which given the nature of PRD is a bit of a joke.'

'Let them rant all they want is my opinion,' Farren said. 'They're on thin ice in any case. They can't attack PRD and they know it, plus they'll still handle all of the funerals that would have taken place on PRD so it won't ultimately cost them. No, it's hardly an issue for us; it's trivial. Let's just get on with the PRD update.'

Jon did as he was bidden and presented the latest status report on PRD planning. As he went through the preparations he cited, more than once, key areas of responsibility that had now been taken back 'in-house' by the government for its own agency teams to deliver.

'Hang on, Jon. It seems as if we're being reduced to bit-part players in all of this,' said Farren. 'This must have badly hit our revenue projections for PRD. What's going on?'

Jon, looking slightly uncomfortable, replied: 'I think it's quite standard for the government – they're control freaks, and they see this as their gig. And they're right up to a point. Yes, we had been hoping to get more income from various aspects of the event, but at least our exposure is reduced if they're taking it all on themselves. Remember how often they change their minds about things?'

'Or they think we're not capable of delivering,' said Farren.

'I don't think that's the case,' said Jon, his face reddening a little. 'It's just the way they are.'

Graeme, having prepared the updated financial report, answered Farren's question. 'I calculate a shortfall on projected income to the tune of a quarter of a million pounds following the re-allocation of work by the government. It will hit hard against projections, but it's not calamitous.'

'Calamitous to whom?' said Farren, irritated at the rest of the board's somewhat cavalier attitude to the company's financial fortunes.

'We'll still make a profit this year, an OK one at that,' said Jon.

'Yes, Jon, but what's the point of working our arses off to go backwards?' enquired Farren, whose sense of positivity was being eroded by the second.

'Well, if you'd have taken a bit more interest, maybe we'd not be in this position now,' Jon replied. Graeme and Peter once again exchanged looks at Jon's effrontery, and Jon's face blushed a still deeper shade of red as he realised he had overstepped the mark.

Farren fixed Jon with an obdurate stare. 'That's not really the sort of comment I'd expect from my director of operations whose responsibility it is, and I quote, "to make the trains run on time". I may also remind you that the revenue forecasts, which we now learn are a quarter of a million light, are *your* forecasts.'

Jon said nothing in reply, merely shrugging his assent.

Farren closed the line of discussion: 'Maybe, Jon, it's a topic we can take up outside of this board meeting?'

Annie Brooks sat in the reception of The Steeple ahead of her meeting with Farren Mortimer. Given his commitments, and his recent bereavement, it had taken two months for Annie to get through the door. As she waited she watched the huge plasma screen in front of her streaming infomercials for the various products and services the group now offered.

As usual she had made an effort to look her best for the meeting; she had gone, with no sense of irony, for a killer little black dress with a Chanel boucle jacket flecked in black and white. She knew she looked stunning – she was dressed for battle after all.

Farren had instructed his secretary to book Annie in for a one-hour meeting slot after his board meeting – he knew he had to play the game following Adlington's pointed introduction. His encounter with Jon hadn't exactly put him in the right frame of mind for this meeting, but he knew he had to go through with it and get it out of the way.

After initially meeting Annie, Farren had been rather intrigued as to how this ex-model had managed to make such a noise over speeding regulations where so many victims' families and supporters had failed in the past. The marketeer in him was impressed. He also knew he'd be asked to help in a number of ways – he would decide how far that assistance would extend once he'd met her properly.

Farren had googled Annie Brooks after meeting her at the Forum and was delighted to find a selection of images of her sporting lingerie and swimwear from her modelling days. Not very classy shots, it must be said, but there was no doubting she had a frame on her. He couldn't also help noticing, sprinkled among the mainly HASTE issued material, a few comments – some of which were bordering on libel – hinting at a less than conventional career path. There was more than a suggestion that the veracity of Annie's official biog on the HASTE website should be taken with a bushel of salt. Farren wasn't perturbed in the slightest at this as he knew that in the popular media culture of 'build 'em up and knock 'em down' this was just a standard rite of passage – he'd had his fair share of detractors himself.

When Annie was ushered into his office – the original sacristy of the church – Farren welcomed her politely and determined to keep all thoughts of the board meeting at bay for at least an hour.

He was immediately struck by how attractive she was – not a classical beauty by any means, but clearly a woman who was determined, possibly too determined, to not leave anything to the imagination. Annie Brooks didn't do mystique or subtlety.

'Farren, it's so good of you to see me. I know how difficult it must have been to squeeze me into your diary,' she said as she seated herself on the leather sofa running the length of the office. 'I have to say, what beautiful offices you have.'

'That's very kind – we like them,' replied Farren as he had a thousand times before.

Annie had a lot to get through, so once settled, she started on her pitch. 'I know how stacked out you are, Farren, so I'll get straight to the point in what I'd like to ask you.'

Farren was immediately struck by this confident style. 'Oh, please, feel free.'

'I don't know how much you know already about the work of HASTE and what we're trying to achieve, and why I set up the charity in the first place?' she simpered.

'Oh, I'm well up to date – hard to miss, Mrs Brooks, and if I may say so, a very well executed campaign.'

'Oh, call me Annie, please! "Mrs Brooks" makes me feel about fifty years old!'

'No chance of you being mistaken for that.'

'Why, thank you! Anyway, the point is I need funding to help me continue the work I've started. Now, don't look so alarmed, Farren – I'm not asking you for a donation. What I

137

had in mind, so I'll cut to the chase, is if we could hook up with your Forever in our Minds site and run a donation scheme on your pages? You know, pop-up ads wherever a motoring accident is mentioned, which would allow people to click through to our donation page or text a donation to HASTE. People could ask for donations instead of sending flowers, that kind of thing.' Annie didn't wait for Farren to response, but continued seamlessly now she was in full flow. 'There's almost 2000 people a year killed on the UK roads and over 200000 injured – we think it would be good for you in a corporate sense to get into bed with us on this one – it's a real PR opportunity.'

Exactly the same scheme HASTE had punted before, as Farren suspected it would be, only now the proposition had reached the upper levels. 'Well, that's certainly an interesting idea,' said Farren, 'and I can see the possibilities...'

'I can feel a "but" coming on...'

'No, please, don't feel that. It's just that I will have to run this by my marketing team. We've not tied up with any charities before so I'd want to ensure it worked for us, and more importantly, didn't open us up to millions of similar requests from other charities asking the same. That could get messy.'

'I think having an exclusive arrangement of this type would work tremendously well,' replied Annie. 'In fact, once you'd linked up with us you could cite us as your preferred partner exactly so you wouldn't have to deal with any other charities.'

Farren smiled – Annie was either well briefed, or a bloody good hustler. It was like negotiating with a lap dancer – and Farren had experienced enough trips out to Spearmint Rhino and the like in his agency days to recognise the similarity. The temptress who, having dulled the victim's senses with the opium of desire, would control the entire negotiation with the mug punter. The word 'no' eliminated from his vocabulary, he would find his wallet considerably lighter by the end of the evening without anything tangible having changed hands. In fact, yes, that's what Annie's whole demeanour reminded him of: a lap dancer.

'That's a really valid point,' said Farren in order to prolong the hope. He didn't want to say 'no' outright – he'd get round to that after it looked as if they'd given it a lot of thought. 'Is there anything else you'd like to cover at today's meeting?'

'Actually, there is. As Nigel – the Under Secretary of course – mentioned, I'd be really interested in talking to you about my overall campaign strategy. As a marketing guru you'd be invaluable to our aims. I know it's a big ask, but if you could spare some time to give me some advice I'd be very grateful. We are saving lives after all.'

'Well, put like that, how can I refuse?' Farren realised that, on this point at least, the word 'no' had been skilfully disarmed from his vocabulary too. 'Of course I'd be happy to help. It would have to be in an informal way as I can't really get tied up in too many things at the moment, but it wouldn't be a problem for me to give your approach the once-over and possibly make some top-line suggestions.'

'I can't tell you how delighted I am to hear that. If we're going to keep it informal, then maybe I can treat you to dinner and we can take it from there?'

'Why not? That would be a pleasure.'

As Annie left The Steeple she chalked up another win. Surely, with a bit of persuasion, she could convince Farren to run the donation scheme, and get a free marketing audit at the same time. She loved her work.

Farren chuckled to himself as Annie departed. She took some beating did Annie Brooks. What a performer. Yes, she'd certainly learned the art of negotiation in a lap bar or worse. He'd play along for now to keep Adlington sweet, but he wasn't going to fall for the oldest trick in the book, not with her anyway.

Following the morning's board meeting and his shoehorned session with Annie Brooks, Farren next rushed to Bocca Di Lupo in Soho for his lunch with Kieran McDonaghy to be updated on the shooting schedule for *Made Men*.

Kieran was even later than he was. As Farren nursed a sparkling water his thoughts returned to Jon's performance earlier in the day. The little shit, trying to have a go at him when he couldn't do his own job? Insubordinate cretin. There was no doubt about it – Jon was becoming a problem. Once so positive and dependable, he was fast becoming the subversive in the camp. *'Well, he isn't going to get away with this,'* thought Farren. *'I'm going to have it out with him.'*

Despite the 'fresh positive start' approach of the morning Farren couldn't escape the fact that the shortfall in projected income would actually make this financial year less productive than the previous year, despite the increased turnover and profile, as overheads and head count had soared in the last twelve months. He recalled the adage one of his old agency bosses used to preach: 'Turnover is vanity, profit sanity.' How true that was, and his spirits began to sag once again at the thought that AMOLAD was turning out to be a huge albatross around his neck.

Kieran arrived in a flurry and Farren immediately snapped back into his professional persona to greet the rising television celebrity.

'Farren, grand to see you,' gushed Kieran. 'And I'm sorry for your loss.'

'Thank you, that's kind of you.' replied Farren. 'But we're getting back to normal now; keeping busy helps.'

'Well, you're going to be busy on this for one, for sure,' Kieran said as he beckoned the waiter to come over to take a fresh drinks order. 'It's all coming together now.'

Once they'd ordered a variety of small sampling plates covering the length and breadth of rustic Italian cooking, Farren listened as Kieran outlined the plans they'd drawn up for the *Made Men* programme. Normally, this task would have been the responsibility of the production team, but Kieran had insisted on taking it on personally in order to get closer to his subject and 'build rapport'. More importantly he wanted to make sure Farren hadn't 'lost it' over his dad's funeral.

As Kieran enthusiastically briefed him, Farren took in how the director was to place a fair amount of emphasis on the anthropological aspects of death and mourning as well as the historical and religious context – it sounded like an intelligent treatment for the programme, not some sort of gushing tabloid feature.

Kieran excitedly hailed how the *Billy Liar* film clip was still in, and how this had led them to identify a number of other classic film clips they thought depicted the traditional British attitude to death and bereavement in an apposite and recognisable manner. 'You know, to lighten it up, and to ram home the point that, at least until you came along, we were all a bit stiff upper lipped about it all,' said Kieran between a mouthful of courgette flowers with mozzarella and honey.

'Well, you're not stiff upper lipped, as you're Irish,' said Farren, beginning to warm to the programme outline.

'Well, that's true, but we're just as traditional and superstitious in a way, so on the same page,' replied Kieran who was thoroughly relieved at the way the proposed programme treatment was going down with its subject. 'No need to worry about Farren,' thought Kieran. 'He's still all there.'

Relaxing, Kieran went into overdrive on what film clips they were looking at, from *Citizen Kane* to *Hamlet* and from *Harry Potter* to *Wuthering Heights*. Farren couldn't help but take in Kieran's performance, because that's exactly what it was, a performance. The Dublin dynamo hardly paused for breath as he spoke, continually waving his arms around to make a point, swearing like a trooper and enthusiastically punching Farren on the arm every time he appeared to agree with him. Kieran seemed capable of eating, drinking and conversing simultaneously almost without pause, and on top of this still managed to check his iPhone at least every thirty seconds for emails, tweets and texts.

Farren watched in fascination as the whirling dervish of a presenter multi-tasked. Farren used his own iPhone slavishly, but he'd never seen anything like this – Kieran's command of his smartphone was the telecoms equivalent of handling air traffic control over Heathrow, even allowing for a French controllers' strike.

Finally, having finished his blood orange granita with almonds and mint, Kieran excused himself to go to the gents. Just then Farren heard a faint buzz and was alerted to the fact that Kieran had left his mobile phone under the dainty man bag positioned next to his place setting. Farren was surprised that Kieran could be parted from his phone for as long as two minutes and, curious as to the level of activity he'd seen on it over the past hour, couldn't resist sneaking a quick look.

Casually leaning forward and picking up the handset he could see a message displayed on the screen: "*@getalife @wappinglie Dead good piece on mr eulogys dads funeral. LOL although no laughing matter.*" As a confused and surprised Farren studied the screen the message disappeared from the locked screen. He immediately put the phone back under Kieran's bag. What did the message mean? What was the piece on Mr Eulogy – him – and his Dad's funeral that was referred to in the tweet? He didn't know who @getalife was, but he could see it was a direct message to @wappinglie, not a re-tweet. That would mean...

Kieran burst back into restaurant and collapsed back into his seat. 'Great lunch, Farren, plenty of progress I think. It's all looking good.'

Farren smiled warmly, and stood up. 'If you don't mind Kieran, I'm going to have to dash. Lots to catch up on.'

'Absolutely, of course, you must have,' replied Kieran. 'Listen, just leave the bill to me, and I'll catch up with you next week. Great lunch again. Onwards and upwards.'

Farren shook Kieran's hand, nodded and made a quick exit into Archer Street. Turning round the corner, he headed straight for the nearest coffee bar. Ordering an espresso he sat down and pulled out his phone. Clicking on his Twitter app, he searched for @wappinglie. He knew of @wappinglie's reputation, but had decided a long time ago not to follow too many accounts so had never really read her. Finding it, he checked the timeline to see recent tweets, scrolling down until he found the link to @wappinglie's blog from the previous Friday – 'Mr Eulogy fails screen test at Dad's send-off.' He read the account in grim faced silence, each line a sickening kick in the teeth.

Kieran McDonaghy was @wappinglie, and pulling off pretending to be a woman at the same time. The devious, crafty, duplicitous git. Farren finally put the phone down and collected his thoughts. How bloody two-faced and slimy was Kieran to have written that, particularly when he was being so unctuous with him over the programme. Typical journalist. Still, it was bloody clever to have created such an alter ego, and he'd obviously managed to maintain his cover.

He pondered how he should handle it. People had said plenty of negative things about him and AMOLAD before so another attack was nothing new, although this blog did exceed previous standards of poor taste. No point in appealing to a journalist's sense of fairness, and to be truthful, Farren needed Kieran to do a good job on him on *Made Men*. For now he needed to sit on it. He swiftly clicked on 'set up new account' and created a new identity that couldn't be attributed to him, @justfishing, before making @wappinglie the first account to follow. Now he'd keep track of what @wappinglie had to say for himself – or herself.

He pressed back against the unyielding rigidity of the plastic chair. Christ, what a day, and he'd come into it determined to 'get back on the horse' so to speak. His heart sank once more as he felt the albatross around his neck weigh down a fraction heavier.

Suddenly his mobile rang. It was Mum. Why was she ringing? She didn't normally call during the day. He clicked the answer button, but before he had the chance to even say 'hello', she spoke: 'Farren, it's Mum. Something very important has come up and you need to come home as soon as you can.'

'What is it, are you alright?' asked a panicked Farren, fearing yet more bad news.

'Best discussed when we meet. Can you get here for tonight? I wouldn't ask if it wasn't important.'

His albatross having gained yet another few extra pounds, an apprehensive Farren could only say: 'Yes, of course. I'll be there.'

As Kieran waited for the bill in Boca di Lupo, he reflected on a successful lunch. Thank God Farren seemed to have suffered no ill effects from his recent bereavement. Everything was still 'go' for *Made Men*, and there was no doubt that Farren was being supportive and cooperative with the production's overall approach. If only the same could be said of some of the other subjects.

Kieran felt a little guilty though. He wondered if Farren had seen the @wappinglie blog? He'd not set out to pan Farren; it's simply that he had felt a modicum of frustration when Farren had turned down the production company's request to cover the funeral as part of the *Made Men* shoot. When the junior researcher's report from the funeral came back in, he'd found it hard to resist the temptation to give it the @wappinglie treatment – it had just been a bit of fun. And hadn't he had the highest number of hits ever with that blog?

If he had been born 50 years earlier, they would have said Kieran had ink in his veins. In 21st century Britain, however, Kieran could be more accurately described as being electronically hardwired into the media circuit board.

Kieran had started @wappinglie as an idle joke, in response

to a less than flattering hatchet job on him by The Voice newspaper. Complaining about the story wouldn't get him anywhere, so he hit on the idea of creating the pseudonym to poke fun at the machinations of the tabloid and its publishing group by posing as someone who may actually work as a journalist in the national news media. Kieran soon learned that it was far easier to create interesting and amusing tweets under a nom de plume than it was to carefully construct his own @kieranmcdonaghy posts.

Having access to news feeds often enabled Kieran to make @wappinglie the first to let followers know of breaking news items; this, consequently, helped spread the word and increased the number of followers. @wappinglie's true appeal though lie in the colourful opinions presented by its author, depicting an on-the-edge reporter who championed true journalism, railed against the excesses of the media, wannabe celebrities and-on-the make parliamentarians, and presented, at the same time, a running commentary on a somewhat chaotic and louche lifestyle. Nobody knew who @wappinglie was and Kieran was careful to keep the identity of this contrived persona concealed. In fact, to the feed's growing army of followers @wappinglie was actually a sassy female reporter.

Naturally, running his own Twitter account, Kieran had to be careful not to mix up the two identities or expose the true authorship of @wappinglie. He always, always double-checked accounts before posting. Tweeting while drunk was an even bigger challenge, but Kieran wasn't working in the media for nothing, and could hold his booze. He hadn't compromised @wappinglie's identity yet. Or so he thought.

Kieran couldn't help but marvel when the number of

followers for @wappinglie overtook his own moderately successful Twitter account. Kieran shrewdly recognised that, the cult of celebrity being what it was, anonymity actually had far more appeal in the long run. Kieran built on this by creating a serious and thought provoking blog site for @wappinglie's views, and then extended the brand with a range of @wappinglie merchandise which became a must buy for the growing army of followers – nobody would ever have been interested in Kieran McDonaghy mugs and t-shirts. What had started as a diverting sideline for him gradually began to assume more and more importance in his overall career trajectory.

Deciding to post a tweet before he left, he let @wappinglie's 93,265 followers know: *'Lunch cancelled due to bully of a news editor. Doorstepping at short notice without thermals. Need hot macchiato now! Brrrrrrr.'*

PRD minus 152.

CHAPTER SIXTEEN

If It Be Your Will

Farren worried all the way up the M1 and M6 as to what could be wrong. It wasn't like Mum to make dramatic phone calls and summon his presence. This was serious. Could Mum be ill? She'd shouldered a lot in recent years, and the strain must have been enormous. Everybody focused on Ernest because of his illness while Agnes just carried on giving, giving, and giving. Had her body simply capitulated to goodness knows what now one of her main reasons for living had gone? Maybe she'd been ill all along and not told anyone? He prayed he was wrong; he couldn't bear to lose Mum as well as Dad, but he'd heard how some couples that lived together for years often expired within short order of each other. No, let it be something else.

Could it be the will? Hardly, he would have thought. In any case, Farren was an executor so knew everything, such as it was, automatically went to Agnes. Even if Ernest had experienced a last minute change of mind and tried to leave everything to the local cat rescue, it wouldn't be legal. No, it couldn't be anything like that.

Or maybe a complication with Ernest's cause of death? Farren had wondered if they might do a post-mortem on Ernest given the nature of his ailment, but no, that hadn't been deemed necessary. But what if the GP had questioned the Health Authority over this now the burial had taken place? Could it be something like that? As he passed Manchester Airport, he steeled himself. Whatever it was, he would soon know.

Agnes met him at the door, and ushered him into the kitchen. 'Thanks for coming, love. Hope I didn't scare you.'

'Well, you did a bit.'

She boiled the kettle and made tea as they indulged in small talk, both ignoring, for now, the elephant in the room that would soon be loudly trumpeting its presence.

Finally, they were ready.

'What is it Mum? Is it you? Are you all right?'

'No, Farren. It's not me. I'm as well as I could be under the circumstances. I miss Ernest, but that's not why I called you.'

Farren looked imploringly at her, urging her to get to the point.

'No, love, it's you. I think your real father may have shown up.'

Agnes shocked herself at the brevity, the directness, of this communication. All day long she'd tried to work out how to break the news gently to Farren, but, as per her frankness in asking Michael Morrison outright about Linda Wilson, she'd done it again.

Farren was speechless. For years he'd wondered about his true parents, who they were and what had happened to them. Very early on he'd learned from Father Culshaw that nobody knew who his real father was and that his mother was dead – Farren hadn't had the nerve to ask the parish priest how he knew that. While he thought that such an account was just a bit *too* convenient, he'd by and large bought into that version of events. He had become aware of his parents' – his adoptive parents' – reluctance to address the subject, so had learned not to raise it with them, and if he couldn't discuss it with them then who could he discuss it with? He'd long thought about tackling Ernest and Agnes over what more they could possibly know, but stayed his hand as such enquiries may have been interpreted as an act of betrayal, a rejection of the couple who had brought him up. Outwardly he had accepted the official line, but inwardly he'd never given up the hope, no not hope – more the possibility – that some day he may discover more information. As AMOLAD grew, he'd thought at one stage of hiring a private detective to discover who his true parents were, but where would he start? It could only be with Ernest and Agnes. Besides, the truth may be as simple as had been stated. Worse still, if that wasn't the truth, what would the real story reveal and would he really want to find out?

Finally, he broke the silence with the obvious question: 'Who is it?'

'Oh, Farren, I'm so sorry. It's been a bolt from the blue and I didn't know how to tell you, but the thing is we can't be sure until we do a test.'

'A test? OK, I see. But who is it?'

'He doesn't want you to know until you have a positive test – it's for your benefit; just in case he's not your father.'

'For my benefit? Mum, you are going to have to tell me more than this.'

'All I can say is that this man has told me that he spent a night with your mother, the night it appears she got pregnant, and all the signs point to the baby being you.'

'My mother? You've found out who she is too? This has all happened in the last few days?'

'Oh dear. Look, let me tell you what I know.'

Agnes then proceeded to give Farren an abbreviated account of what Father Culshaw had told her and Ernest, both at the beginning and eight years previously. How she and Ernest endured countless agonies over whether to tell Farren or not. Not being able to identify the father, and the mother being dead (Agnes was aware of how she'd just brought Farren's real mother to life for all of thirty seconds before killing her off again) they'd not gone any further with it. She confessed her unease that maybe Ernest and herself had short-changed Farren over the past eight years when they could have done more to act on the information they'd received. She studiously didn't mention she had Linda's letter at this point as she still had to protect Michael Morrison's identity until they had the test results. Michael had taken over from Ernest as her collaborator-in-chief in this carefully planned encounter with Farren – they had to be 100% sure.

'So now, to be absolutely certain, you should do this DNA test and then we'll know once and for all.'

'What I don't understand is how he's just popped up now? How did he find out about me, and why didn't he try to find me before? And my real mother was around and I could have seen her. Why didn't she make contact?' asked Farren, not unreasonably.

'He's only just found out about the possibility of you being his son himself. It's very complicated. The important thing is to see if he is your father, and then he can tell you more. You do want to find out, don't you?'

'Yes. I do. I've a lot of questions. A bloody lot of questions,' replied Farren. 'What do I have to do?'

'We have to take a swab from the inside of your cheek. He's already done his. Then we'll send them off to a lab to see if they match. It will take four days, and then we'll know for sure.'

Farren felt a wave building that he knew would soon envelop him in blackness. He quickly excused himself from the kitchen table to seek refuge in the bathroom until the storm passed.

Lying in bed in his old bedroom later that night, Farren's mind was still racing. He should have been told. He instinctively guessed that he still wasn't being told the whole truth – why, after all, was his 'dad' making contact with Agnes and not him directly? At first Farren couldn't understand why they were conducting this charade over the DNA test? Or maybe it was sensible to establish the facts first? Could this just be some random guy claiming paternity? Stranger things had happened – he was in the public eye after all. Yes, he had to concur that they had to be sure – what if he was introduced to a person claiming to be his dad only to discover that he wasn't – that would be worse than this uncertainty.

On the other hand, if this person *was* his real dad what would that mean for both of them? What would he be like – thin, fat, handsome, ugly, pleasant, obnoxious? Presumably he worked still, but what as? He'd at least established from Agnes that he was a widower and he didn't have any children, so no brothers and sisters for him. He'd also learned that he was a Mancunian. Was he successful and happy? Had he achieved in life? Was he a red or a blue, or neither? Did he actually want a son after all of these years?

Then there was his poor old Mum. He believed her that she and Ernest knew nothing about his parents when he was adopted, but they'd found out enough, surely, to tell him eight years ago. Bloody Father Culshaw – he'd never liked him, acting like the Holy Pontiff himself the way he went about sticking his nose in everywhere. He'd probably known the full story all along, but he was dead now so no point in conjecturing any further in that direction.

His real mum was dead, a nut job by the sounds of it. Had he inherited those genes? These thoughts pursued each other around and around his head well into the early hours of the morning, and he had to get up at 6.00am to make an early start back to London.

Would all be revealed in four days? In a fitful sleep he dreamed that he was seated on a TV studio set opposite four men all dressed in dark suits and wearing bags on their heads. Three of them wore a number on their lapel – 1, 2, 3; the fourth wore a badge that said 'Unknown'. A slick presenter, looking remarkably like Kieran McDonaghy, held an envelope in his hand and was telling the studio audience that it contained the truth about Farren Mortimer's dad – was it number 1, 2 or 3, or worse still would the result say the hunt has to go on?

'I'm about to reveal the contents of this envelope which will put Farren out of his misery and solve the biggest puzzle of his entire existence. Or could the findings simply throw him back on the scrapheap of uncertainty for the rest of his life? Farren, I'm ready if you're ready. Audience, are you ready? Join us after the break....'

PRD minus 151.

CHAPTER SEVENTEEN

Hurt

'You shouldn't get so worked up, darling. It's just not worth it.' Becky Bell's right ear was ringing from the stream of invective about Farren Mortimer she was receiving down the phone from an irate Jon.

She slowed down her pace on the step machine at the ladies only gym where she was a member. 'You're just having a bad day, darling. Calm down. You *can* be a little over-sensitive at times.'

After a pause: 'Well, yes, he does sound like he's getting worse from what you're saying, but he's only just come back to work after his father's funeral so maybe he's still getting back into things?'

She wiped the perspiration from her face. 'I don't want you to do anything rash, darling. I just want you to be happy.' Why did he always ring her when she was in the gym? She paused for a drink of water. 'Are you sure you're not doing anything wrong to upset him?' All she heard in response to her innocent question was a further stream of invective, this time aimed at her. Then the line went dead.

'Just wanted to catch up on how things are going, Nigel, particularly on this People's Remembrance Day initiative.' The minister had summoned his Parliamentary Under Secretary for Social Responsibility for tea.

'It's all going swimmingly, Minister. All in hand,' replied Nigel as he dropped two sugar cubes into his porcelain cup of Earl Grey.

'There was a certain difficulty at the Forum I believe, over the former PM's somewhat premature obituary?'

'Ah, well, yes, but that had nothing to do with PRD, *per se*.'

'I understand that a fake memorial page appeared on the AMOLAD site, which doesn't look good, you must admit Nigel, as they are our advisers and consultants in all of this?'

'That's not strictly true, Minister. The fabricated in memoriam site didn't actually appear on the AMOLAD owned site – it was merely a hoax designed to *look* like it was from there.'

'Well, that's the same difference as far as most people are concerned.'

'It was taken down quickly, and most of the media didn't make a direct link.'

'Nigel, these are mere details. I have to point out to you that the PM, for one, was less than impressed at this unfortunate gaffe.'

'Really, Minister, it was outside of anyone's control. It was apparently the work of some rogue street artist who has been making a habit of attacking AMOLAD.'

'So you *could* have foreseen something of this nature happening?'

'Not exactly, Minister. But I do take your point. In fact you'll be pleased to know that since the spring conference I have been more than robust and have pulled various aspects of the implementation programme away from AMOLAD and assigned these tasks to our roster of agencies. Taking precautions, you see.'

'Well, as long as you're sure Nigel. You don't need me to remind you that the PM is now taking a particular interest in this event. Nobody wants a cock-up, least of all you, Nigel.'

'Absolutely, Minister. I fully understand.'

'You're nothing but a bloody tart. You don't give a shit about me and Donny. All you're interested in is your precious "career". God knows why I married you – I must have been mad.'

Stuart Brooks was agitated. He'd been unhappy with his wife and the mother of his child for a while now. Since he'd first helped Annie get this HASTE thing off the ground, it had taken over. At first he'd been delighted that she was doing something positive about the appalling accident that had nearly claimed their son. He was pleased that it energised her and gave her a purpose. As things had progressed though, he couldn't help but suspect that this was all about Annie. She now saw herself as some sort of Mother Teresa figure, a crusader for justice, a reformer. What rubbish.

Deep down Stuart knew that the accident was a golden lottery ticket for Annie who was determined to build a celebrity career on it. She was jetting here, appearing there, and was never out of the media. He should have been proud of her appearance at the government conference but all he could feel was the gulf between them growing wider and wider. Not all of the media coverage about Annie was complimentary either. Some papers had been trying to dig up stories about her earlier modelling career while others had been painting her as a ruthless bimbo.

What was also troubling Stuart was that Annie was spending an increasing number of nights away from home – God only knew what she was getting up to with her new circle of acquaintances. The lads at training would take the mick every time she was in the paper, and his own mother was telling him he needed to get a grip on Annie as she was neglecting both him and their son.

For Annie though, used to conflict throughout her life, her husband's entreaties were falling on deaf ears. 'Go stuff yourself. You're just jealous 'cos I'm better known than you now. Who are you? A little footballer with a little team, who soon won't be able to play.'

'You're a cow, Annie. An A1 cow. You've not answered my question about whether you're sleeping with anyone, have you? Is having a go at me your way of admitting it?'

'Don't be ridiculous. I'm not sleeping with anyone. I can't believe how negative you're being when I'm trying to, well, save lives. How bloody selfish can you be?'

'Me? Selfish? You? Saving lives? Talk about brass neck. All you've saved is a shit career that was over before it began. Well, enjoy your moment in the sun, but don't expect me and Donny to be here waiting for you when it all goes tits-up. Because we won't!'

In Smudger's studio, a gigantic eighteen-stone tub of lard going by the name of Malcolm Storm sipped his diet Coke as he gave his mystery client the benefit of his advice. 'You need to broaden your range, Dazza, is what I think. I mean the stuff is flying out, and we're charging what we like for it, but believe me, interest has a habit of coming and going in waves. You've got to be a bit more David Bowie – kill off Ziggy while he's on the top, and become the Thin White Duke instead.'

'He did "Aladdin Sane", "Diamond Dogs" and "Young Americans" between Ziggy and the Thin White Duke,' replied Smudger, not exactly warming to his agent's metaphor.

'See, exactly my point. Ch-ch-ch changes!'

'Can we drop the Bowie thing, Malcolm? I'm not finding it helpful.'

'Yeah, OK, but the point is, and let me reiterate, you have to move into different phases, evolve your canon if you want to call it that. Otherwise you'll end up repeating the same style of work forever like Lowry or someone. Sixty years of bloody matchstick men, and that isn't commercial, I can tell you. Look at Hirst, look at Emin – no sooner done a theme then, bang, off to something else before anyone can work out if it's any good or not.'

'I do have a broad range of work,' protested Smudger. 'And it's very varied in terms of the media I use. And it *is* good.'

'Yes, well, that's true, but you've been banging on about the same subjects too much is my view. Take AMOLAD – a great laugh, I know, but it's time to be worldlier, more global. Take on governments, regimes and tyrants. Go international – that's where the big money is.'

'I don't do *that* much stuff on AMOLAD,' said Smudger by way of defence.

'Try asking them that!' said Malcolm. 'I don't know why they get up your nose so much anyway.'

'I just think everything they do is crass. Life isn't a reality TV programme and everybody doesn't have to be famous. I can't stand that kind of shit.'

'Whatever. All I'm saying is that while you're in the box seat you should be planning your next move; call the shots. Don't put yourself in a position where you have to react.'

Smudger, feeling like he'd just been told off by his infant school teacher for wearing the wrong colour shoes to assembly, reluctantly recognised that there was a salient point being made.

'I'll think about it,' he said.

David Fleming, the producer of *Made Men*, was conducting an update meeting on the series and was making his feelings clear about the script and schedule for the Farren Mortimer programme. 'All it is, is that's it's looking a bit, you know, light. There's plenty of interest in there, but we need more on him; he's the subject, and I'm still not getting the real man – what makes him tick, what gets him out of bed in the morning. I think we need to know.'

'I think he comes across really well in it,' ventured Kieran, conscious that any criticism of his first foray into serious TV was perforce a criticism of himself.

'Yes, he does. And that's just it – he comes across as being *too* nice. There's no edge to him. We should have more controversy – after all, he's ruffled a few feathers, so let's see more of that.'

'But I thought that *Made Men* was meant to laud these British entrepreneurs, to praise their achievements, their singular thinking, commercial savvy and determination?' said Kieran.

'Absolutely, but it will be bloody dull television unless we inject a bit more dirt into it – that's what the public wants to see. Bloody-mindedness, cunning, calculation and ruthlessness is what makes a good entrepreneur, and I want to feel I'm seeing that side of Farren Mortimer in this programme. So that's what I want to see more of here. OK, everybody?'

Nobody dared to offer a contradictory view, particularly Kieran who thought he might already have said too much.

PRD minus 149.

159

CHAPTER EIGHTEEN

Father and Son

'It's come.' It was Friday morning and Agnes had called to tell Farren that the envelope containing the test results had arrived. How were they going to handle this? As it turned out, in a not altogether different way from the dream that had disturbed Farren's sleep the previous Monday evening. He was to drive to Didsbury where he and Agnes would open the envelope together. The contents would then dictate the next course of action.

All week long Farren had tried to put the matter to the back of his mind, but with scant success. He was excited, but at the same time he was frightened as to the possibilities the truth may engender. And what if it was all a false dawn – what then? Would he be let down, or actually be happier with the status quo?

That evening, the usual preamble of tea and trivial chitchat having been conducted, Farren and Agnes got down to business. There was no humour or levity in their demeanours; they knew how serious the implications of what they were about to learn were for both of them.

Eventually, Agnes started. 'Well, shall we?'

'Yes,' replied Farren. 'Go on.'

Agnes handed him the letter. 'You open it. I think you should.'

Farren took the A4 ivory envelope, paused, took a deep breath and slid his finger under the flap before withdrawing the contents. He stared at the paper, and read it slowly. He blinked as he assimilated the meaning of the words printed out on the blue and white letterhead.

Finally, Agnes could contain herself no longer. 'What does it say? Are you related or not?'

Again, a long pause: 'Yes, it's a positive match. You can tell me who is he now.'

Agnes, continuing the TV theme of the evening's proceedings, said, 'he's going to introduce himself. He's outside.'

Farren was somewhat taken aback by the suddenness of this potential introduction, not having thought that Agnes and his mystery father could have gone to such elaborate lengths over the 'reveal'. 'You're joking, aren't you?' he said.

'No, love. I said I'd call him when we'd opened the results. Do you want to see him? If it's too much, we can wait. He understands.'

Farren didn't really need to think about it for very long – why wait another few days after all these years? 'No, I'm ready.'

'But before I do, I will tell you who he is, because you've already met him so it will be a bigger shock than you thought.'

'I've met him? But I thought you said he didn't know about me?'

'He didn't know about you, but it turns out that he's local, and has met you, recently as it happens. Your father, I mean Ernest, and me know him too.'

'Who?'

'It's the undertaker who did Ernest's funeral, Michael Morrison – he's your natural father.'

'Michael Morrison? The undertaker? My father? How can that be possible?'

"Farren, I'm as shocked as you are, but it's a long story, and I think it's only right that he should tell you himself. Shall I call him?'

Farren was struggling to think straight but knew there was only one answer to Agnes' question. 'I need to know. I need to know everything. You'd better call him.'

Barely two minutes after Agnes had telephoned Michael, Farren heard the knock on the door. Michael had actually been parked up around the corner, waiting to be called in from the wings or sent home without an audition depending on the results of the test and Farren's decision whether to see him or not. Agnes went to the door while Farren sat motionless at the kitchen table. He was about to meet his real father, a father he hadn't realised existed, a father he'd never known, and a real life father to replace the stand-in father who'd just died.

Following the sound of a muffled conversation in the hall, Agnes held back as Michael entered the kitchen. 'Hello, Farren,' said Michael as he extended his arm to shake his son's hand. 'I realise this is a bit of a shock after all of these years. I hope you're not mad at me.'

Farren limply shook the hand of the amply proportioned newcomer in front of him, and replied. 'I'm not mad, just confused. I want to know everything you can tell me.'

Over the next two hours, the three sat in the kitchen and tried to construct the jigsaw of Farren's beginnings from scratch. The night of the conception, the loss of contact, Michael's ignorance of the pregnancy and birth, Father Culshaw's intervention, the later revelation about Farren's real mother, the letter implying Michael Morrison's identity, the decision to let sleeping dogs lie, the eventual realisation of the truth following Agnes' inquisition of Michael Morrison after Ernest's funeral.

It was an enormous amount of information for Farren to take in, but he remained calm as he listened, asking a succession of questions as both Michael and Agnes exchanged the narration. The atmosphere was one of seriousness and formality rather than celebration – all three were wary of going too fast or being over-presumptuous of the others' feelings at this point.

Eventually, Michael brought proceedings to a halt. 'Your head must be spinning, Farren. Agnes and myself have at least had some days to get used to the idea. I'll leave now, and hope we can meet up again soon? I know I'd like that. I didn't know I was a father, and I'm as shocked as you are. But I do know that I'm as delighted as any man could be to make a discovery like this, and if I can be a dad to you in the future, nothing would give me greater pleasure.'

As Michael drove home he reflected that it had all gone rather well. He was a dad! It was true. He couldn't believe it. As he'd sat in the car earlier, around the corner from the Mortimers' home, he'd felt ridiculous. What was he doing skulking there, playing silly games of 'Surprise, Surprise?' And what if Agnes had called and said he wasn't Farren's dad? He and Agnes had discussed how to play this evening, and couldn't come up with any better alternative. Still, thank goodness, it had gone all right.

He'd wondered what to say on being introduced, but all his thoughts had fled from him as soon as he was led into the kitchen to meet Farren. He'd been a bit clumsy there, he thought, but too late to change it now. Farren had been fantastic under the circumstances – he thought he might have given him a hard time, or been resentful or angry with him, but he'd been calm and collected; not effusive, but not condemnatory either. Michael knew that he could hardly call himself a father in anything other than biological terms, but he still felt a surge of pride at his achievement. He couldn't believe he was a parent, but he was, it was official, and he had to get used to that idea.

Michael had delicately skated over the details of the fateful night – he had to maintain decorum of course so had merely inferred that he and Linda had been intimate at the party. In essence his part in the recital was restricted to relating the events of that frosty December evening long ago.

Michael had been very careful not to mention AMOLAD in any great detail – politeness precluded him from talking about their coincidental professions, particularly as Michael recalled some of his earlier thoughts on AMOLAD's activities before he knew Farren was his son. He'd been careful not to chunter on about the family business he was now the sole survivor of – well, no, that wasn't true any more either. Fancy that, he mused; Farren had somehow continued the family tradition, giving it a modern twist. No, he instinctively knew that there was a potential clash there and conflict of any description was to be avoided as they got to know each other.

Neither was said much about poor old Looby; there wasn't an awful lot to say about her at the moment because they had so few facts. At the back of his mind though Michael had already resolved to find out more about Linda Wilson, the mother of his son, as soon as he could. With Father Culshaw being dead it wouldn't be easy, but he knew where she went to university, what course she did, and now the psychiatric hospital where she had sent the letter from eight years previously. Yes, but first things first, he had to build a relationship with his son, and to see what Farren wanted to do about that too.

Tonight was the start, and he felt optimistic that Farren would want to continue his bonding with him. Smiling to himself, he turned his car CD player on – *I Believe in You* from *After The Gold Rush* by Neil Young that he'd bought again on CD that week.

Agnes felt shattered. She'd continued talking to Farren for an hour or so after Michael had departed, but had felt compelled to go to bed to rest after the stress of this monumental day. It had not been a good day for her; it had not been a good week, a good year, or a good decade for her. Life was conspiring against her, and now she had to face this latest development over Farren's parentage without Ernest. If Ernest was here she knew he would be now be telling her 'I told you so.' She'd let the genie out of the bottle and now there was no way of getting it back in there.

She knew she should be pleased for Farren to discover he had a real dad after all of these years, but couldn't help but feel resentful that at the very moment she needed her son for support, this Johnny-come-lately had popped up out of nowhere to compete for his attentions. Well, he'd not so much popped up as been summoned by her. She knew she was being a silly old fool, but only up to a point, and this coming on top of everything else made her feel even more forlorn and isolated than she could possibly have imagined.

She'd watched Michael and Farren closely at their 'reunion'. Michael Morrison looked like the cat that had got the cream. He'd tried hard to contain himself which probably wasn't difficult for him as he didn't look like he ever let his hair down, but there was no doubt about it; he was cock-a-hoop.

All these years and he'd not known, and now all of his Christmases had come at once. No bringing up the boy, no looking after him from being a baby, no responsibility at all – here you go, instant son. And she was going to be the loser.

As for Farren, he'd been remarkably composed, but she knew he must be strained to snapping point. This was a terrible shock to him, how could it not be? But he'd handled himself well. Was he happy at this discovery? That was still hard to work out, and in any case he'd need time, but he didn't look unduly downcast at the entry of his real father into his life.

Agnes had filled in most of the evening's details – how Farren came to them, Father Culshaw's role, their belief that his mother was dead and the father unknown, and the dilemma they'd faced when Father Culshaw had given them Linda's letter and brought them up to date. She'd watched Farren survey the letter, largely without any outward show of emotion. In fact, when he'd read it the only thing he'd said was: 'I was called Fred? Can't see me going back to that.'

The evening had ended with Michael inviting Farren to spend more time with him once he felt up to it. It was good that he'd not pushed on that and left it open-ended. Farren's decision on whether to see him again soon or not would speak volumes over how all of this was going to turn out.

As she turned the light out she whispered to the blackened room: 'It's done now, Ernest. No matter what we think, it's done.'

Farren sat on the garden bench at the rear of his mother's house. He wanted some fresh air and time to think over the events of the night. He had met his real father, a man who had been brought back from the dead. A day he'd never imagined would come to pass, and now he had to cope with it. It was a strange old tale – that was for sure. A one-night stand, a secret birth, a less than regular adoption, a mother whose life was clearly blighted and the machinations and interventions of Father bloody Culshaw.

His real dad was a big bloke – out of shape. Farren wondered if he'd look like that at his age. But he could recognise the physical resemblance now he knew to look. Michael was a bit old-fashioned, but to be truthful Farren was grateful he hadn't been gushing all over him – at least he'd been spared that aspect of the standard TV reveal format. Michael had also given him space, hadn't insisted on planning the next ten years of his life now they'd been reunited – that was sensitive, and welcome.

But what to do now? Did Farren want to see more of Michael, his dad, and build a life with him? It struck Farren that Michael was alone in the world too, with no family other than him now. Farren had Agnes of course, but that was different. To Farren there wasn't any question – he wanted to learn about his wider family, where he'd come from and how his own make up was informed by these factors, as they surely were. He also wanted to find out more about his mother.

He thought of Agnes upstairs in bed – what a shattering few weeks it had been for her. He had initially been annoyed at her for having kept back the secret for eight years, but understood now that this hadn't been for selfish reasons. In fact, if it wasn't for Agnes, he'd never have known the truth anyway. He knew she was troubled by the revelation of Farren's true parents; she wasn't exactly warm towards Michael Morrison and he discerned that she felt she was being usurped. He would have to keep an eye on that and ensure she didn't feel like she was being pushed out, particularly as she was so vulnerable following Ernest's death.

Ernest – what would he have made of it all? He clearly hadn't wanted to know or to delve any deeper. Farren suppressed his rising resentment as he wondered what must have been discussed between his adoptive parents. Well, Ernest had been wrong – he shouldn't have tried to brush it under the carpet. But what was done was done, so no point in raking it over, especially now when he'd only been in the ground for two weeks.

And who, literally, had put him there? Michael Morrison, the funeral director. His real dad had seen off his adoptive dad. Farren hadn't really said much to Michael about the unusual nature of his profession. Michael could have turned out to be a doctor, a dentist, a teacher, or a traffic warden, but no, he was an undertaker. How weird was that? In the same way that Farren hadn't said much about it, he'd noticed that Michael hadn't dwelt on it or on what Farren did for a career either. But how bloody incredible? Not for the first time recently Farren felt the weight of AMOLAD on his shoulders – bigging it up it to Kieran McDonaghy was one thing; explaining it to his dad may well be another, particularly as he was now trying to justify it to himself.

No matter, he'd deal with it all in time. Looking up at the clear night stars he thought how, under the very same stars back in 1972, he'd been conceived in a one-night stand just down the road at a student party in Withington. Un-bloody-believable.

PRD minus 147.

CHAPTER NINETEEN

Late For The Sky

Eight days after meeting Michael for the first time Farren followed his Sat Nav to Heald Green where he was to see his father again. Agnes had declined to join them, saying they needed some time on their own, so Farren had arranged to go on and visit her afterwards.

Michael's semi-detached home was modest and rather lacking in any concessions to modern style, but did have a spectacular position in that planes landing at Manchester Airport half a mile away appeared to scrape the roof tiles as they passed overhead every ninety seconds. Farren found the sensation a little disconcerting, but Michael assured him that it was something to which you could soon get accustomed. 'Like having a dad or a son, maybe?' suggested Farren who had considerably lightened up over the intervening week following the discovery of his origins.

Michael, reassured by Farren's offer to visit this Saturday (the call being made the very day after they'd met for the first time), was also feeling more relaxed – jovial in fact. He was also slightly relieved that Agnes was sitting this meeting out.

Both had looked forward to seeing each other again, and having got the initial greetings out of the way were keen to discover more about each other – they had a lot to catch up on after all.

Michael dug out the family photo album as a starting point as he told Farren his life story. Besides that 'one mad night' it was as conventional a life as could be imagined. Destined in childhood for the solemnity of the family trade Michael's worldview extended to one horizon – his apprenticeship and induction into the family business. That succession being self-evident it had encouraged Michael to learn to toughen himself up – tolerating being the butt of others' 'Addams Family' and 'Munsters' taunts at school would have been an open invitation to bullies to terrorise him if he hadn't.

At the very time when England started to swing, twelve months before the Summer of Love, and on the cusp of the permissive society, Michael took to learning his trade with enthusiasm. In particular he discovered he had a gift for empathising with the bereaved in their darkest moments of need.

At the same time as his career was set into motion, Michael's thoughts, as young men's do, turned to the opposite sex. He didn't have too many girlfriends; given the Morrisons' close association with the Catholic church in the city, the only girls Michael seemed to get dates with were well brought up left footers who at least had respect for his profession and standing, and, of course, they knew his business prospects weren't going to die out any time soon. By the age of 21 Michael was going steady with Carmel Kilpatrick, a year his junior and a secretary at SELNEC, the regional bus and transport company.

Michael and Carmel enjoyed an old fashioned romance,

insofar as they certainly weren't swinging or permissive in their view of courtship – they suited each other very well in that regard. Inevitably, both families began planning for the inevitable wedding day, which nothing was to derail, not even an unlikely encounter with a mystery girl that Michael was never to forget.

Michael's story then jumped swiftly over the next forty years. Marriage, work and that was about it, until Carmel passed four years ago.

Farren reciprocated with his potted life history, telling Michael all about his upbringing, schooling and university days, and his early career in advertising.

He self-effacingly admitted he'd never been singled out as one to watch when he was younger and how he'd preferred to quietly tick off the appropriate academic boxes while honing his interest in music and football. These pursuits, together with a healthy appetite for drinking, figured highly in Farren's outlook on life by the time he went to Leeds University to study English. Farren told Michael how his first breakthrough was landing the position of Ents Secretary at Uni. A labour of love, Farren learned to spot upcoming bands, and discovered he was a natural when it came to selling out gigs at a profit (his predecessor had merely used the position to book the bands that made up his own rather esoteric record collection). It had been fun, but he realised later that this pastime had also doubled as a business induction course.

His hustling experience as Ents Sec served him well – Farren fell into the world of advertising on graduation, initially back in Manchester and then in London and shot up through the ranks quickly, helped by switching agencies once or twice.

He got to work on a diverse number of accounts for beer, chocolate, soft drinks and pizza until the fateful day when Fond Farewell Funerals appointed his agency. 'The rest is history,' he laughed.

The two of them were getting on famously, and relaxed further into each other's company as the afternoon progressed. As Michael's family album contained numerous prints of Morrison family groups posing next to hearses and outside the funeral home, the topic of undertaking couldn't be avoided altogether.

'Five generations of undertakers, that's amazing,' said Farren. 'I suppose that I'm the sixth generation if only I'd known it. How spooky is that?'

'Well, yes, you could say that our respective professions aren't entirely unconnected,' said Michael diplomatically.

'But how is business these days?' asked Farren. 'Surely you're getting squeezed out by the big chains?'

'Well, yes, Farren, we are, and to be honest it's not been good in recent years, but what can I do? A while back they'd have bought me out for a good price. Now I'd have to take what I could get – either way it's not a fitting end to a business that's served its community for over 100 years.'

'I thought you handled Ernest's funeral really well.'

'Thank you. It was a straightforward job, but every funeral to us is a special case. No matter how many times you do this, you never forget the pain that the family and congregation are feeling. That's the point. Not like the bloody conveyor belts some of the big groups seem to be running. I've even seen logjams at the crematorium as they try and turn too many funerals round in too short a time. It's all about money these days.'

'What's it like being an undertaker? I mean how do people react to you?'

'I know what you mean. The unwelcome guest at any party. Well, you get used to it. I've heard all of the jokes, have done since I was a lad, but the thing is no-one thinks it's a joke when we're needed, when we have to help them through their grief. Death doesn't really hit home until it's under your roof, affecting you personally. But you must understand that, doing what you do?'

'I thought I did, but to be honest, at Ernest's funeral I realised I knew very little about bereavement really, and I'm supposed to be the government's bereavement adviser.'

'Yes, I'd read that. In fact I've read quite a bit about you in the last two weeks – hope you don't mind?'

'No, but don't believe everything you read – most of it's made up or muckraking.'

'So why are you the bereavement czar?'

'It's a gimmick for the government basically, just their latest fad. I fitted the bill for PR purposes; well at least I do for the time being. I thought it was great for the profile – that there would be no harm in it, but like most things like that it's so bloody contrived.'

'Can't you get out of it?'

'Well, I can't resign if that's what you mean. I just have to present a report and recommendations later this year, and I don't even write most of that – it's all for show. Once that's done, I can slip away, my job done. I've also got PRD later this year, so that's a pressure job.'

'You've stirred up a bit of a fuss in the undertaking world with that, haven't you?'

'So it seems. But it's not only that; they've been against us from the start. I suppose that includes you, Michael? Were you anti-AMOLAD before you found out who I was? Maybe you still are?'

'People are spending money on films and things that they might have spent through us in the past, but the big chains have done more harm than you. Not that I'm having a go or anything.'

'No, it's interesting to talk to you about it. To be honest, there have been times recently when I think I've bitten off more than I can chew.'

'Really? It all looks like a fantastic success in the stuff I've been reading. Are you sure it's not just Ernest's death affecting you? It hits a lot of people that way, where what was important yesterday is trivial today, or they think their lives are meaningless. It does pass.'

'No, I'm aware that can happen, but it's not that. I've been feeling this way for a while. Yes, the business is successful and it's high profile, but I'm wondering now what it's all about? When I started it, it was just like getting my own plaything – I could do what I wanted to do. No idea was too ludicrous, and I could use my marketing skills to hype everything up. It was a classic ad man's dream – no client to say "no", or "it's too risky" – just come up with ideas and launch them. It was a game really, one that really took off.'

'Is it out of control now?'

'Not in a business sense, but I think it's going to peak this year. It's just like a big machine that needs more and more fuel to run. Staff start taking things into their own hands, mistakes happen, you cop flak from the media, and you have to run around sucking up to politicians and the like to keep things ticking over. The fun has gone out of it for sure.'

'But people are still buying your ideas, so they must want them?'

'At the moment, yes, but who knows next year, or the year after that? It's not that – it's more a question of the appropriateness of what I've done. I sometimes look at the on-line memoriams and the biovids and, I know I shouldn't say it, but some of them appal me with their crass sentimentality and sanctimoniousness. Mock grief – it's just hypocritical. And I started it. I sometimes think I've declared war on decorum.'

'Farren, you shouldn't get wound up about it. I think you're being a bit harsh on yourself. It's just the culmination of what you've been through in recent weeks. Listen, how about another cup of tea?'

Farren was surprised at how easily he was able to unburden himself and talk to Michael so candidly about his innermost thoughts, and he felt the albatross lighten slightly as he acknowledged his concerns to another for the first time. Yes, he felt much better, and Michael was a very sympathetic listener.

'You know, Michael, it's been good to talk to you about this, but I do need to ask you one thing and it's a bit embarrassing.'

'Not a problem. What is it?'

'It's just that if the media get hold of the fact that I've discovered my long-lost dad and that he's an undertaker, they're going to be all over us, and most of it won't be kind. I hate to ask, but can we keep this strictly between us and Agnes for the time being while I work out the best way of handling it?'

'That's fine by me,' replied Michael. 'I'd had the same thought as well.'

As Farren bade farewell to drive over to see Agnes, he promised to come up again the following week. For the first time in his life Farren felt like he truly belonged.

PRD minus 139.

CHAPTER TWENTY

Free Bird

The clapperboard announced that this was the third time they'd run this shot. Kieran McDonaghy was in a cemetery, a funeral taking place behind him in the distance as he recorded his *Made Men* show intro: 'What goes down has come up with a multi-million pound business for bereavement entrepreneur Farren Mortimer. He's the man who has stripped away the shroud from centuries old funeral traditions in the UK. How did he get on to this dead cert? Let's dig a little deeper.'

'Cut. OK, we'll take that one, Kieran. Right, can we have Farren for the promenade?' As the early autumn light started to fail, the director was already worrying about completing the outdoor shots on his crammed filming schedule.

Farren and Kieran were to stroll around the graveyard chatting before going into the church to do an interview in the pews just in case any of the audience missed the point.

The shoot being in Kensal Green Jon had also turned out for the day, saying it would be interesting to see how the programme was put together so he could report back to his government contacts ahead of PRD. Farren had asked Jon to join him that evening for dinner, as they'd not had a chance to have a good talk in recent months. Jon wondered if this would be the evening he would get the sort of deal he thought he deserved?

Jon soon become bored with the endless setting up and retakes. Much to the annoyance of the production team he resorted to making wisecracks, got caught in camera shot requiring a re-shoot of one scene, and was generally a nuisance. Farren had to suggest to him in the end that maybe it was a better idea to not waste any more time there and meet up later. Jon, knowing he'd been given his marching orders, sulkily obliged.

When they met up later that evening at Rules in Covent Garden there was an air of apprehension as the two got to spend their first hours together for some time. Both opted for the potted shrimps followed by the steak, kidney and oyster pie and as Farren consulted the wine list, Jon pondered when would be the best time to come out with his pitch for an increased share package.

But it was Farren, having ordered the Domaine Rossignol – Fevrier Bourgogne, who kicked things off. 'I'm glad we've been able to get together to have a catch up, Jon, because I think we need one. I can't help but notice that you haven't seemed too happy recently. I think it's been affecting your performance and your attitude to work and I'd like to get to the bottom of it. What's the problem?'

Jon, clearly not expecting this opening, was immediately put off guard. 'Problem? Nothing that I'm aware of – in fact, I thought it was *you* that was experiencing problems.'

'What problems would those be, Jon? I'm not sure to what you're referring?'

'Well, with your dad's death for one. And before that – you seem to have lost interest in the business. In fact, that's what I wanted to talk to *you* about tonight.'

'Well, it's an intriguing observation, but to be honest we're not here to discuss me. I want to discuss you. And I think I have a right, don't you?'

Jon suddenly felt undermined and defenceless – he could hardly say 'no' to his boss. He'd not seen this coming.

Over the potted shrimps, Jon had to endure Farren's summary of his Director of Operations' behaviour over the past few months. His flippant attitude, his cock-up over the forecasts, the lost revenue from the PRD projects the government had taken away from them, Jon's persistence in trying to dream up new concepts which, frankly, were off kilter with AMOLAD's original principles. It was a hatchet job, delivered with a concise and cool detachment by his boss.

'Or do you think I'm being unfair?' said Farren finally, signalling that the litany of accusations had now been exhausted.

Jon, who by now had drunk the majority of the bottle of wine on top of his large gin and tonic aperitif, could have opted for injured pride and amazement that his efforts were valued so lowly by Farren, but unfortunately discretion was not uppermost in his thinking as the blood rushed to his head. 'I can't believe what you're saying. I really can't. If it wasn't for me, the business would be in the shit and you know it. I'm the one who's been holding the company together for the past year as you've been off gallivanting around, hobnobbing with politicians, doing your TV programme. Who's doing PRD? I am, and without me that would crash and burn too.'

'You seem to have rather a rather inflated opinion of your role, Jon. You're supposed to be doing PRD – it's your primary task at the moment. As to your view that you're somehow running everything, well, that's news to me, and would be to the majority of your colleagues I suspect. Unless, of course, you've already been canvassing them on this?'

'I think it's fairly evident to everybody what's going on,' said Jon as the steak, kidney and oyster pies made an appearance.

'Interesting. Well, it may be evident to you, Jon, but it's not to me, so can I suggest that we get back to the points I've just raised about your performance, and also, can we please try to keep this civil?'

Two hours later, back at home, Jon was seething as he told Becky how the dinner had gone. He poured himself a large whisky and lamented the shoddy way in which he'd been hijacked over the cool white linen of the Covent Garden eatery. '"What's the problem?" he asked me. Well, yes, there *is* a problem. With you, Mr Bloody Wonderful. I can't believe the way he treated me. He's off his head. I could bring that business down in a flash if I wanted to, and I just might well do that.'

Becky was alarmed at this turn of events. 'Are you sure he was as critical as you're saying? You're not misreading him are you?'

'No, I'm bloody well not. He had a go at me over all sorts of things. He just can't face the fact that he's losing it. He thinks the business is all down to him.'

'He owns the business, Jon. It is sort of down to him. You didn't say anything you'll regret did you?'

'I'm not bothered about him. He can't do anything, not while I'm in charge of most things.'

'Honestly, Jon, you have to be careful. He could sack you.

You've always got on so well, and you love the job, and it's really well paid – you shouldn't get worked up like this.'

'I'm telling you now; I'm going to show him how important I am to this business. I'll show him.'

As Jon reached for the whisky bottle for a top up, Becky decided it was time to impose a curfew. 'No, Jon, you've had enough to drink. Come to bed – things will look better in the morning.'

Farren had enjoyed better nights out, that was for sure, but at least his suspicions had been confirmed. As his taxi made its way towards Highbury Grove, he took stock of the evening's conversation. Despite falling down on the job in some pretty salient areas, Jon seemed to think that it was he, not Farren, running the business. He'd actually said so. This was a pretty odd way to hand in a resignation thought Farren.

Jon had a great job, was well paid, and was given his head – probably too much leeway as it turned out. Why was he kicking off like this?

Or did Jon have a point? Was Farren spending too much time away from the business? Well that was rubbish for a start, as it was Farren who remained the creative and driving force behind the entire operation and it was he who made sure it was profitable. Jon in particular would have them bankrupt if left in charge.

Had Jon picked up on Farren's growing crisis of conscience over the activities of AMOLAD, was that it? No, there's no way he could have discerned that. The bottom-line reality was that Jon had let power go to his head, and was acting out some form of fantasy. The trouble with that, as Farren had observed in his agency days, is once you get an individual thinking he or she is indispensible and bigger than the business, you're effectively dealing with a terrorist – a malcontent whose ultimate fallback if they don't get their own way is to remove the pin of the grenade and take everybody up with them.

With PRD now only a few short weeks away, just how dangerous was Jon to AMOLAD?

PRD minus 45.

CHAPTER TWENTY-ONE

It's The Same Old Song

'Annie, just blow him out and stay with me. I can't tell you how exceptionally randy I'm feeling.' Nigel Adlington was in a state of longing as he met with Annie Brooks at the Langham Hotel for an early evening drink. Annie was due to hook up with Farren Mortimer in an hour for her 'working' strategy planning dinner.

'Don't be silly, Nigel, it's taken me six months to nail him down and you yourself said how important he could be to me,' replied Annie, by now well used to Nigel's neediness.

'He won't mind,' pleaded Nigel, but now Annie had Farren in her sights she wasn't going to lose the opportunity to pull the trigger.

'Well, it wouldn't be very professional of me to duck out now, so the answer is "no", Nigel – I can't change plans at the drop of a hat. It will make the next time we're together all the sweeter for the wait.'

Nigel looked less than convinced. It had been a brutal day, and he could have done with some comforting – the type of stress alleviation that Annie was so adroit in dispensing. Nigel had been glad to get away from his Cheshire home after the weekend from hell spent with his wife and children. Not that it was the boys, Adam and Teddy, who were the problem; it was Emma who had been on the warpath. He'd endured her normal carping about how he was never there, how she felt like a single mother, and how she was at the end of her tether looking after the boys and the home while he just checked in and out like the house was a hotel. She'd accused Nigel of treating her like a skivvy and never paying her any attention. Well, he was used to that and merely reverted to donning the metaphorical tin hat.

However, on the Saturday evening, after dinner and a DVD, a slightly tipsy Emma tried to reintroduce some intimacy into their non-existent sex life after they'd retired to bed. Nigel, appalled at the prospect, tried to defend his lack of interest as being down to tiredness and working too hard, but Emma, not a million miles from the truth, immediately interpreted his lack of libido as being down to the fact that he was 'getting it from somewhere else.'

All day Sunday she laboured the point: 'Who is she? Is it your secretary? It's as clear as the nose on your face,' and so on as she lamented the turning point in their otherwise perfect marriage. Faced with a defence that consisted mainly of 'don't be silly' and 'I'd never do that', she'd upped the game, telling Nigel that when she found out who it was she was going to divorce him and take him to the cleaners, adding, 'how would your constituents like that, Mr Bloody Perfect?'

Nigel's metaphorical tin hat wasn't nearly adequate enough protection against this fusillade. He miserably counted down the hours until he could once more slink away to London to gain some respite from this domestic doghouse.

The Monday hadn't been much better. He'd not heard from Emma, thank God, but he had been given an awkward time over PRD by the Minister who, not for the first time, felt the plans lacked cohesion, public appeal, and more importantly, voter buy-in. Nigel had tried to defend himself again these charges but his, 'well, I think, Minister, that the plans have to be taken in context,' and 'I take your point, Minister, but I'm confident that you'll be impressed when the overall campaign is rolled out,' cut as much ice as his excuses to Emma had twenty-four hours earlier.

On asking the Minister for guidance on specific areas he thought may benefit from additional attention, Nigel had been left in no doubt. 'Here's the thing, Nigel. Your name is on this. A lot of people are getting twitchy about this PRD event, and you don't want to go down with the ship if it sinks, do you? Let me just say it needs a bit more life.'

'It needs a bit more life?' thought Nigel. Was the Minister having a private joke? He felt the noose tighten around his neck as he recognised that he was being set up as the scapegoat. No help or support, just a brutal reminder that if it didn't go well, he was on his own. If it did go well of course, then he'd have played a major part in a key government initiative.

Subsequently, Nigel cancelled his dinner meeting with a lobbying firm and called Annie – he needed some comforting and was most insistent that she dropped everything so they could get together that night. On being told by Annie that she was booked up for the evening, he'd entreated her to at least meet up for half an hour beforehand –please, please, please. Not wanting to make him angry, Annie finally relented, but she could guess he just wanted to moan and she didn't really want to have to listen to it all. She was glad it was just going to be a quick drink.

'Things are getting complicated at home,' said Nigel

looking around to ensure there were no eavesdroppers. 'I think Emma suspects that I'm having an affair.'

'We're just having a bit of fun, not an affair,' said Annie. 'But in any case, why does she suspect?'

'She tried it on in the bedroom on Saturday night. I couldn't face the prospect of it, so it all kicked off.'

'Bloody hell, Nigel, you can't do that. Course she'll think you're at it somewhere else if you won't do the business. It's an obvious admission you're up to no good. "You're playing away" is all you're going to get if you pull the "I'm stressed out" excuse.'

'That's what she said; exactly that,' said Nigel, stunned at Annie's hitherto unseen insight into female psychology.

'Well, you're going to have to give her a good seeing to, calm her down, or she's going to start having you followed or something,' advised Annie.

'Good God, I don't know if I could,' said Nigel, starting to feel a little queasy at the thought.

'Nigel, she's your wife, and if you're not giving it to her, then of course she's going to suspect. Take some Viagra – I can get you some if you want; just sort her out every so often, and she'll shut up.'

'But what about us: won't you mind?' asked Nigel.

'Don't be silly,' came the reply. 'God, Nigel, you can be a bit naïve at times. I'm married too in case you've forgotten. Go on, call her to say sorry, and do your duty when you're next home. You can think of England, or me, if it helps. You're going to have to.'

Nigel looked crestfallen. Did he have to? Annie was so cold-blooded about it all. He had thought it meant more to her. Part of the reason he'd not wanted to have sex with his wife was out of some sort of commitment to Annie – now she was telling him to just get on and do it, like it was no big deal.

But maybe she was right. If he could summon up the willpower to make that part of his marriage acceptable to his wife, it could make life a whole lot easier. Emma had never been that interested in sex if the truth be told – it was only after receiving no interest from him that she'd suddenly developed an appetite, probably more to test him than anything she actually felt.

'Look, I've got to dash now, Nigel. I'm late,' said Annie. 'Go on, get on the phone, apologise, send some flowers, and sort her out this weekend. You don't want to make a bad situation worse, OK?'

'I suppose not,' said Nigel as Annie headed for door.

'A lady's prerogative,' said Farren as Annie apologised for being late. Annie again looked ravishing, if not a little flushed having dashed there in heavy traffic. Except Farren knew that wasn't the case having spotted her downstairs in the bar, huddled up in a corner with Nigel Adlington, when he was on his way into the hotel. Their body language suggested that they weren't discussing business. '*As I suspected,*' thought Farren with a smile as he waited fifteen further minutes for Annie to appear – '*they're at it*'.

Farren had suggested Roux at the Landau in the Langham Hotel for dinner as it felt to him to be more businesslike than social if anyone spotted them together. Quite why Adlington and Annie risked being seen there was bit of a mystery, but Farren had noticed before that people who were having affairs often considered themselves to be invisible.

Farren was hungry, but hearing Annie's order to the waiter

he made a quick adjustment to his choices when his turn came – he felt he could hardly tuck into the fois gras starter followed by the chorizo filled rabbit leg with Scottish langoustines main after she'd asked the waiter what vegetarian dishes he'd recommend. Their grilled marinated courgettes and green acquerello rice risotto with asparagus and morels having been ordered – Farren had opted for the same as Annie – he was relieved that she was at least up for a bottle of wine with the meal. Time to go through the motions.

'I'd really like to hear about the core objectives of HASTE and where you see the organisation going in the future,' said Farren who had decided that the easiest way of getting through the evening was to get Annie to do most of the talking.

At the prompt, Annie went into overdrive as she outlined how HASTE was changing attitudes, harnessing growing support and saving lives. Her messianic zeal was noticeable, as was the number of times she used the words 'I' and 'me'.

Farren, long practiced at listening to agency clients wax lyrical about their latest revolutionary principle or game changing product, dutifully nodded in the right places and looked suitably impressed.

What *was* evident to Farren about Annie's strategy was that there wasn't one. HASTE was clearly a means of putting Annie Brooks in the media and keeping her there. In fact he thought she'd gladly have sacrificed poor little Donny under the wheels of the nearest ten-ton truck if it meant gaining more media exposure.

Farren had seen it all before with campaign martyrs, looking for free agency support for their crusades, but all the time wanting to talk about me, me, me. As she continued to hold forth well into the main course he mused that where

Annie had got it right was that she was a footballer's wife and looked like a footballer's wife in a classic WAG sort of way. He watched her perfect lips shape the words she'd only recently learned such as 'collateral damage', 'campaign creep' and 'inertia', and couldn't help but think about his earlier impression of her as some sort of super-charged lap dancer – the one who was determined to make more money than the other girls over the course of the night.

'So, Farren, what I'd really be interested in is your views as to how we can do this better, take our message wider, and achieve real change?'

She'd stopped, and now it was Farren's turn. 'Well, before I do that, can I suggest another bottle of wine? I know it's a Monday, but what the heck?'

'Only if you promise to drink most of it,' said Annie, taking this as a sign that she was doing well, and that he didn't want to break the spell she was casting.

'The first thing that strikes me,' said Farren after ordering another bottle of Sancerre, 'is that you're not being specific enough in your aims.'

'Oh, but I thought I was,' said Annie, taken aback slightly that anyone could conceive that the strategy was anything less than perfect. When she'd asked for help, what she'd really been inviting was praise for her outstanding efforts, not an actual critique.

'Yes, you're stating that you want change through slower suburban road speeds, but my impression – I'm talking objectively here – is that you'd be better lobbying for a *specific* law change. You know, an "Annie's Law" type of thing that would impose a minimum two-year ban on drivers who break suburban speed limits more than once – no exceptions. It would spark a fiercer debate, and give you an end game.'

Farren had her at 'Annie's Law'. What a concept. Her name enshrined in the campaign. Why had her people not come up with this?

Farren continued. 'The way to make it stick is to use more research. I don't think you use enough from what I've seen. Stats, yes, but you really need to take the pulse of the nation and use that as ammunition – you know, "do you think we should have stricter road safety laws in order to save lives" – that sort of thing. It's always going to be a "nine out of ten agree".'

Yes, she got it – Nigel was right that Farren was a clever marketeer. The future direction of the campaign was suddenly clearer to her, and she was the one to lead it on to the next level. Annie's Law. That had a real ring to it.

'I can really see where you're coming from with that, Farren – that's really insightful. I like it. I like it a lot. I'm going to take that up with my people and see how we can develop it.'

'Well, it's just a suggestion, but it did strike me as being one way to go,' said Farren knowing that his work was done, on the strategy side at least.

'Have you had any more thoughts on the donation scheme idea?' asked Annie, wondering if her evening could get any better.

'You're going to have to bear with me on that, I'm afraid,' replied Farren. 'I'm still awaiting our evaluation report from the marketing team. They're a little busy at the moment with PRD as you can imagine.'

'Oh, I understand completely,' gushed Annie. 'All in good time. I really appreciate you considering the proposal.'

'Not at all,' said Farren who had already decided that hell

would freeze over before he allowed HASTE to splash itself over his testimonial pages like an outbreak of herpes. He'd let her down gently in the near future by telling her it didn't align with their model and he'd sweeten the pill by pointing her in the direction of some other poor sods she could bother.

Nonetheless, Annie was triumphant. Glowing with success and her intake of Sancerre, she immediately felt grateful to Farren for his fascinating advice and his undoubted mastery of the marketing medium. He wasn't bad looking either. Still inside her cloak of invisibility, she couldn't stop herself when the time came to leave. 'Farren, it's been a fantastic evening. Thank you. I've learned so much. I don't know about you, but I'm staying in town tonight. You'd be very welcome to join me for a nightcap.'

Farren had half been expecting this, but having it on a plate was one thing, whereas cheating on the Under Secretary of State was another. Never mind lap dancer, Annie was a first rate hooker, and he wasn't going to go there. Far too dangerous. 'I'd love to Annie, but unfortunately I've got a 6.30am start tomorrow. I've enjoyed it too. Maybe some other time?' What was that old newspaper maxim about making one's excuses and leaving?

As Annie's taxi disappeared down Regent Street, Farren was relieved as he pondered his lucky escape from the boa constrictor grip she was looking to exert on him. '*God help Adlington*,' he chuckled to himself as his taxi pulled up.

Annie didn't want the night to end. She'd had a ball. Annie's Law – it was a genius idea. She felt excited and for a second she contemplated calling Nigel and going round there, but then thought 'sod that' as he'd only be earnest and pathetic. Flicking through her mobile phone address book she found the number of her former agent's best friend who had looked after her when she first came to London. On a whim, she called it. 'Hi, Gavin. Guess who? Tiff. Long time, no see. Fancy partying?' No point in wasting a night out in London. Especially when you're dressed like a stealth bomber.

PRD minus 14.

CHAPTER TWENTY-TWO

Death Of A Disco Dancer

Jon had a lot to get off his chest as he strode into Farren's office on Friday afternoon.

'Got a minute, Farren? It's important.'

The moment of truth had arrived – was Jon going to toe the line, or was this the moment when the pin was removed from the grenade? Farren didn't have to wait long to find out.

'Farren, this is very difficult for me, but the thing is, I've been approached by a headhunter with a very attractive job offer, and I wanted to know where I stood with you before I made my decision.'

'I see,' said Farren. 'Go on.'

'Well, it's just that when we had dinner at Rules last month you seemed very unhappy with my work. I was upset to be honest, and it unsettled me. So when this offer came in I had a look at it, which I normally wouldn't have bothered with.'

'So you were approached by a headhunter rather than the other way round?'

'Yes,' lied Jon.

'Who's the job with?' asked Farren.

'Fond Farewell Funerals. They want me to be their development director.'

'You mean they want you to copy AMOLAD and take us out of the market?'

'No, it's not like that, Farren, they just want to kick on is all, and they see me as the man who can help.'

'So you've accepted?'

'No, not yet. I wanted to know what my future prospects were here first.'

'Well, where do you think you stand?'

'I'd been hoping to be given a bigger incentive, more shares, to keep me tied in here, but now I've begun to doubt whether that's your intention. That's why I've come in to ask you.'

'What are they offering you?'

'It's a very attractive package, more money than I'm on now, and with a rising share incentive. It's a wonderful opportunity, but of course my first loyalties are to you.'

'Of course. So what you are saying is that I need to give you a better package of salary, shares and responsibility so you don't sod off to Fond Farewell and try to shaft us? Is that a fair summary?'

'No, Farren, I don't think that's fair. You know I don't really want to move, but it's too good an offer not to consider. You know how it is. I'm just interested in how you see it, that's all.'

'Right. You're going to have to give me the weekend to get my head around this, Jon, if you don't mind. There's a lot at stake for both of us. Thanks for telling me. I'll speak to early next week.'

The pin extracted, Jon slunk out of Farren's office with a smirk on his face.

'What did he say when you told him?' asked Becky as she

and Jon tucked into their Friday night Chinese takeaway treat.

'Not much, but he didn't look best pleased.' Jon gnawed at the flesh of his salt and pepper spare rib before adding, 'In fact, he looked mightily pissed off.'

'Are you sure he can't do anything to you?' asked Becky, unsettled at Jon's carefree gaiety as he recounted the afternoon's events to her.

'No, he's between a rock and a hard place,' continued Jon. 'He either has to give me a deal, or he knows that Fond Farewell and me will take him to the cleaners. He can't afford to lose me.'

'But if Fond Farewell wanted to get in on what AMOLAD do why don't they just buy him out?'

'It would cost millions to do that. But with me, and my inside knowledge, we can overtake them within two years – put them out of business. Plus I'm more progressive than Farren, so we can really build a dominant market position. I've got it all worked out. That's why F3 are prepared to give me a slice of the future profits.'

'But you've liked it at AMOLAD and Farren has been really good to you. It might not be like that at Fond Farewell.'

'I've been good to AMOLAD too, and look where it got me. No, I can't lose on this one. You get one shot at playing your ace, and I've just played mine. You'll see.'

'So you're going to leave, even if Farren gets back to you with a better offer?'

'That's right, I am. Can't wait. I just want to see how low Farren can grovel first,' laughed Jon as moved on to his sweet and sour chicken. 'Get out of that one, Mr Eulogy'.

Becky didn't look too sure.

As Farren drove north to Manchester, he was cursing Jon and his attempt to shanghai him and the business. He'd suspected as much of Jon, but now he had to make a decision. There was no doubt that Jon had approached Fond Farewell directly, as he'd gone straight to Farren all those years before. This time, instead of a quirky video, he'd no doubt given them a spiel about how he could build a model to outstrip AMOLAD in double quick time and got the pound note signs rolling round in their eyes. All right in principle, but still a long way off actually achieving it.

Jon was a number 2, and would screw up in a lead position, that much Farren knew. He was too egocentric, headstrong and uncommercial for a start. He had some nerve trying to hold him to ransom, especially after all Farren had done for him, but no doubt he was telling anyone who'd listen to him that 'business was business'. Well, yes, it was business and losing Jon wouldn't be the end of the world for AMOLAD.

Farren had always known that, eventually, someone would try to take them on in the market. He'd not really seen Jon as the Trojan Horse before now, but now he'd played his hand there was no doubt about it. Did Jon really think Farren would beg him to stay and offer him golden handcuffs? Well, there wasn't a chance of that – the priorities for Farren right now were to get PRD over and done without mishap and after that do a damage limitation job to ensure Jon couldn't harm them as much as he no doubt intended to. Jon was going, but he'd have to manage him out of the door carefully.

Did Jon have anything else on Farren that would cause him problems? No, he was clean. Jon would know about the arrangement with Nigel Adlington back in the day, as they'd discussed it before the PRD pitch, but surely he couldn't use that? After all, Adlington would come off worse than Farren if the story got out, and Jon would have to be careful over whom he chose to make an enemy of, especially as he'd be chasing after Adlington for Fond Farewell at the first opportunity.

Something like this had been on the cards for a long time. It didn't make it any easier to handle of course, but AMOLAD had enjoyed a good long run and been unchallenged for quite a while. F3 thinking they could run AMOLAD down with Jon at the helm was a long shot for them – the easiest entry to the market would have been for someone to make a bid for AMOLAD itself. After all, it was a privately owned company, and Farren had received expressions of interest before, but not, it must be admitted, from a funerals company.

In fact, Farren could solve this little problem by activating a sale to a third party, even including F3. Maybe the timing was right? That would be one way out. He thought about how unsettled he'd been in recent months over the direction the business had taken, the sniping, the cock-ups, being treated like a brush salesman by the government and its lackeys, not to mention the distinct lack of staff loyalty. He thought about how increasingly uneasy he was feeling over the crass sentimentality and crocodile tears AMOLAD encouraged, and how Ernest's funeral had shown him the true face of bereavement. What had he said to Michael? *I sometimes think I've declared war on decorum.*

Was it time to get rid of the whole shooting match? It could well be. Plus, he thought as he slid his credit card in to the barrier machine at the M6 toll road booth, he would make sure he got even with that little shit Jon somewhere down the line.

Farren stayed with Agnes on the Friday night, and did his

best to keep her spirits up. It wasn't easy. Not only was she still in mourning for Ernest and missing him terribly, she was clearly feeling territorial over Farren and his new relationship with Michael. She'd asked Farren more than once if he was seeing Michael when he came up on a visit, and her tone hadn't seemed overly approving.

Over the past three months Farren had made regular trips back to Manchester and was building a good rapport with Michael as well as keeping an eye on Agnes. Farren was careful not to appear too keen in talking about Michael in front of Agnes as he appreciated that she may be feeling sidelined, but there was no doubt about his developing feelings towards his father – he was looking forward to seeing him again the next day.

On Saturday morning Farren drove over to Michael's, ducking under the flight arrivals as they buzzed the Heald Green suburbs. This was the pair's tenth meeting since they had found out about each other.

Farren and Michael had planned a trip out to the Peak District for lunch, and both were looking forward to the outing. However, when Farren arrived, Michael had disappointing news for him – he'd been called in to handle a collection that morning which would delay their departure. 'Are you sure it's all right with you, Farren? I can't really turn these jobs down.'

'No, not at all. It's your business. I understand.'

'Would you like to wait here and read the paper while I attend to it? I'll be around an hour and a half.'

'No. Listen, why don't I come with you? I can stay in the car most of the time. It will give me a chance to see where you work too, while no one is about. Is it a house call or the hospital?'

'It's the hospital morgue – an unidentified corpse that the council have asked me to handle. It happens more than you think.'

'What do they want you to do?'

'Remove the body, and arrange interment. They can't cremate as that destroys DNA, so they're always buried just in case they need to be exhumed.'

Farren was intrigued. It was something he'd not really thought about before. 'Do you get many like that?'

'The odd few. The council gets the responsibility when they're found. After a year of holding the body, if there's no identification, they release it for burial – they normally give them to me to sort. So, I keep taking them. All part of the service sort of thing. By the way, we'll be taking the van for this one.'

Half an hour later they arrived at Wythenshawe Hospital where Michael gently guided the anonymous looking vehicle into the morgue's loading bay.

The mortuary attendant glanced at the paperwork and ushered the two of them inside, Michael pushing the trolley. Farren was struck by the silence and the blandness of the location, before chastising himself for thinking it would be any different. It was a morgue, after all, and local councils and Health Authorities were always going to favour function over aesthetics for such a facility.

Farren watched in silence as Michael went about his duties. No small talk with the attendant and total respect for his charge as he checked the ID and handled the body bag, all with an air of dignified efficiency. They were done within five minutes and heading back to the Morrison Funeral Home in Parrs Wood.

Neither spoke as Michael drove; the air of quiet reverence continued as if they were at a funeral itself. After a fifteen-minute drive, Michael turned off Kingsway to a row of shops. At the end of the row, immediately next to the side road leading to the rear of the parade, stood the double fronted windows of Morrison Family Funeral Services. Michael turned the van into the side road and pulled up at the rear of the building before getting out to unlock the double doors at the rear of the premises. Communicating solely with nods and gestures Michael directed Farren as they removed the body bag from the vehicle into the preparation room.

Only then did Michael break the spell of tranquillity. 'Are you OK?'

'Yes,' replied Farren. 'Thanks. I was going to ask, who is the deceased?'

'There's no name, obviously, but it's a young girl, around twenty years of age they reckon. Cause of death, heroin overdose.'

'And no-one can identify her?'

'Sadly not. She was found in a car park down by the Rochdale canal where it runs through the city centre. No ID, no match on the DNA register, no trace on the missing persons bureau. Just a poor, lonely, lost soul.'

'Surely somebody knows she's missing?'

'Possibly, but no-one has come forward, and all the enquiries have drawn a blank. She's been in storage, but they can't hold on to her for ever, so it's over to us now.'

'What will you do?'

'We'll bury her in a cardboard coffin in a common grave

on Monday. The only trace of her then will be a cross saying "Unknown Female".'

'That's terrible.'

'Yes, it is. But like I said, this does happen more than you'd imagine. Would you like to see her?' Seeing the look of surprise on Farren's face at this invitation, Michael quickly added, 'Sorry, didn't mean to shock you. I only meant to say goodbye to her. I do normally – there's nobody else to.'

Taking a deep breath Farren looked at the body bag, and then back at Michael. 'OK. We should say goodbye. Somebody should.'

Solemnly, Michael unzipped the body bag a sufficient distance to reveal the face and neck of its occupant. A halo of dull blonde hair edged the white sheen of the girl's face, the purple tinged eyes and mouth bestowing a supernatural air. Her features betrayed the fact that alive she had been thin and angular of feature, scrawny almost. There were no obvious signs of distress; she looked peaceful, as if in a deep sleep.

Farren regarded her, and felt the strain mount behind his eyes as he took in the piteous sight. Not knowing what to do he awaited Michael's lead once more – was he going to say a prayer or something? Michael merely joined Farren's gaze towards the young girl and then gently spoke. 'Whoever you are, you were loved by someone somewhere along the line, and I hope you may be still. Somebody's daughter; rest in peace.'

After an enquiring glance at Farren to check he too had finished his valediction, Michael quickly re-zipped the body bag, wheeled the trolley into the chiller, and said: 'Right, we're done.'

Ninety minutes later, in the bar of the Stanley Arms near Wildboarclough in the Macclesfield Forest, Farren and Michael sat over their pints of Marstons Pedigree awaiting their bottom-of-the-oven lamb.

Farren was still coming to terms with the morning's unexpected diversion. 'Michael, I don't think I'll ever forget how you saw that poor girl off. It was really moving.'

'Well, I hope anyone else would have done the same. She was obviously lost when she was alive, but she was a human being and deserved some dignity at the last. Were you OK with it though, Farren? I thought for a minute I may have overstepped the mark asking you along.'

'I'm fine. No, it was an eye-opener for me. It just shows up what I've been saying about what I do for a living and all this government crap I'm tied up in. It all seems so inappropriate when you see what we saw this morning.'

'Well, this morning wasn't the norm, so don't start thinking it was.'

'Yes, but what we do and persuade people to do somehow seems to, well, trivialise that poor girl's death.'

'We just had a job to do, and she needed us because she had no-one else to remember her.'

'Yes – no-one to remember her, or put up an online testimonial or produce a biovid. That was… well, so final.'

'Death is final, Farren. However you dress it up.'

'That's what we do isn't it? Dress death up. It makes me feel ill thinking about it.'

'Don't get it all out of perspective. I shouldn't have taken you along.'

'But think about it – that could have been Linda – Mum – couldn't it? She died of an overdose, and we still don't know anything about her. She could have ended up in a body bag like that with no-one knowing who she was.'

'She didn't because at least we know that Father Culshaw found out about her death through the authorities. We don't know yet about who else may have known, but she won't be down as an "Unknown Female" at least.'

'You know Michael, I've been thinking about getting out of this game altogether. Today makes me think it may be about time.'

'That's not why I took you, Farren. Please don't think that.'

'No, it's not you. It's been getting to me for a while. The whole business was fun to start with, but I never thought it would, well, get so out of hand. It's not just that though – I'm beginning to think the critics are right – we're turning bereavement into a freak show.'

'There are always people who criticise new ideas,' said Michael, trying to be positive about Farren's perceived persecutions and by now convinced that he had set all of this in motion in inviting Farren along on a call, particularly so soon into their relationship.

'Until recently I never worried about what detractors said. But what if they have a point? What if Smudger's right? Where did you stand on it before you met me? I bet you were against AMOLAD. Most undertakers are.'

'It doesn't really matter what I think about it, in the same way that it doesn't really matter what I think about us joining the Euro or whether we should have invaded Iraq. Everybody went over the top after Diana, and it all stems back to that really. All you did was tap into that, and give them what they wanted.'

'But not what they needed. I've seen that with Ernest's funeral, and this morning.'

'Listen, Farren. If it's getting you down, can't you do something about it? Sell it or something?'

'I was thinking about that only yesterday. But if I sell it, then it's only going to continue with somebody else feeding the frenzy, isn't it? You should see some of the schemes and ideas I've had to stop.'

'Well, I can only imagine. But it's very much part of the way people carry on these days, isn't it?'

'Yes. And I'm to blame. If I could undo what I've done, I think I'd do it like a shot.'

'I'm sure you'll do the right thing,' said Michael. 'If I can help you, Son, you know I will.' It was the first time Michael had called Farren 'son'.

'Thanks, Dad,' said Farren. 'I know you will.'

PRD minus 9.

CHAPTER TWENTY-THREE

Hey Hey, My My (Into The Black)

At precisely 21.49 later that Saturday @wappinglie was the first to get a sniff of the exclusive being run in the Sunday Splash the following day. The feed's rising number of 98, 928 followers was duly alerted to the impending publication with a message that read: *'Another one forgets to destroy the negatives– tomorrow's Splash leads with Annie Brooks porn shots.'* A link conveniently took readers to a facsimile of the Splash's front page which featured a photograph of Annie Brooks caught in a provocative embrace with a handsome young stud. Both were completely naked.

The headline read: *'Annie Road Up'* followed by a sub-head of *'Campaigner exceeds the limit in Thighway code porno snaps.'* On zooming in on the body copy Tweeters could read the following:

> *'Road safety campaigner Annie Brooks was saying anything but "slow down" to her boy racer companion when it came to romping naked for a lurid under the counter magazine porno shoot. In a series of snaps that will shock the denizens of supporters of her HASTE road safety initiative the campaign figurehead, using the name of Tiffany Wilkes, can be seen engaging*

in a number of depraved sex acts, wearing provocative lingerie, handling a variety of sex toys and acting out sex fantasies with various items of food.

The explicit photographs, obtained exclusively by the Sunday Splash, were taken four years before her marriage to Championship footballer Stuart Brooks.

Mrs Brooks launched her HASTE campaign to reduce urban speed limits following a hit and run accident involving her son, Donny, now aged six, two years ago.

The publication of these highly controversial images is bound to embarrass sponsors and supporters of the high-profile campaigner who recently appeared as a guest speaker at the government's spring conference.

Turn to pages 3, 4, 5 and 6 for the full story.

View the full series of photographs on the Sunday Splash website.

Kieran couldn't believe his luck at getting a tip on this one. With a few more tweets like this @wappinglie could double its number of followers in the near future.

Nigel and Emma Adlington both woke up happy on Sunday morning. Each had a smile on their face as they cast their minds back to yesterday evening's lovemaking. As Emma went to bring him breakfast in bed and the Sunday newspapers, Nigel stretched out his arms above his head and yawned in contentment. He'd quite surprised himself; it wasn't like being with Annie, obviously, but it hadn't been that bad. In fact, not bad at all.

At that second, his mobile phone rang. The curse of being

an Under Secretary – it was almost impossible to turn it off. He reached across to the bedside table and picked up his BlackBerry to see who was calling so bright and early. As soon as he saw the caller name displayed he snapped to attention and answered: 'Yes, Minister?'

'Nigel, I take it you've seen the morning papers?'

'Er, no. Not yet. Why?'

'Why? I'll tell you why. That bloody speed campaign woman you put on at the spring forum is all over the Sunday Splash with her bits out. A porno shoot they've dug up. Makes us look bloody silly, Nigel. No doubt about it.'

Nigel's sunny disposition evaporated in an instant. 'I had no idea. How could I? Is the Splash actually linking her with us?'

'Of course they are. When was the last time we featured a pornographic model on the conference platform? I want you to keep us clear of this, Nigel. No contagion. Cut any links with her organisation; check where else she may be connected to us. I want a call PDQ from you with an update.'

'I'll look into it straight away,' said Nigel adding, somewhat unconvincingly, 'Thank you for letting me know.'

At that precise moment Emma breezed into the room with a tray of boiled eggs, toast and tea perched on top of a doorstep full of newspapers. 'Have a lie in, Nigel, while I see to the boys. You need to keep your strength up, after all.'

As soon as she'd left the room, Nigel tore at the pile of newspapers to find the offending article. He didn't have to look for long. There, in common with two and a half million other readers, he could see the snap of Annie *in flagrante delicto*. He quickly skimmed the story, rolled his eyes to the ceiling and groaned. 'Shit, shit, shit.'

Farren Mortimer, alerted by @wappinglie's tweet on his arrival back in London the previous evening, had already read the story about Annie Brooks as he headed against the rising wind to Soho to view the rough edit of his episode of *Made Men*. '*No surprise there,*' he thought as he read the salacious details – it had been obvious to him that she was too hot to handle, and a murky past was almost guaranteed.

Was he amused or titillated over Annie's treatment in the media (because by now other papers were running it, and she was trending on Twitter)? No, because he knew how the papers worked and that anybody in the public eye was fair game. Leave *schadenfreude* to others – it could be him next week, albeit not for anything approaching the scale of Annie's peccadilloes. But then, others might disagree.

She'd certainly been naïve to think that she could get away with playing the saint while those photographs – and no doubt plenty of others – were biding their time to make an entrance and steal the scene. How many times had he seen similar suspensions of disbelief when it came to people assessing their media vulnerability? At least AMOLAD wasn't linked with her, so thank goodness for small mercies. Adlington would be having an uncomfortable morning though.

Kieran had already arrived at the Wardour Street Studio where post-production on *Made Men* was taking place. It had been an unexpected invitation from Kieran to allow Farren to view the offline edit, basically the rough outline of the programme before the final production. Editorial approval had never been mentioned; maybe Kieran was so proud of the programme he couldn't wait to share it with its subject?

As the staff busied themselves and coffee and croissants

were brought to the edit suite, an upbeat Kieran entertained Farren with jokes and anecdotes about his time as the showbiz correspondent on the Daily Tablet. 'At least I can get to bed earlier these days,' he laughed. 'It was manic. Nobody should have to do that shift for longer than a year.'

Changing the subject Kieran then said: 'Did you see that Annie Brooks in The Splash? How bloody funny is that? And not a bad looking girl too. I bet it's carnage at Chez Brooks this morning.'

Farren wondered if the view being expressed was that of Kieran McDonaghy or of @wappinglie?

Finally they viewed the edit, or rather Farren watched the screen while Kieran anxiously scanned Farren's face for his reactions. Farren felt the most unusual sensation as the assembled footage unfolded. It was like they'd turned the tables by doing a biovid on him. Or maybe it was *Citizen Kane* that came to mind? Nevertheless, he remained impassive throughout, so much so that Kieran thought he'd make a first-rate poker player as he gave no indication whatsoever as to whether he liked or disliked what he was seeing.

At the end, Kieran was beside himself trying to find out what Farren thought of it: 'Well?'

'Are you giving me the opportunity to change it or just seeking my opinion?' asked Farren.

'Your reaction, really. Are you pleased with it?' Kieran implored.

'All I can say is – I wouldn't change a thing,' was Farren's reply.

Annie Brooks was distraught. She was sheltering in the kitchen of their four-bedroom detached home in Radlett, the blinds pulled down to exclude the world without and to deny the lenses of the paps who were hanging around outside. She'd turned her mobile off, and had pulled the home phone from out of its socket.

She and Stuart had joined in a blazing row the night before when the full extent of the exposé had become apparent and he had stormed off to his parents with Donny. She couldn't really blame him.

The first indication of the shit-storm to come had been a call from the Splash mid-Saturday evening. 'Would she like to comment, and put her side of the story?'

No, she bloody well wouldn't.

'It would help make sure all the facts are right if you'd speak to us; it's in your best interests.'

I don't think so.

Christ, how could she have been so stupid? She knew instinctively that it was Gavin who had sold the pictures to the Splash. She knew she'd been showing off when they had got together, giving it the big 'I am'. Of course, if it was Gavin, he could have done it anytime, but she knew that she'd unwittingly let him know the optimum time to cash in on her had arrived. All she'd fancied that night was a bit of fun; after all she'd been in a great mood and up for it. All the time being so bloody naïve that something like this wouldn't happen.

If she thought hard about it, and she did now, what else was out there? She shuddered at the recollection of some of the shoots she'd taken part in when she was younger, films as well as stills. She'd erased them from her memory by and large, but nothing is ever wiped permanently from the digital blackboard. It wasn't even a question of this story being tomorrow's fish and chip papers – those images would be

210

available and accessible at the click of a mouse for ever, just seconds away from being viewed by every perv, loser and schoolboy across the globe.

She shifted uneasily as she stared into her cup of cold coffee. She'd been doing lines of cocaine with Gavin as well. She'd not done much of it for years and it was a real buzz after a long gap – 'for old time's sake' as Gavin had said. What if he had photos of that, from his phone or something? Was that going to be next week's front page? Why, why had she gone back to that scene? She'd thought it was just for one night, just for a laugh, but now it was going to be with her for every day for the rest of her life.

What was Nigel going to say? Would he even talk to her again? He had his position to think about after all. Had she blown that too? She already felt she knew the answer.

Annie had no friends to speak of, nobody close enough to come round and rally, comfort and support her. She had no family other than her husband and Donny and Stuart had made his feelings very clear. No one to turn to; nobody to help. She was on her own.

Suddenly, she stood up. *'Sod it,'* she said to herself. Turning her mobile back on, she ignored the missed calls, messages and texts that had amassed there and rang Mal Jones, the owner of the PR company she used for HASTE.

'Mal? Annie Brooks. I presume you've seen the papers? Right. Can you get down here in an hour? I'm not taking this lying down. I'm a victim in this and we've got to start our fight back. I've done nothing wrong. In fact I've overcome hundreds of obstacles to get where I am. I'm a survivor. Should I be crucified for that? Exactly. We've got to see where we can find some positives in all of this.'

211

Smudger and his mates were in the pub having a few pints before they headed off to The Den to see Millwall play Leeds United, always a big game. It was blowing a gale and the lads were concerned that the match would be ruined with the ball behaving like a beach ball in the high wind. Smudger liked his football, and loved the whole set up for a match day when all of his concentration could be focused on the game. It wasn't just the ninety minutes of course – that was just part of it. It was meeting up, having a few pints, enjoying the craic with the guys in the pub and the rituals of the day like getting to the ground two minutes before kick off that made going to a game so special. And, if Millwall won, it was the icing on the cake.

Besides one or two of his hoodies who were sworn to secrecy over his identity, no one knew that he was Smudger the infamous street artist. Dazza merely described himself as a commercial artist when asked what his line was, and nobody could accuse him of being untruthful.

This was his day off, his leisure time, and normally he had little trouble in just relaxing and enjoying himself. But the smallest reference or incident can spark a memory or a chain of thought, particularly in an artist's mind, and that's what happened today.

As Smudger took his seat prior to the start of the game the announcer called for a one-minute silence to honour the memory of the famous former Manchester United and England captain Chris Matthews who had died that week. While the Millwall fans were dutiful in their observance, all that could be heard from a section of the Leeds fans crammed in to the upper section of the North stand was a chorus of: 'We hate Scum'.

Scum. Smudger thought of his father. His bullying, drunken, psycho dad who had made both Darren's and his mother's life a misery. Incredibly, when his dad had been murdered eight years ago in a gangland feud, his mother had wept and wailed; Darren had put this down to some form of Stockholm syndrome. He certainly didn't share her views – he was glad the bastard was dead. His dad's pals had paid to have a biovid produced for the funeral, which had been like a society event at the time. Afterwards his mother had watched the film endlessly – a shambolic homage conjuring up an apparition she could fall in love with again and again, all played out to the track *Going Underground* by the Jam.

Smudger's flashback triggered the thought: *'I've not come up with anything for PRD yet and it's only two weeks away.'* He made a mental note to get on to it in the morning, before joining the irate home fans in the loud booing and abuse being directed towards the Yorkshire visitors.

One hundred and thirty miles north, Muriel Bell, Jon's mother, was driving her Ford Ka back home to Belper along the A517 from Ashbourne. Her husband Graham had gone to Pride Park that afternoon to see The Rams take on Cardiff City so she'd taken the opportunity to visit her sister. As she headed for home to prepare a late Sunday post-match dinner she reminded herself to stop and pick up some horseradish sauce as they'd run out. She'd already prepped the vegetables to accompany the joint of beef she'd bought the day before.

The high winds of the morning had now whipped themselves up into a strong gale, and Muriel gripped the steering wheel with all her might as she apprehensively peered through the rain lashed windscreen. As the car was buffeted from side to side she turned the radio off to help aid her concentration. Muriel wasn't a confident driver; she normally only ever drove to the shops and to work at the infant school where she was a classroom assistant two days a week, rarely exceeding a five mile radius around her home. Nevertheless, the roads were relatively clear, and she knew that if she kept her focus and drove steadily she'd be back home within half an hour or so, and could have the dinner on the table for when Graham returned.

As she climbed out of the valley at Turnditch she contemplated stopping for a while as the tiny car struggled against the headwind, but she persevered, the sooner to get home. Gamely she negotiated the next five miles until she came in sight of the garage around the corner from their house. '*Made it,*' she thought as she parked the car up on the forecourt and got out to buy the overlooked condiment.

At that moment, a huge gust of wind dislodged the revolving 'Car Wash' sign situated next to the garage entrance and propelled it in an upward trajectory and with considerable force in the direction of the unsuspecting Mrs Bell. As the sign cracked against the back of her skull, all went black. Muriel would roast no more potatoes; her journey had reached its end.

Farren spent Sunday evening at home. He was in no mood for TV, or even reading the newspapers. He couldn't even be bothered to turn any music on. He hadn't eaten all day except for a croissant at the studio and could only find a large bag of salted peanuts in the kitchen cupboard by way of sustenance. As the wind beat at his windows he opened a bottle of Sangiovese – 2 x bottles for £8.99 at Sainsbury's – to pass the evening. The events of the weekend were pre-eminent in his mind, and he needed to take stock.

The rough edit of *Made Men* he'd seen that morning had been a discomforting experience. He should have been pleased with it because although it gave some space to opponents of his ideas and techniques, there was no doubt about it – the programme was exceptionally favourable and flattering. The use of classic film clips had been inventive and entertaining, and Farren knew that he'd held up his end of the bargain by looking and sounding like the consummate, professional entrepreneur he was supposed to be. Kieran was a good presenter too. Farren knew he'd have been over the moon about the programme a year ago, but now he felt embarrassed and rather abashed over the profile; he felt a sense of shame in his depiction as some sort of magnate of mourning – was that really him? The truth was that there was nothing wrong with the programme as such, nothing he could object to or ask to be removed. No, the problem was that it *was* accurate, and he'd not liked what he'd seen in the mirror.

Farren also had to deal with Jon tomorrow. He'd have to go, but Farren would first need to speak to his solicitor over the details. Also, it would be important to keep the lid on any announcement until after PRD. Jon had picked his timing carefully for maximum damage, but the primary objective now was for AMOLAD to get over the PRD dateline without mishap. Farren figured he'd probably get Jon to do a further month, allowing them to get PRD out of the way without getting the government twitchy about senior personnel changes. He'd then enforce five month's garden leave on Jon before he could join Fond Farewell.

Leaving Jon in the company for a further month was

risky, as God knows what he'd try to steal in the way of plans, financial information and such like, but he assumed Jon would have already appropriated whatever he thought important. Farren could keep an eye on that and on Jon for the next few weeks – what he couldn't afford was sending Adlington and his crew into a blue funk as he knew they were pretty much at that level already. He could really have done without this, and he couldn't predict with any certainty how Jon would react, but there it was – that was the plan.

Still, the most disturbing aspect of the weekend was the haunting image of the 'Unknown Female' who had prompted his subsequent admission to Michael, Dad, that he was 'contemplating getting out of this game altogether'. The comment had surprised Farren too, because while he'd been cogitating with increasing frequency about what AMOLAD did and the impact it may be having, he'd never actually told himself he was going to quit, but the way he'd said it to Michael made it sound like he'd reached a conclusion. Had he made a decision?

Deep down he knew he had. He'd had enough of it, and it was time to get out. He knew it wasn't managing the business itself that was the problem. Areas where many business people succumbed to pressure while running a company, such as planning, accounts, creativity, working with the team and marketing were, by and large, meat and drink to Farren. But in his soul he *knew* that what he'd unleashed upon the population was an abomination of taste and an infraction of humanity. He'd given grieving a makeover and the result was grotesque – the silent accusations of 'Unknown Female' had only reinforced what he already suspected.

Could he bring himself to let AMOLAD go? He had no

doubt about it. After all, many artists destroyed their own work when they disowned the ideas or the inspiration they had originally invested in it. 'Every act of creation is first an act of destruction,' Picasso had said. OK, he wasn't an artist, so how could *he* destroy his work? He couldn't erase it, paint over it, burn, rip or slash it like an artist could.

More importantly, in disowning his work he had to make sure that nobody else wanted to claim it. As he'd told Michael yesterday, if he sold the business, someone else, like Jon or Fond Farewell, could well take it to new heights of vulgarity. No, if he really wanted to call a halt to the circus, then he had to bury AMOLAD deep and make sure that the lid was nailed tight shut. He had to discredit it to such a degree that it could never rise again.

PRD minus 8.

CHAPTER TWENTY-FOUR

Grace

Farren woke early the next morning. He felt somewhat queasy after consuming a large bag of peanuts and a bottle of red wine the evening before, and he hadn't slept at all well as he'd grappled with the challenge of how to despatch AMOLAD into the long and lonely night.

At around 4.30am in the morning a surprising figure popped into his head as he wrestled with the conundrum – one Annie Brooks. Only yesterday she had demonstrated how easy it was to fall from grace; that was a personal ignominy, so was it the same he was reaching for? Was that the way to go?

Surely HASTE was all washed up after the Splash exposé? HASTE wasn't quite the same as AMOLAD of course, but if he ended up being similarly fried in the media, what effect could that have? But he hadn't dirt on him in the same way that she had. Or had he? Everybody had a skeleton rattling around in the cupboard they'd rather keep quiet about. What was his? What would look bad in the press for him and threaten to crush his career? There were many things he'd done that he wasn't proud of, but anything strong enough to make the front page? Suddenly, a connection formed in his mind:

Annie.

Adlington.

PRD.

Farren.

They *were* interlinked in a way. He with Adlington; Adlington and himself with PRD; Adlington and Annie. Where did *he* fit in with Annie? He didn't, but could he square this circle in some way to bring the house crashing down? As he had tossed and turned, the germ of an idea began to intrude into his semi-consciousness. Could it work, or was he just clutching at straws? He'd dozed off not knowing if he was scheming or dreaming.

At 7.30am, showered and weary, Farren called into the greasy spoon at the end of his road for a reviving egg and bacon sandwich and a mug of tea. This was his normal default remedy before going to The Steeple after a late night. On this particular morning it also afforded him some space for unravelling the myriad thoughts that had been chasing around his brain for the past few hours.

The first decision he made was to give a codename to his act of destruction -'Operation Picasso'. Farren always gave his plans a project title as a means of solidifying his intent – this was going to happen. His mood was strangely positive as he recapped his thoughts. The decision was made – he was going to scuttle AMOLAD, never to surface again. But how? What was his plan going to entail?

There was no doubt that if the media knew about Farren's financial support for Adlington prior to his election that would certainly light the blue touch paper given the sensitivity over MPs' funding and expenses. That Adlington had championed both PRD and Farren once in office looked like an obvious pay off. That hadn't been the original plan, and

Adlington would argue that the funding wasn't illegal but Farren knew Adlington had never disclosed the donation; in any case, everybody would assume that there was no smoke without fire.

Farren reflected as he sipped his Darjeeling that if it came out about Annie and Adlington's affair at the same time, then anything the Under Secretary said would ring hollow. His word would be undermined and PRD *would* look like it had been a crony commission – Farren, AMOLAD and PRD would be discredited too. All Farren had to do was provide the evidence and leak it – he could work on the 'how-to' during the day. But was it enough?

As he dipped the last remnant of his bread into the yolk congealing on his plate, Farren knew there were still holes in the plan. He still had to find some evidence that Adlington and Annie were entwined for a start. Also, say he could do that and anonymously seed it to the media, while that may spell curtains for him as well as Adlington, would it actually put an end to the social fad he'd spawned? PRD would be compromised, yes, but would it stop the biovids that were now almost porn in his eyes, the memorial events that were fast becoming a convenient excuse for a piss up, and the maudlin bad taste that now dominated 90% of the online memoriams being posted? Probably not.

In fact this stratagem may even play into Jon's hands – he would not only swan off to Fond Farewell to continue the supply line, but with the chief rival having been taken out altogether, it could actually aid him. No, Farren needed to come up with something in addition if he really wanted to be sure of making the public recoil against the excesses of conspicuous mourning.

As he drained his tea and made to depart, his mobile rang. It was Jon. Farren looked at his watch – talk about keen. Couldn't he at least have waited until he'd got into the office to discuss Farren's thoughts about his job offer?

Farren answered the call with a neutral, 'Morning Jon, you're up early.'

'Farren? It's Jon. I'm afraid that I have bad news.' Farren froze – what had gone wrong now?

'My mother was killed in a freak accident in the high winds yesterday. I'm up in Derbyshire now. I'm going to have to be away for a day or two.'

Farren was genuinely shaken at the announcement. 'Jon, I'm so sorry to hear that. That is desperately sad. Are you alright?'

'As you can imagine, we're all very shocked. Dad's devastated, and we're getting our heads round it still.'

'What happened?'

'It's ridiculous really. She was hit on the head by a sign that got blown into the air at the local garage. Something as simple and stupid as that; she was killed instantly.'

'That really is tragic, Jon. Awful.'

'I know. A complete waste. I'm sure I'll be in during the week – just got to get things organised here.'

'Listen Jon, you've got to stay up there and do what you need to do. Don't worry about things here. Take as long as you need.'

'Thanks, I'll let you know what's happening when I know.'

'OK. Do that. Speak later – and my sincerest condolences.'

Farren was taken aback at Jon's call. He returned to the café counter and ordered another cup of tea over which to absorb the news and to assess the implications. Poor Mrs

221

Bell. He'd met her once when she was down visiting Jon in London and thought she'd been very pleasant and chirpy. She could only have been in her fifties – no age at all. A petite and attractive woman, and clearly proud of her son. At least with Ernest he was much older and they'd been prepared for his death, but Mrs Bell's accident was a crushing shock to her family. He could only feel for them in their loss.

Obviously there had been no mention of last Friday's conversation from Jon. Farren thought it would suit him that Jon was otherwise disposed this week – one less thing to worry about as he worked on 'Operation Picasso', and at least the government wallahs couldn't complain about Jon's absence under the circumstances (well, they would in all probability, but nothing to be done about it).

Jon's future also took on a new complexion too. Farren's earlier plan to make Jon work through PRD and then put him on garden leave may have to be revised – now he was planning to scupper his creation it wasn't that important. Jon may even change his mind about leaving now – he'd not formally resigned after all. Farren reminded himself that the most important thing he had to do was to ensure that Fond Farewell, or anyone else for that matter, did a volte-face on the thought of jumping into AMOLAD's grave.

Farren ruefully recalled the conversations he'd had with Jon when Ernest died and Jon's total insensitivity to his bereavement. Perhaps Jon would have a better idea now of what he'd gone through.

And that's when Farren came up with his master plan to sink AMOLAD once and for all.

Kieran sat in the production meeting for that evening's *Feet Up* show and could hardly believe his ears. 'Annie Brooks wants to do an exclusive interview tonight?' he said in amazement. 'She sure has some balls.'

'Clearly she does, but this will be a massive ratings booster for us, so we're going big on it with half the show,' replied the producer.

'Who's doing it, me or Jenny?' was Kieran's next question. He was keen to trump his co-presenter on this scoop for the show.

'I'm putting you up against her, Kieran. Viewers detect a bitchy edge when it's female to female in interviews like this – your job is to appear totally non-judgemental.'

'I see that, but we can't give her *too* easy a ride,' replied Kieran.

'No, not at all. But we have to remember our audience and our time slot,' said the producer. 'Her PR hasn't asked for any conditions, just the opportunity for her to give her side of the story. In my experience that means you'll just have to wind her up and let her run. She'll hang herself without you having to do too much.'

'I'm with you,' said Kieran, who was already optimistically looking forward to the prospect of a live TV meltdown on his watch.

Nigel Adlington closed the door of his office to gain a minute's peace. The past 24 hours had left him somewhat shell-shocked. He'd instructed his team on the party line for Annie Brooks – 'nothing to do with them' basically – and was grateful that there were no further plans in the pipeline to have any future dealings with her organisation. He'd briefed the minister that they were 'without taint', and hoped that was that. However, one major problem remained – Annie.

Annie had texted him on Sunday afternoon, entreating him to call her. He'd sent her one text saying he was at home and it was impossible to call her, and he'd be in touch Monday. He didn't want to call her, but realised he couldn't just cut her off as she had too much on him. His reply hadn't stopped Annie texting him throughout Sunday evening, the general tone of which was 'you'd better not desert me now'. The consequences for him if he did were not articulated but nevertheless he felt vulnerable and ill at ease. She was hard-boiled, that was for sure.

He asked himself, time and time again, how had he fallen for the oldest trick in the book? She was a porn princess, nothing better than a high-class hooker who'd seen him coming and snared him good and proper. Now his career and his marriage stood on the very brink because of his weakness. If anyone got wind of his affair with her he was toast. If he ignored Annie's pleas she'd take him down with her, of that he was now sure. What should he do?

He had to speak to her, had to make sure. Reluctantly, he picked up his mobile, scrolled to 'HASTE' in his contacts list and hit 'call'. What was he going to say?

'Nigel, thank God you've called. I can't believe what the bastards are trying to do to me.'

'Hello, Annie. Yes, I've seen the coverage – this puts us both in a rather sticky position, doesn't it?'

'It hardly puts you in a sticky position, Nigel. I'm the one copping the fallout. Nobody knows about *us*.'

'But, you see, if it came out, then it would be disastrous.'

'But it's not going to come out, is it, Nigel?'

'Maybe it would be better if we kept a low profile for a while, didn't see each other, you know, just until things blow over?'

'I need your support, Nigel, now more than ever. You can't leave me to do this myself.'

Nigel tensed still further – she wasn't going to go quietly. 'Annie, I take it the photographs were genuine? It's not a trivial matter.'

'I've been stitched up. All that was years ago. I'm the victim in all of this. You don't know about my life and what I've had to overcome. I've nothing to be ashamed of.'

'No, of course not, it's just that…'

'I'm not crumbling at the first sign of trouble. I'm a fighter – that's why I'm going on *Feet Up* tonight to give my side of the story.'

Nigel couldn't believe what he was hearing. 'Is that advisable, Annie? Wouldn't you be better actually avoiding the media for a while? Don't fan the flames by extending the debate?'

'It's all sorted. I know it's the right thing to do, but can we meet up afterwards?'

'Well that may be difficult, and it could be risky – you could get followed by photographers…'

'Nigel. I need to see you, and I'm not going to take "no" for an answer. You're in this with me now whether you like it or not.'

Nigel, well and truly snookered, could offer up nothing but: 'come to the flat at 11 tonight, but be discreet.'

'See you then – of course I'll be discreet. Thanks Nigel. It means a lot to me.'

As a cold sweat broke out on Nigel's brow he felt powerless, weak and pathetic. Why hadn't he simply refused to see her? Could he try to reason with her tonight and put some distance between them? Would money do it? He knew that was most unlikely. He had a nauseous feeling in the pit of his stomach that his fortunes were now yoked to hers whether he liked it or not.

Having dealt with Nigel, for now at least, Annie continued with the tasks in hand. She was on fire, calling contacts right, left and centre, telling the HASTE team that yesterday's coverage was merely a hiccup and instructing her lawyers to sue the Sunday Splash for breach of privacy. By mid-afternoon, she was at her PR company's offices being prepped for her interview on *Feet Up*. The team, now led by the boss, Mal, were stressing that she should put the emphasis on her work and achievements with HASTE, remind viewers of the support she was receiving from her family and circle of friends, and underline the vulnerability of disadvantaged teenagers who could, like her, fall into the exploitative clutches of unscrupulous people if they weren't careful. A few tears wouldn't go amiss either. They were aiming for a sympathetic hearing, which is why they'd opted for *Feet Up* in the first place. Annie nodded, and reminded them that she did know what she was doing. The truth was, she couldn't wait to get started.

Now she had spoken to Nigel, she felt greatly comforted. She'd been worried that he would try to ignore her, but he'd been OK really under the circumstances and she could bring him round fully tonight. Besides, he knew and she knew that she was better on the inside of the tent pissing out than outside the tent pissing in. As long as no one knew about him and her, she could control him.

She still had to plan how to dodge the paparazzi tonight in order to get to Nigel's but she'd come up with something – in a perverse way she was enjoying being on the offensive rather than the defensive.

Her phone buzzed for the umpteenth time, and she was surprised to see Farren Mortimer's name on the display. She immediately answered.

'Hello, Annie. I noticed you were in a spot of bother and just wondered if I could do anything to help?'

'Why, Farren, that's absolutely fantastic of you. Thanks. I really appreciate that. As you can imagine, there's plenty of people queuing up to put the boot in.'

'Thought there might be – that's why I called. Is there any way I can help, maybe with my comms team or something?'

'I think I've got most of it under control, but I'd always welcome a friendly expert view.'

'What are you doing this evening? Perhaps we could meet?'

'I'm on TV tonight, but yes, why not, afterwards, about nine?'

'On TV? What are you on?'

'*Feet Up* – I'm doing my side of the story.'

'At least they'll be sympathetic – good choice.'

'That's the plan.'

'Can I suggest you come round to my flat after the show then? It's not far. I'll text you the address.'

'Thanks, Farren. I may have to take a detour or two to shake off any paps, but I'll make it.'

'Great, see you later. Break a leg on *Feet Up*'.

Annie smiled for the first time that day. Fancy Farren calling to offer help? At least there were still some gentlemen left in the world.

Farren's next call was to Michael, who was just back from the common grave having buried 'Unknown Female'.

'Remember on Saturday, Michael, when I said I was thinking about getting out of AMOLAD and you said you'd help me if you could?'

'Yes, of course I remember, and I meant it too.'

'I think I've come up with a solution.'

'That's good news, then. What are you going to do?'

'I need your help, Dad. I really do. I can't do it without you.'

'I'm sure you could. I'm happy to do anything I can, although I really can't guess what you've got in mind.'

'Can you get down to London tomorrow evening to talk it through? It's really important to me that I follow through now.'

'I think I can manage that. You know I'll do anything for you,' said Michael softly. 'As long as I don't have to break the law, mind.'

'I'll tell you everything tomorrow.'

Nigel left for home in mid-afternoon, claiming he felt a little peaky. He certainly looked it so his colleagues bade him farewell and hoped he'd perk up for tomorrow. In the flat, he sat on the sofa and willed a solution to his predicament to jump into his head. *'Come on, you're supposed to be the one in charge,'* he urged himself. *'Come up with something.'*

Try as he might, Nigel could only see disaster ahead of him – what could he do to get rid of her and to secure her silence? His mood wasn't improved at seven o'clock when, against his better judgement, he turned the television on to see Annie's interview. He was hoping that she might be able to play it all down, to emphasise that the Splash's cruel treatment was water under the bridge and she wouldn't be deterred from moving on with her important work. Annie, however, was a volatile interviewee, who didn't so much participate in an exchange with the presenter as embark on a stream-of-consciousness rant. The interviewer Kieran McDonaghy hardly said a word – he didn't need to, as Annie was up and running for most of the twelve minutes duration of the feature.

Nigel shrank further and further into his sofa as Annie howled at the moon on the Bang & Olufsen 42 inch HD screen in front of him:

'There's people out to get me.'

'This is a tabloid ambush.'

'Is a youthful indiscretion worth more than saving lives?'

'I've dedicated my life to helping others and this is how I get rewarded.'

The presenter finally got a word in and steered her towards the photographs that had appeared in the Splash:

'They're nothing.'

'I was forced to do it.'

'I'm just a victim as surely as any other sex slave in this county, but I managed to escape.'

'Are you going to kick me because I managed to get out of that scene? Or would you rather I was still being exploited?'

On her seemingly turbo-driven quest for fame and media coverage:

'You tell me one charity that doesn't need to keep awareness high?'

'I've sacrificed a lot to keep HASTE in the limelight, but do I get any thanks?'

'What charity work do you do, Kieran?'

Finally, what next for Annie?

'This won't stop me – just watch.'

'I've got plenty of influential supporters who aren't going to see all my work go to waste.'

'I'll have the last laugh – you just wait and see.'

Finally, the hell for Nigel was over as Kieran linked to a feature on the annual UK gurning championships. What had possessed Annie to go on live TV and debase herself in that manner? Christ, she came across as a demented fishwife with a serious messiah complex – she was seriously off her trolley. And she was coming round to his place next.

Should he contact her and tell her he was tied up? That would only make things worse. He was in her power and he had to do something about it. Otherwise the game was up.

Annie arrived at Farren's 15 minutes earlier than planned. She'd left the *Feet Up* studios hidden in the back of an anonymous looking Renault Clio driven by her PR executive shortly after a blacked out Porsche Cayenne had drawn the majority of the assembled photographers' attention. She hadn't really expected the ruse to work, but could come up with nothing else. In the eventuality there was less of a press pack outside than she'd expected due to a film premiere in Leicester Square taking place at the same time. After a forty-minute meandering journey Annie was dropped off near a car her assistant had parked in Islington for her earlier in the afternoon. Looking around, and satisfied she wasn't being followed, she headed for Farren's address, first calling him to let him know of her impending arrival.

Farren ushered her into his hall, and they made their way to the kitchen.

'Did you see the interview?' asked Annie.

'Sorry, not yet, just got in myself,' lied Farren who'd squirmed in astonishment watching her inept display on TV. But that wasn't the purpose of her visit. 'Bet you could do with a drink?' asked Farren.

'Would kill for one,' came her reply.

'How did it go, anyway?' Farren asked.

'Oh, you know. Not bad. I think I got most of my points across.'

'Good, well, that's the important thing, isn't it?' said Farren, trying to mask his incredulity at the rhinoceros hide she wore in place of a normal epidermis.

For the next hour Farren dispensed sympathy as well as Sangiovese, making sure that Annie felt the lack of neither. He wondered if, out of gratitude, Annie might make a predatory move on him, but there were no alarms – no doubt she was still stupefied by the events of the previous two days. He prattled on about having a clear comms message and the importance of momentum. It all seemed over her head, so he added: 'But you already seem to have everything in-hand, if I may say so, so you hardly need any further help from me.'

Annie was confused. She'd come along expecting revelationary advice of some sort, but he was waffling all over the place. Had he got her round because he fancied her? '*Well, not tonight mate, I'm not in the mood.*' She started looking at her watch, calculating she'd have to leave at 10.30pm at the latest to get to Nigel's.

Finally Farren took the hint. 'Listen, Annie, I think you're doing everything you can in the circumstances, and now I'm keeping you from home.'

'It's good of you to say so, thanks. You're right – it is about time I was going,' replied Annie.

As she got her coat and they made their farewells at Farren's front door, he suddenly gave her a friendly kiss on the cheek. 'Everything will turn out for the best, Annie, I'm sure,' he said as he gave her a friendly hug to let her know she wasn't without friends. Across the road, hidden from view, a leather-clad motorcyclist snapped a series of photographs of this fond embrace between the two good friends.

Making his way back to the kitchen, Farren checked his Twitter feed. At 19.42 @wappinglie had posted: '*like watching a car crash in slowmo. Annie drives off the middle of the road into the ditch on prime time TV.*' In addition to a YouTube link to the interview there was a useful hash tag, *#madasahatter*, to help continue the Twitter debate on Annie's TV appearance. Farren gave up reading after a minute – it was fair to say that Annie's TV performance had become somewhat of a *cause celebre*, and for the second day in succession she was trending.

Nigel Adlington had made his mind up. He had to be firm with Annie. This just wouldn't do, wouldn't do at all, for him to be associated with her. They were both grown ups, had enjoyed their fun, and now it was time to call it a day – there it was, there was nothing else to say.

He had to get a grip of the situation. He wondered how she'd take it; her performance on TV didn't fill him with confidence that she'd quietly concur. He poured a stiff Glenmorangie, straight, to give him courage as he waited for her call to tell him she was outside. When she eventually arrived, Nigel buzzed her in and waited for her arrival at his apartment door.

Annie went to kiss him and Nigel looked decidedly

awkward as he allowed the briefest of contacts before heading off into the kitchen at pace. At that point Annie knew exactly what to expect.

'Did you see the interview on TV?' she asked Nigel.

'Yes, I did as a matter of fact. Maybe it would have been more advisable to just let the story die?'

'What do you mean?' asked Annie. 'I thought I did OK.'

'I take it that you've not checked the Internet since, Annie? I'm afraid that the interview didn't go down at all well generally – quite the opposite in fact.'

'They can all sod off as far as I'm concerned. I don't give a shit what people think. My biggest priority now is us.'

Nigel grimaced. It was now or never.

'Listen, Annie, don't you think, with all this trouble, we should knock it on the head, at least for a while?'

'Are you dumping me now as well, Nigel?'

'Well, it's not like that is it? I think we both know perfectly well where we stand. Things are just a bit too hot now, that's all.'

'Hot for me, you mean. Not for you. You didn't seem to think we needed to cool things last week, did you?'

'Come on, Annie. You know the story in the paper yesterday changed everything. I've got my position to think of, you understand that.'

'And what about my position, have you thought about that? Where's the difference?'

'Annie, I'm a member of parliament, an Under Secretary. If I get implicated in this I'm dead meat, never mind what will happen at home.'

'You've used me, Nigel, used me from day one. And now you're throwing me on the rubbish heap.'

233

'Annie, it's not like that at all. Be reasonable. Don't get upset. Come and have a drink and we can discuss it.'

'Stuff your drink, Nigel. You've exploited me as much as anyone ever has. At least the others weren't as hypocritical as you. I'll do you a favour and go if that's your attitude.'

With that Annie made for the stairwell and down to the front door of the apartment block, but not before issuing her Parthian shot: 'It will catch up with you like it caught up with me, that's all I can say.'

Panicked at the intimidatory nature of her words, Nigel chased after her, catching her at the front door. He grabbed her hand and pleaded to her.

'Please don't be angry, Annie. It won't do either of us any good. Let's not do anything we'll regret.'

'Easy for you to say, Nigel. Now let go,' she said as she pushed him away and scurried off down the steps.

Their short but decisive meeting concluded, both were left with the uncertainty as to what would happen next.

Neither was aware of the motorcyclist, hidden behind a car parked across the road, snapping off their leave taking at five x frames per second on his motor driven Nikon.

PRD minus 7.

CHAPTER TWENTY-FIVE

Where To Now St Peter?

All the way down on the train to Euston Michael had been trying to guess what Farren had decided about AMOLAD. He couldn't figure how he could help, but he was glad to have been invited down to share the moment. Maybe Farren was just looking for moral support, an endorsement of his plan – whatever it was, Michael was there for his son.

In only a few short months, Michael's life had transformed. He couldn't believe his good fortune in discovering he was a father, and he was immensely proud of his emerging relationship with Farren. After the initial shock of finding out about Farren he'd initially worried that his son may not want to have anything to do with him – he wouldn't have been surprised at that outcome. Farren had done his best though to meet him halfway in the relationship; he gave the impression that he was as glad to have found Michael as he was to have found him.

Michael had also been afraid that they may not see eye to eye over AMOLAD but it was obvious, without Michael having to push the subject, that Farren was having some serious misgivings over aspects of his business. The previous weekend had proven that – Farren was really beating himself up about it. Michael hadn't intended to make him think that way; in fact he'd been cautious over even seeming to convey disapproval. If he was being honest with himself, he knew that it wasn't his influence that had led Farren to the point where he wanted out.

Michael was glad Farren had decided AMOLAD wasn't his future, because, deep down, Michael felt that the Gadarene rush towards conspicuous mourning that AMOLAD had led and cashed in on was an aberrant departure from centuries of funereal custom and decency. Michael may be old and traditional, but he didn't consider himself to be against progress. However, he did feel that the way some people now 'celebrated life' was more akin to a Blackpool hen or stag do; a sign of a greater moral breakdown and a blight on modern society that prized vapid ostentation and indulgence over spirituality.

Now Farren was going to get out and do something new. Not for a second did he worry that Farren was doing the wrong thing – he felt admiration at his decisiveness, at how he was prepared to walk away from his own creation. But how was he going to walk away? And how could Michael possibly help him to take that step? He'd find out soon enough.

Michael arrived at Farren's at 7pm. He thought the area Farren lived in was 'a bit cosmopolitan', but once inside the house found himself impressed at the layout, fixtures and fittings of his son's sumptuously designed period dwelling. He noted too how clean and tidy it all looked – Farren clearly had a cleaner.

After depositing his bag in his bedroom for the night and a quick tour of the house, Michael settled in the kitchen while Farren busied himself over preparing dinner. As his son had opted for cassoulet au confit de canard, two jars of which he'd bought ready made, together with a foil tray of dauphinoise potatoes, similarly pre-prepared, it was merely a case of heating the food for the requisite length of time.

As Farren poured the accompanying Brouilly, Michael was impressed at his son's culinary accomplishments – the meal was a far cry from what Michael would have been eating at home on a normal Tuesday evening. The two were at ease and light dinner table conversation flowed naturally between them – it was as if they'd known each other for years.

Eventually, the dinner plates having been cleared away into the dishwasher and two espressos having been extracted from the Miele built-in stainless steel coffee machine, Farren signified that they had arrived at the serious part of the evening.

'You're going to be shocked at what I've got to say, Michael, but I can't see any other way out without doing something drastic.'

'So you've decided you're definitely getting out?' asked Michael.

'Yes. That's not the problem; it's *how* I get out that's the issue.'

'Well, unless you sell it the only option you've got is to close it down, isn't it?'

'I can't do either of those because I have to make sure I don't risk someone else just carrying it on after me.'

'But how can you guarantee that? People seem to like what you do, so how can you stop somebody else copying you?'

'They wouldn't copy AMOLAD if the public lost its appetite; if they woke up to the fact that what we do is crass. And to do that we need to shock people. Knock it on the head once and for all.'

Michael looked perturbed. Drastic? Shock people? Knock it on the head once and for all? What on earth was Farren thinking of doing?

'I've come up with a plan, in fact it's a twin plan, but the only way I can do it is with your help, Michael. No-one can know about it other than me and you.'

'Are you sure you're not going to do something crazy, Farren? You don't want to do something you'll regret.'

'I already regret what I've done. Now I think I can put it right.'

Michael was beginning to feel very uncomfortable over what Farren had up his sleeve, and how he, of all people, was to fit into the plan. But in his wildest dreams he could never have conjured up the scenario that Farren now outlined and his own fantastical role in its execution. As Farren spoke, Michael felt faint and frightened at what he was hearing. Farren's plan went against everything Michael had ever stood for; it was outrageous – surely he couldn't be serious?

As Farren concluded outlining his plan, he looked Michael squarely in the eye and said: 'You think I've taken leave of my senses, I know, but believe me, if I could do this any other way, I would. And I can't do it without you.'

Michael, initially lost for words as he replayed the key points of Farren's outrageous contrivance in his head, finally spoke. 'Farren, we can't do this. We just can't. The price is too high. You'll be marked for life and I can't do what you're asking of me. We could both go to jail. It's too extreme; really, it is.'

Farren, calm and unperturbed by Michael's reaction, continued. 'I didn't expect you to say, "yes" straightaway. It *is* extreme, and there are risks, but if you think about it, it's a

238

sacrifice that's worth making. I can get out of the business, and I think it's a fairly safe bet to assume that no-one will be rushing to take my place. The public's appetite for these forms of mourning is bound to wane after something like this.'

'Yes, but your reputation will be shot – is it worth that? And you're forgetting that you're asking me to do something that I could never do in a million years.'

'Reputations are disposable these days – I can always get another one. But the main thing is that nobody will link me or you to this – I'll be the captain of the ship that's just hit the iceberg, and you'll be the anonymous fireman in the engine room shovelling the coal.'

'You make it sound easy, but what if I got caught?'

'We have to make sure you don't. If we pull it off, and we can, then we'll have solved all of our problems in one fell swoop.'

'I don't know, Farren, I really don't. It's actually more extreme than what you want to stop.'

'Yes, it's shocking, but in that respect it's justifiable, an atonement that wipes the slate clean. I know I'm asking a lot, but I can't ask anyone else. If only the two of us know, then we're safe.'

A million thoughts went through Michael's mind. His son had asked him for help to slew off his old life and start again. Surely a father shouldn't refuse? But what he was being asked to do was outrageous and hard to justify. Could he even bring himself to do it, even if he said he would? What would a refusal to assist mean for his relationship with his son – would it be over before it began? Was it even fair of Farren to ask him?

The two talked intently for the next three hours, with

Farren going over the plan and explaining his rationale in the most passionate of terms. The more his son spoke, the more Michael recognised Farren's need to extricate himself from AMOLAD in this way; his desire to put it behind him. Farren wasn't coercing Michael – he was desperate for his help, and within the outline of his plan there was a perverse logic that would achieve his objective.

Finally, just before midnight, Michael made a decision. 'God forgive me, Farren, but I'll do it.' A relieved Farren, sensing the end was in sight, gave his father a hug of gratitude. Fortified by more coffees, they then spent the next two hours discussing in detail the execution of the plan.

PRD minus 6.

CHAPTER TWENTY-SIX

In My Hour Of Darkness

PRD was now only four days away, and Farren was needed at Millbank to meet with Nigel Adlington for a final catch up session. Jon hadn't been seen all week, and wouldn't be until PRD itself now as his mother's funeral was to take place the following day, on the Friday.

Farren wasn't exactly looking forward to seeing Adlington, but consoled himself with the fact that he wouldn't have to be doing this type of meeting for much longer. In the event, the two didn't dwell overmuch on the planning and media exploitation for PRD as much of this activity was now firmly under the control of the government's agencies and therefore outside of AMOLAD's remit.

Instead, Adlington seemed keener to get Farren's input on his preparation for his appearance that evening on the current affairs and debate TV programme *The Next Question?* which was filmed in front of a live audience. As well as getting the opportunity to remind everyone about the government's achievements in office he was there specifically to trail the inaugural PRD.

Although Adlington was acting chipper, Farren knew that he must be under enormous strain, not least from the Cabinet to make sure PRD was a success; still, he put on a good front, as, Farren supposed, all politicians are trained to do.

Adlington was also in a somewhat conciliatory mood, telling Farren: 'I know that we've rather taken over the running of this event, but I won't forget that it was your inspiration that made it possible. Next year, I'll try to ensure you get a bigger piece of the action.'

Farren nodded appreciatively at the Under Secretary's consideration.

'I believe that you have a bit of a TV special yourself this Sunday,' added Adlington, who dreamed of receiving such media attention himself.

'Oh, yes, *Made Men*,' replied Farren. 'I may have to miss it though as I've got a couple of things on.'

Adlington looked surprised that Farren could miss his own one-hour TV special, before realising he was joking. 'Ah, yes, very good, I'm sure.'

Afterwards, as Farren headed to The Steeple, he wondered how many hours since he'd started working he'd wasted in meetings like that, where nothing actually happened. Having worked in advertising, he concluded that it must be at least half of his lifetime.

As soon as he arrived at The Steeple his secretary brought a package into his office that had been left at reception by a courier. As per usual, security had opened the pack, and while there was nothing dangerous or threatening inside, the contents were, nevertheless, slightly perplexing. Inside the cardboard box were a party hat, party poppers and streamers, and a handcrafted card saying: 'Coming Up for the People's Remembrance Day party.'

Puzzled, Farren instructed his secretary to alert their government contacts and the police – was this Smudger's way of telling them he was planning something for PRD? He'd pulled similar tricks before, and PRD was too obvious a target for him to miss. As Farren anticipated, there was no sender, and the leather-clad courier had merely asked for the receptionist's signature before leaving.

Farren drew a line under the incident, telling his PA: 'He may just be taunting us but we can't spend all day worrying about what may never happen. In any case, we haven't got a clue what it means.' He had other things to be getting on with.

As soon as he was ensconced in his office, Farren took out his mobile and accessed the newest Twitter account he'd surreptitiously set up, @whistleblower. Then, he direct messaged @wappinglie the following: '*You should know about Adlington, Mortimer, Brooks love triangle and secret AMOLAD funding that landed PRD. For details follow link.*' He then DM'd a second tweet to the same address: '*password: theyreallatit. Your access closes at 1300.*' Part one of 'Operation Picasso' was underway.

Precisely two hours later, a flustered and excited Kieran McDonaghy sat down with David Fleming, the producer of *Made Men*, for an emergency meeting.

'David. Don't ask how I got this, but I've got hard proof that Nigel Adlington has been shagging, or conducting an affair, with Annie Brooks of HASTE. That she's also at it with Farren bloody Mortimer too, and, this is the best bit, that Mortimer secretly funded Adlington's parliamentary campaign six years back, for which, bingo, Mortimer gets PRD gifted to him. Now, is that enough dirt for you?'

The producer tried to appear calm. 'All rather salacious and interesting, Kieran, but can we prove it?'

Kieran brandished the printouts from the link he'd accessed ninety minute earlier. 'It's all here including photographs of Adlington and Annie Brooks, and Mortimer and Annie, but more importantly there are internal AMOLAD documents covering the funding of a profile campaign for Adlington called 'Adlington Cares' when he was trying to get into Parliament for the first time.'

David maintained his reserve. 'I do need to know where you got this from – it could be an elaborate forgery designed to discredit.'

'It's no spoof, David.' He picked up the photos of Farren embracing Annie at his front door, and the print of Adlington holding hands with Annie outside of his apartment block. 'OK, it's an anonymous tip off, but these photos don't lie – how incriminating can you get? And the day after her exposé in the Splash, and her meltdown interview with me? These were taken last Monday, which I can verify as she's wearing the same clothes and coat she wore to the *Feet Up* studio. Plus, I've checked online about Adlington and he *did* run an 'Adlington Cares' campaign the election before last. It looks bloody kosher to me.'

'And you are the perfect recipient of this information as our special goes out on Sunday, before PRD, and of course, you interviewed Mrs Screaming Nutcase three days ago.'

'Precisely,' replied Kieran, ignoring that the information had actually been leaked to @wappinglie. That, he'd put down to coincidence. 'It's obvious, David, that someone high up in AMOLAD has a grudge against Farren Mortimer, but the main question is, how are we going to use this to best effect?'

David hardly required much prompting on what to do next. 'We're going to get our learned friends on the case to spell out our parameters, and then we're going to re-cut the programme because this is now an entirely different proposition. Then, and this is the most important bit, we're going to blitz this in the media to make sure that ten million viewers tune in on Sunday. I can feel awards in my water, Kieran, I really can.'

So, too, could Kieran who couldn't believe this gift had landed on his, or rather on @wappinglie's, plate.

Annie was full of trepidation as she contemplated her sixth night at home without Stuart or Donny being there. Stuart was being very hard line, refusing to come back from his mother's, and Annie was missing them both more than she ever thought possible. The nanny, superfluous to requirements, had been packed off by Annie leaving her to enjoy her own company. Except enjoyment was the furthest thing from her mind as she bounced around the empty house.

Despite her fighting talk, she was beginning to realise how quickly one could be cut asunder by so-called friends and associates. Stuart had deserted her, Nigel had dropped her like a hot potato, and her phone had gone largely silent.

Her interview on *Feet Up* had created an almighty stir in the media and she had been shaken by the degree of hostility and scorn she'd received from all manner of journalists, bloggers and the public; she felt like public enemy number one. Her HASTE dream was teetering on the brink following the defection of staff and sponsors during the week. Even her PR company had resigned her account, Mal Jones saying she ignored his advice on Monday and he wouldn't work for her again – how much lower could she go? And still, in the back of her mind, an uneasy nagging thought kept persisting: *'What else have they got? What's coming next?'*

She turned on the television, and tuned in to *The Next Question?* Not so very long ago her team were angling to get her on the programme, and she always liked to see how the panellists performed. There, to rub salt into the wound, was Nigel, looking masterful, if not a little smug. How quickly he'd dumped her when the going got rough. He'd been like virtually every man she'd ever met – after one thing, and then heading for the hills as soon as they had no further use for her. She'd told herself after Monday that she'd get even with Nigel, but knew she would only be inviting further media controversy for herself if she kissed and told. Well, she could keep that possibility saved up for a rainy day.

As she hung on to every word Nigel uttered, she found her spirits flagging lower than at any point during the week. Nigel waxed lyrical about social responsibility, sense of community, paradigm shift and self-help agenda, causing Annie to chide herself for having ever thought she could conduct herself with that level of intellect and composure. She'd have been terrified at having to come over on live TV as insightful and confident as Nigel now did. And to think she'd had him eating out of her hand. She'd never climbed as high as that before, and now she was back down at the bottom of the heap.

In Highbury Grove Farren was also watching Nigel Adlington as he oozed into the nation's living rooms. He knew that by now Kieran McDonaghy and his team would be hard at work in ripping himself, Nigel and Annie to shreds. It would be done on the grounds of public interest, but would nevertheless maximise every lurid detail to sate the nation's voracious appetite for scandal and shame. He wondered why the English hadn't yet improved on the German word *schadenfreude* – for a country with such a rich literary history surely we should have come up with our own word by now?

He felt calm. There wasn't long to go now before the storm broke. He'd maybe get some signs tomorrow, some journos gathering information and checking background facts while pretending they were doing PRD stories and then, on late Saturday, he'd get the call to tell him what was in store and would he care to comment? Late Saturday so he had scant opportunity to do anything to halt the onslaught. Kieran would have lined up an exclusive, probably with the Splash again, and would ensure he was the first to break the news via @wappinglie. Other newspapers, TV and radio stations would lift the story from the Splash's early edition, re-vamp it and run it on their front pages too. There wouldn't be anyone in Britain who didn't know about their strange *ménage a trois* and the 'alleged' behind the scenes PRD deal by Sunday lunchtime.

At the same time, Kieran and his team would be re-editing the *Made Men* episode for Sunday night, no doubt going with a live intro for extra topicality and urgency. They'd probably triple or quadruple the audience they'd originally anticipated. And all eyes would be on Nigel, Annie and Farren.

Farren was serene as he waited for the blow to fall. The hare was off and running and Farren could do no more. But this was only a part of the picture – for his plan to really work Farren knew that Michael needed to come through on his mission. He reached for his well-thumbed copy of *Edward II*, and turned to the quote he never thought would actually apply to him:

*"**Young Mortimer**: Base Fortune, now I see that in thy wheel there is a point to which when men aspire; they tumble headlong down. That point I touch'd, and seeing there was no place to mount up higher why should I grieve at my declining fall?"*

PRD minus 4.

CHAPTER TWENTY-SEVEN

Come Home

Farren wasn't far wrong in his estimations of what was going on behind the scenes as PRD edged still closer. Calls were being made, backgrounds were being checked and verifications triplicated as Sunday's bubbling dish of shame and humiliation was brought to the boil. Newspaper and broadcast lawyers were, for once, justifying their outrageous fees and everybody in the know was caught up in a fetid frenzy of collusion as they played their parts in the offensive – the type of story for which they'd joined up in the first place.

The Splash had sourced a picture, from the Manchester Spring Forum, of Adlington, Farren and Annie together at a cocktail reception. As if this wasn't exciting enough for the picture editor, Annie's scarlet velvet dress, making the most of her attractive décolletage, was an unexpected bonus.

Tracking down the 'Adlington Cares' campaign was a relative doddle, and the newspaper was dedicating a double page spread to all of the ads and fliers, leaving no-one in doubt that Adlington did, in fact, care very deeply about crime, health, education and welfare. His pious pronunciations on the sanctity of family life and his common sense values were a priceless gift.

The AMOLAD documents were checked out, and stacked up. Farren Mortimer's ambitious growing company had picked up media space invoices from the newspapers that had run the ads, and the print bills for the fliers. There was also a belt and braces piece of evidence in the form of a helpful internal memo from Farren Mortimer to his fellow directors saying the investment was a punt worth making if, as expected, Adlington was elected. The expression 'bang to rights' was trumpeted more than once as the journalists went about their work.

The Splash had a minor problem, however, as they'd planned to run their drug exposé on Annie that weekend, courtesy of Gavin and a number of reliable witnesses whom he'd produced with remarkably little difficulty. Eventually, they decided that it would make next Sunday's lead anyway, and took the risk they could keep it under wraps for a further seven days.

Baccarat Productions were in overdrive with their last-minute edit, bringing in the entire PR team for the weekend, agreeing to do a live studio introduction to the programme and weighing up whether to use an alternative title for the programme of *On the Make?* This was the big one.

Kieran, the source of this windfall, strode masterfully around the edit studio as he helped make decisions on what was in and what was out.

The plan was to hit the ten o'clock news bulletins on the Saturday evening, and then ride the escalation of the story that would ensue. @wappinglie was, of course, planning to go out with news first, at 9pm, but Kieran wasn't going to be troubling anyone with that particular item of scheduling. Everybody was buzzing and excited by the investigative zeal in train; serving the public interest was what they did, and this week they were serving it better than ever.

Saturday daytime passed relatively uneventfully for the three protagonists of the unfolding drama. Farren had stayed in London to be on standby for any PRD emergencies, but was untroubled by his team all day. Adlington was home for the weekend and enjoyed a trip to Manchester Opera House with his wife and two sons for a matinee performance of the boys' favourite, *LazyTown*. Annie had finally persuaded Stuart to agree to talk things over, and was expecting him home that evening after his away game at Watford. Donny remained with the in-laws.

For both Annie and Nigel, there was an incipient sense of optimism, a growing belief that, touch wood, the worse was over, and that things may start to pick up from this lowly point. Annie insofar as she hoped to persuade Stuart to have her back and the decision she'd made to fade into the background for a while, and for Nigel, a relief that he seemed to have got away with it, and shaken off Annie once and for all.

At teatime Farren headed north to spend the night with Agnes. She was going to be the person most affected by his treatment in the media, and he thought it appropriate to be on hand to personally comfort her when the balloon went up. Having agreed with Michael to make no contact with him until Sunday night, Farren considered himself ready. His transition from hero to zero was about to commence.

At 21.01, @wappinglie seismically triggered the tsunami that would engulf Adlington, Farren and Annie in its wake. The tweet read: '*Breaking: Adlington, Mortimer, Wilkes implicated in love triangle, plus illegal AMOLAD funding that landed PRD contract. More to follow.*'

And more to follow there was as Kieran continued to pull the levers and stoke the twitter traffic, trending well into the next week.

As soon as Farren read @wappinglie's first tweet, he sat Agnes down, and said, 'Mum, I've something to tell you.'

As he explained the situation to her, it almost seemed plausible; he'd known this politician, had offered help, and he couldn't help it if the politician hadn't declared the funding as he ought to have done. AMOLAD certainly hadn't hidden the contribution in their books, so they had nothing to conceal. Getting PRD had nothing to do with any deal, it was won on merit. As for this woman Annie, he'd met her three times and he certainly hadn't had any form of relationship with her. All of this was a typical tabloid muckraking exercise aimed at the politician Adlington, and Farren was the unfortunate collateral damage.

Annie had made a big effort for Stuart that evening, cooking them a meal of ribeye steak and salad and making sure that there were bottles of his favourite Tsingtao beer in the fridge. She was determined to be humble for a change, to express regret for the humiliation she'd visited upon both of them, to convince him the story was an unwelcome flash from the past, and to seek forgiveness. Such meekness didn't come naturally to Annie, but she had grasped that the stakes were now too impossibly high to lose everything she had. Stuart initially responded with sarcasm and disbelief, but after getting it off his chest, he began to mellow. Maybe it hadn't been her fault after all, and it had all happened before he'd met her. What was marriage for if he walked out on her now? That would only make her a victim twice, and Stuart was bigger than that.

Just as Annie thought she may be winning Stuart over, and was contemplating launching a physical manifestation of her undying gratitude and eternal love on him, her phone rang. It was Mal Jones from her PR company – or ex-PR company to be more accurate.

'Annie? Mal Jones. I take it you've not heard from the newspapers?'

Annie felt the force of his words pick her up and throw her against the wall. Surely not again?

'No,' she croaked. Then, in a forlorn grasp at non-existent straws: 'Do you mean *today*?'

'Yes. Listen, I'm not ringing with good news. Basically, the Splash is running a story that you're involved in a love triangle with both Nigel Adlington and Farren Mortimer. And apparently the two of them have dodgy dealings together on this PRD bank holiday contract. Annie, it's bad. It's going to go absolutely nuclear.'

Annie was incapable of assimilating what she'd just heard, never mind begin to construct a response.

'Annie? Are you still there?'

Annie, fighting back the tears that had started to form, grunted to signify that she was still on the line.

'Well, I don't know what truth there is in any of this, and I'm not going to ask. I only thought it the right thing to do to give you the heads up as soon as possible because it's going to be another media feeding frenzy.'

Finally, Annie managed to speak. 'Can you help me? Please?'

'Sorry, Annie. You're on your own. I think we both understand that. If I can give you one piece of advice though it's lie low, keep out of it. Adlington's the main mark. Sorry to have ruined your evening.'

Stuart was staring at Annie with the look of a priest about to hear a rather long confession. 'Don't tell me there's more, Annie?'

'Stuart, you won't believe what they're saying about me now.'

And with that, Annie broke down, her spirit extinguished and her appetite for battle quelled.

The Adlingtons were spending a cosy Saturday night in together. The boys were in bed, and Nigel and Emma were planning to catch up on their DVD box set of *The West Wing*. As they settled down for the evening, with cheese, grapes, crackers and a bottle of Amarone, Nigel also received a disturbing phone call that was to shatter all of the certainties he had hitherto held to be dear and true in his life.

'Nigel, you bloody fool. You have let us all down tremendously.'

Nigel, unaware of how he'd let them down tremendously, could only say, 'Minister, I have no idea what you're talking about.'

'No, well, you will before the night is out, so let me be the first. The Sunday Splash is running a story that you've received underhand funding from AMOLAD. Secondly, that you've cooked up a payback deal by giving them PRD, and thirdly, that you and Farren Mortimer are embroiled in a sordid "love triangle" with that bloody pornographer HASTE woman. I think that's quite enough to be going on with, don't you?'

Nigel glanced at Emma, hoping she hadn't picked up on the tone of the conversation. 'Absolutely, Minister. I see. Yes, that's rather difficult, I concede.'

'Just cut the flannel, Nigel. We have to deal with this, and I warn you, I want the facts from you, not more bullshit. The director of communications will be calling you in five minutes to be briefed. Do that, then tell Emma before she hears it on the news. I'm sending a car for you and we need to convene in conference ASAP. No ifs or buts. Be ready to go in half and hour and don't speak to anyone but me or comms.'

The line went dead. Nigel turned to Emma and said, 'I may have a bit of a problem on my hands.'

Farren watched the ten o'clock news with flat detachment: he knew the beginning of the end for AMOLAD was underway. Agnes was upset and taken aback at the tone of the reporting, but pacified to a degree by Farren's cool defence against the accusations being levelled.

When the first calls started to come in from the media and his own press team, Farren was decisive. He would give a press briefing the following morning at The Steeple when he would scotch these allegations once and for all.

Annie sat on the floor amid the debris of her kitchen. After Stuart had walked out on her for the second time in a week, she had flown into a hysterical rage and smashed every glass and piece of crockery within reach. For a brief second she'd even thought of ending it all, but for now all she could do was lament the pass to where her actions had led her.

She was as confused as much as she was hurt. How had the news about her and Adlington got out? And as for the preposterous suggestion that she was involved with Mortimer? That was just ridiculous. The photographs of her she'd seen online from last Monday looked less than innocent, but they didn't tell the real story by any means. Had Nigel and Farren cooked up a dirty deal on PRD between them? Even if they had, what had it to do with her that she should be dragged into the story? She knew that in losing Stuart she was paying an almighty price for her recklessness. She dragged herself out of the kitchen and curled up on the settee, where she cried herself to sleep.

Nigel's meeting with the minister and the director of communications was a peremptory and businesslike affair. Facts were at a premium. Had he received any funding from AMOLAD? Had he declared it? Had he agreed any form of reward or incentive for the donation? Had he slept with Annie Brooks? Did he have anything else he needed to get off his chest? Nobody was really interested in the whys and wherefores; this was a question of damage limitation. After an hour of questions, Nigel was left alone while the others left the room to 'consult'.

Nigel wondered whether to call Emma, but decided against it. On leaving home, he'd told her that he'd been accused of some dreadful things and he had to go and sort it out. He hadn't the courage to tell her what the allegations were, but by now she'd know well enough. The fact that she hadn't called him spoke volumes.

He knew, instinctively, what he had to do, and that was resign. The funding from AMOLAD had been, what, for £20,000? An expensive leg up as it was turning out. It wasn't so heinous a crime he thought – he'd just not declared it. As for Annie, well the picture was merely suggestive of a liaison, but he'd seen enough of how these things worked. As a lawyer he'd often briefed clients that when you're in a hole the best thing to do is stop digging yourself in deeper. It was sound advice.

He would fall on his sword, but would they let him? Normally it would be purely an academic consideration but as his name was pinned to PRD which was taking place in just over 24 hours' time, would it cause more harm to the government if he went immediately rather than hang on for a day or two while they conducted an internal inquiry? He knew that it was the timing of his resignation that his colleagues were now debating in the adjoining room.

PRD minus 2.

CHAPTER TWENTY-EIGHT

The Sound Of Silence

There was hardly room to swing a cat as the assembled media throng crammed into the atrium of The Steeple. Dead on the appointed hour of eleven o'clock Farren, dressed casually in jeans and a white open-necked shirt, strolled in and took his place at the baize-covered table facing the tiers of expectant journalists. To his right sat his press officer, a largely redundant figure as this show was all about his boss.

Farren took a sip of water, before, without the aid of notes, embarking on his statement.

'Thank you for coming here this morning. I think it is very important for me to put the record straight regarding some of the allegations that have been made against me in today's newspapers and, if you will bear with me, I will attempt to cover all of the salient points one by one.'

Farren paused for effect before continuing.

'Firstly, there has been an insinuation that AMOLAD has received favours from the Under Secretary of State for Social Responsibility, namely contract work for People's Remembrance Day, or PRD, through an informal, or pre-arranged, or if you prefer, an underhand deal. I can refute that allegation one hundred per cent and furthermore, in the interests of transparency, I am prepared to open up our files regarding the award of the contract to public scrutiny.

AMOLAD has nothing to defend in the light of such an allegation.'

At this point, his press officer slid a file across the table to Farren.

'Secondly, it has been suggested that AMOLAD secretly funded a profile raising campaign for Mr Nigel Adlington before he ran for parliamentary office six years ago. I want to make it quite clear that while AMOLAD funded such a campaign for Mr Adlington at that time, at a budget of £20,000, we have *never* made *any* attempt to deny or obscure this information. I have copies of invoices received by AMOLAD for media space and printing costs for this campaign and copies of these will be issued to you at the conclusion of this briefing. These costs are recorded as a political donation in our annual accounts for the financial year in question. To my knowledge, it is not unusual for a private company to make donations of this kind, so nothing out of the ordinary has taken place. If, as is being alleged, Mr Adlington did not declare the funding he received then that is a matter for him and his party, not for AMOLAD.'

Two or three journalists simultaneously began to try to ask a question, but Farren held up his hand for quiet, before picking up his thread.

'Thirdly, there have been lurid insinuations that I am, or have been, involved in some form of personal relationship with Mrs Annie Brooks of HASTE. I have met Mrs Brooks on four occasions, including last Monday when I offered her support, ironic as it may now seem, on dealing with the media (pause for laughter). Due to her being harassed by photographers we met briefly at my home and that is the extent of my involvement with her. It is ludicrous that my name and hers should be linked in anything other than a purely professional context.

Let me say that while I refute all of the allegations made today against myself and AMOLAD, it would be a great shame if tomorrow's People's Remembrance Day celebrations were to be tarnished in any way as a result of these unfounded slurs. That is all I have to say. Thank you.'

And with that, Farren got up and left, not stopping to take any questions. The main purpose of the press officer became clear as he was left with the duty of telling the journalists present that was all they were going to get.

Nigel watched Farren's performance on TV with mounting astonishment. What the hell did Mortimer think he was doing? Handing out documents and trying to pin the blame on Nigel? Like a drowning man, Mortimer was dragging him under too. This put a very different complexion on what had been decided in the early hours of the morning.

Then, after considerable discussion, it had been decided that Nigel had to carry on and face it out. Nobody wanted PRD to take place with its prime architect in disgrace. There would be an investigation, and the situation would be assessed when all of the facts were known, but the party line was that they were confident that these allegations held little water. It was business as usual.

However, the party and the public weren't the only people Nigel had to tough it out with – he also had to deal with Emma, who had taken the news of his alleged infidelity less than stoically. When he had returned home in the early hours of Sunday morning, he had found her still up, trying to piece together how her marriage had reached this point. Had she suspected? No, despite her earlier accusations she really hadn't, and still couldn't believe his betrayal of her and the boys.

Nigel denied point blank the issue of Annie Brooks, saying the allegation was a total fabrication, and that he'd only ever dealt with her professionally over her charity; there was no question of any impropriety. He brushed off the photograph saying it was misleading. No, Annie Brooks was a red herring – the real nub of the problem was the accusation that he'd failed to openly declare the help he'd received from AMOLAD all those years back. Emma, unsure and wanting Nigel's claims to be true, asked if he had done anything wrong over AMOLAD's funding.

'I have nothing to apologise over,' said Nigel loftily. 'I'm sure that we will find that it's purely an administrative error somewhere down the line.'

Now, seeing Farren Mortimer move the goalposts, all that had changed. This wasn't going away. Nigel picked up the phone to call the Minister. It was a short conversation. There was no alternative – he was going today. Nigel detected that the minister seemed to be as appalled at Nigel's lack of control over Mortimer as he was over the actual allegations.

At 3pm, Nigel, with Emma in tow, walked to his garden gate to speak to the media who had been doorstepping there since the early hours of the morning. His statement, cleared by the Party office, would vie with Farren's on news bulletins for the rest of the day.

'As you know, I have been the subject of a number of allegations made in today's press. These accusations are totally without foundation. Before I entered Parliament, funding and support in kind was contributed by a number of corporate benefactors. There is nothing unusual in that. The issue here seems to be the question of whether that funding was declared in the appropriate manner. I can tell you that an internal enquiry has already been set up to check that the established reporting procedures for third party donations were followed. I am confident that my team and myself will be fully exonerated once that enquiry is complete.

'As for the suggestion that donations may have procured favours, I won't dignify such an outrageous slur with a response; similarly, nor will I be drawn into a debate on the veracity of other vile insinuations regarding my personal life.

'Both my wife Emma and myself have been shocked and upset at the nature of these insinuations. Despite not having anything to hide, it is with regret therefore that I have tendered my resignation as Under Secretary of State for Social Responsibility due to one simple and overwhelming reason. Tomorrow is the inaugural People's Remembrance Day and I feel that it would be most inappropriate for this significant milestone in the UK calendar to be hijacked or to be overtaken by these allegations. I feel that my decision is in the best interests of people who are looking forward tomorrow to celebrating the lives of their loved ones in a unique and personal manner. I want nothing to detract from this very special day. Thank you.'

As a volley of questions from journalists came flying at him, Nigel held Emma's hand, blithely ignored the baying pack and smiled serenely, panning slowly, for all of twenty seconds, from right to left for the benefit of the photographers. Then he and Emma turned slowly before walking back to the house where they disappeared from view. Even in his blackest moment as a member of parliament, Nigel still found time to give himself an imaginary pat on the back for the noble way he'd handled his resignation.

Annie had some unexpected company as she hid away from the hacks outside her home for the second Sunday in a row. Mal Jones had called to warn her that he was coming up to the house on urgent business. Confused, as she was very much the dumped client, Annie nevertheless let him into the house. Any support, paid for or free of charge, was welcome.

'Hi, Annie. This is all rather a mess, isn't it?'

'That's a bit of an understatement. What are you doing here, Mal? I thought you weren't going to have anything to do with me?'

'Well, that was before I saw how deep a hole you'd got yourself in. It just wouldn't be right not to help you considering what's going down.'

'I'm honoured, I don't think.'

'Don't be like that. Listen, I may be able to help you in quite a significant way.'

'Really? What are you going to do? Shoot everybody outside?'

'No, what I have for you is an offer – now hear me out on this – for an exclusive interview with the Sunday Splash. Get to tell your side of the story and put all of the facts across.'

'You mean a kiss and tell – with those bastards? You must be joking.'

'Very much the opposite, Annie. They're prepared to pay big bucks, *and* they'll give you some protection from the other newspapers at the same time.'

'I've got nothing to say to them. They've ruined my life.

There's no way I'd have anything to do with them. The answer is "no".'

'Annie. I really advise you to think about this. It's how it works, that's all. You've got hell of a story to tell about Adlington and Mortimer and people will pay to hear it.'

'I've nothing to do with Farren Mortimer.'

'By which I take it that you *do* have something to do with Nigel Adlington?'

'I can't do it. I really can't.'

'It's big money, Annie, big money. I can get you 75 grand, depending on the agreement.'

'What sort of agreement?'

'Oh, you know, the details of your relationship with Adlington, what he was like in bed, a bit of a sexy photo shoot – that sort of thing.'

'Do you take me for some sort of tart?' blazed Annie.

'Of course not, but there is something else. Apparently they have pictures of you snorting cocaine – same source as the glamour shots apparently. Think positively, Annie – you can make those pictures history if we factor it into the deal.'

Annie narrowed her eyes and sighed. Photos of her snorting cocaine? She knew it had been a possibility. What new level of degradation would she be letting herself in for if she were to agree? Stuart wasn't coming back, of that she was convinced, and Nigel hardly deserved any consideration after the way he'd treated her. She was on her own now, and would have to make the most of it. Plus, Mal was right that she'd at least get some protection if she threw her lot in with the Splash. More importantly, how could she turn down £75,000? That was serious money that would help tide her over while she got her life back on track again. She also instinctively knew that instead of being the villain of the piece cowering behind her curtains, doing this deal would make her the star of the show once more.

'You'd have to let me read the contract first before I make a decision, but maybe it's something I could consider.'

Mal, who'd not mentioned that he'd be pocketing the small consideration of £25,000 of the £100,000 the Splash had on the table, smiled. Nobody ever turned down that sort of cash.

Kieran McDonaghy looked earnestly to camera as he confided to the millions of viewers who'd tuned in to this special edition of *Made Men*: 'It's fair to say that this is a rather different programme to the one we'd set out to make.'

As the public settled down to see Farren Mortimer's reputation well and truly buried, Michael Morrison had other things on his mind as he climbed into his car. He was going to help his son out.

PRD minus 1.

CHAPTER TWENTY-NINE

One

Michael Morrison was scared. In fact he was petrified. He'd never received as much as a parking ticket in his whole life and now he was about to do something that, if he was caught, would send him to jail. He felt sick at the prospect of what he was about to do. He'd thought of nothing else for the past five days, and now the time had come.

He'd run through the plan countless times with Farren and prepared with military precision. That was the easy bit – what really concerned him was his strength to actually carry it out. Would he be brave enough, or would his resolve fail him at the last?

Every time he felt on the verge of backing out, he clung to the convictions that brought him back on track. Farren needed him to do this; he would be the one to free his son and help him find contentment – what father wouldn't do that? He would be helping to restore dignity to the world of bereavement, his world, by helping to rid it of the vulgar excesses that now prevailed. Sometimes it was acceptable to make a sacrifice for the greater good – this was one of those times. It was a price worth paying.

Michael had ensured the car had a full tank of petrol that afternoon and as he set out from Heald Green, the start of his journey illuminated by the landing lights of the planes overhead, he was composed and ready.

Not wanting to use satellite navigation, he'd studied his road map and knew his directions inside out. In the boot of his car was a rucksack into which he'd packed a pair of rubber boots, a blue Tyvek protective suit, three pairs of latex examination gloves and a Primus camping lantern (which he'd taken the precaution of equipping with fresh batteries) alongside other items deemed necessary for his expedition, including, tucked into the rucksack within its own storage bag, a steel folding shovel.

Leaving the M60 at Stockport Michael joined the A6, which he followed patiently and without exceeding the speed limit for over an hour and a quarter, first through Buxton and then Matlock. Finally, reaching Duffield in Derbyshire at the lower end of the Pennines, he took a right turn off the A6, followed by another quick right until his destination came into view. Not slowing, he continued for another three hundred yards before turning off left down an unlit country road.

Michael pulled up, and turned the car engine and lights off. Maybe because he'd completed his journey without mishap, or possibly because he knew there had been no one on the road since he'd reached Duffield, a surge of adrenalin gave him renewed determination. Now was no time for considering anything other than getting the mission over and done with.

Opening the boot of the car, he quickly donned his protective apparel, and taking the spade, rucksack and the unlit lamp with him, made his way across the field that separated him from where he was heading – Duffield cemetery was only 250 yards away.

Even in the dark, it only took him three minutes to find what he was looking for, aided by the detailed instructions Farren had provided him with two days before. There, on the pathway furthest away from the entrance gate, in front of the western wall of the cemetery and directly in front of a giant Ash tree which had been struck by lightning, lay the freshly dug grave of Mrs Muriel Bell. In the absence of a gravestone, which wouldn't be finished for at least another month, a small wooden cross, together with a plethora of bouquets, confirmed he had arrived at the correct place.

Looking across the cemetery, Michael could see that he wasn't overlooked from the main road; at his back were fields. A three-quarter moon shone sufficient light across the blackened landscape to aid him in his work. He was glad he didn't have to resort to turning the lamp on.

Michael first set about clearing the grave of its floral tributes. Even in his hurry, he gently picked up each beautifully bound arrangement and deposited it carefully to the side. Then, satisfied he had enough room to work in, he unfolded the spade and locked it into position.

As the edge of the spade slid into the soil beneath, Michael was thankful that the freshly turned earth yielded easily enough. Despite that, this wasn't a job that could be done speedily. Michael calculated that working at a steady pace (and he'd need to as he wasn't as fit as he once was) it would take him about an hour and a half to access the coffin below. The first part of the dig was actually easier as he could deposit the earth alongside the grave without too much difficulty. As he excavated deeper the effort of clearing the soil from the enlarging hole grew more and more taxing. Michael would stop every so often and peer around the graveyard to check if anyone was coming, but after he was two feet down he abandoned this precaution and gave his undivided attention to his digging. What had sounded to him like a deafeningly noisy operation when he first struck earth seemed to dampen in volume as his labouring fell into a steady momentum.

As he dug, Michael hummed under his breath the hymn *Be Thou My Vision* that had popped into his head.

Be Thou my Wisdom, and Thou my true Word;
I ever with Thee and Thou with me, Lord;
Thou my great Father, I Thy true son;
Thou in me dwelling, and I with Thee one.

He wasn't meaning to be sacrilegious, but he imagined the recitation provided a charm and a protection against both the night and the deed as he dug; besides, it was the Van Morrison version that was uppermost in his mind rather than the normal church rendition, so it didn't *feel* blasphemous or profane.

Pausing for breath at intervals to take a drink of water from the one and a half litre bottle he'd also factored into his preparations, Michael stuck at the task. Dripping with sweat, he continued to dig, scoop and scrape the soil spadeful by spadeful until, at last, four feet down, he heard a dull thud as the edge of the steel blade found the coffin. Buoyed by this he found a second wind and set about clearing the earth from around the coffin lid until at last he could see the entire surface. A brass plaque, *Muriel Bell, RIP,* confirmed the occupant.

As Michael had predicted, the lid was secured with electro – brass plume screws and washers, and he set about removing all four of them without needing to access the bag of tools he'd brought with him. Now, donning a face mask and crossing himself, he gingerly raised the lid to reveal the supine figure of Mrs Bell, dressed in a smart light coloured dress – he couldn't be sure exactly what hue in the darkness – and wearing a twin row of pearls around her neck.

As Michael mutely begged forgiveness from the corpse for the rude interruption, he threaded a rope through Muriel Bell's right armpit, behind her back and out through her left armpit, dislodging a family album of photographs that had been placed atop her folded arms. Then, tying a giant knot around the front of her chest, he was ready to attempt the lift.

Shaking with trepidation as much as exertion, Michael climbed out of the head of the grave, and curled the two loose ends of the rope around and around his fists; he then took the strain, and slowly, fitfully, excruciatingly edged her lifeless body backwards out of the grave, laying it on the ground. He thanked God she was a slim woman, otherwise he would surely not have been able to manage the hoist.

After catching his breath yet again, he removed the rope from the corpse, delicately picked her up in his two arms and carried her to the grave twenty feet away – there he gently deposited her in a seated position against the headstone. The angel keeping vigil above the granite memorial gazed down on the two figures.

Still he wasn't finished as he went back to his bag and removed the last items he required for his diabolical undertaking. These he arranged on the cold, pitiful and defiled body of Mrs Bell.

Quickly, he gathered up all of his tools, calmly re-bagged them and double-checked that there was nothing left behind.

Ready to leave, he now had but one duty to perform to complete the mission. Taking out a new mobile phone he clicked the camera function on and took a photograph of the grisly tableau. Looking at his screen he could see that he'd captured perfectly the image he had come for – the corpse of Mrs Muriel Bell, the deceased mother of one of AMOLAD's directors, wearing a garish party hat at a jaunty angle and holding a sign on her lap reading: *'Looking forward to getting the party started on People's Remembrance Day.'*

Just over three hours later, Michael was back at home. He'd driven up the M1 and across the M62 back to Manchester – this had added considerable distance to his return journey, but he and Farren believed this would make his car less of an obvious target for any CCTV cameras. At Hartshead Moor he texted the photograph to Farren from the pay as you go mobile his son had given him, before continuing his journey back to the funeral home. Here he incinerated the clothes he'd worn together with the rope, the mobile and the rucksack itself, and put his tools into the steriliser.

Finally, an exhausted Michael fell into bed around four o'clock, but found it impossible to sleep. Could the end justify the means? Had he really committed this atrocity for the greater good? Only time would tell.

When the picture of Muriel Bell popped up on his mobile, a wave of revulsion hit Farren hard. He vowed that no-one but he and Michael could ever know about this infernal act. Texting a blank message back to Michael's normal mobile, he knew that his father would now delete the image he had sent and destroy the mobile on which he'd taken the photo. Farren would only get to work when he received confirmation from Michael that he was safely home.

Around 3.30pm, receiving a blank text from Michael's usual phone, Farren took his pay as you go mobile, again intended for one single purpose, and underneath the shot of the unfortunate Mrs Bell typed: 'Duffield Cemetery.' Next, withholding the number as a secondary precaution, he sent the text to the Press Association.

After that, there was nothing Farren could do but go to bed and try to sleep. The inaugural People's Remembrance Day had arrived.

PRD zero hours.

CHAPTER THIRTY

All Things Must Pass

Trafalgar Day dawned bright and sunny. A year had passed since PRD and in a progressive move the government had decided that the theme for the new November bank holiday date should be rotated annually, the better to reflect diverse interest groups and for the benefit of the citizenry. The set-piece of this bank holiday was to be a parade of sea cadets marching through Trafalgar Square, a practice that had been in effect for a number of years in any event, but at least the cost of staging it was in line with austerity minded budgeting.

On this day, however, Kieran McDonaghy was heading not to Trafalgar Square but to Blackburn where the League of Albion far-right group was holding its own rally on this most auspicious of days. Kieran was hoping to get some lively action for his new current affairs series, *The McDonaghy Report*. His trip would be worthwhile.

Since being bathed in a shower of critical acclaim and winning a BAFTA for his *Made Men* special on Farren Mortimer Kieran's stock had continued to rise – he was broadcast gold. A number of offers had fallen on his agent's desk and the two of them had carefully cherry-picked the formats that would best build Kieran's growing reputation as a presenter and commentator of stature, one who wasn't afraid to tackle the big issues, one could connect with his audience. 'Is it cut-through?' was the question they asked as they weighed up the pros and cons of each offer. Ultimately, Kieran wanted to host his own TV chat show and was currently working on treatments that would reinvent and refresh the tired old format. There was no stopping him.

Neither was there anything stopping @wappinglie. What Kieran had started as a bit of a lark had turned into a successful brand all of its own, spawning a book deal, *They're All At It*, and a TV spin-off series. The number of @wappinglie followers had now swelled to over 200,000, the vast majority of whom had been gained around the time of PRD a year earlier, and they'd stuck. Remarkably, the true identity of @wappinglie was still unknown to all but a few insiders. Kieran had already decided that the next phase of the campaign would be a major reveal – in a twist of genius he was planning to make it look like his secret had been discovered, rather than he'd decided to unmask himself voluntarily.

On arriving at the protest march Kieran donned his protective flak jacket and got right down into the middle of the action. As his crew dodged the bricks being thrown by the anti-fascist protesters, he gasped his intro to the camera: 'Right wing militants parade on the streets of Blackburn on Trafalgar Day under a hail of bricks from anti-march opponents. What would Horatio Nelson make of how his famous battle is commemorated 200 years on? Welcome to modern day Britain with Kieran McDonaghy.'

Trafalgar Day didn't hold the best of memories for Jon Bell, the date marking the first anniversary of the desecration of his mother's grave. The sudden death of his mother followed by the violation of her final resting place still pervaded all of his thoughts. Life had been a succession of difficulties in the intervening period and his wife Becky was at her wit's end in trying to get him to move on.

Jon hadn't worked for over a year and was now, with Becky's prompting, about to set up as an independent consultant offering advice to businesses on branding and digital marketing. At least that would allow him to work from home.

Jon wasn't altogether confident that the consultancy idea was the best thing for him to do, but consoled himself with the thought that if it didn't work out he could always downsize and move back to Derbyshire – in his heart of hearts he was already set on that course.

The police had pursued a few lines of enquiry into the dreadful act carried out at his mother's grave but had got nowhere. The motivation for the outrage remained a puzzle and no-one had claimed responsibility; yet it was an atrocity that had left a lasting legacy on the Bell family.

Would Jon find some form of closure if he discovered the truth? He doubted it, as nothing would ever assuage for him the horror of what took place that grim night.

To add insult to injury Farren had been most supportive towards him after his mother's death, attending the funeral and sharing in the revulsion towards the defilement of his mother's grave, which made Jon's sense of shame all the more pronounced after he'd tried to hang him out to dry.

As Jon carefully placed a large bouquet of flowers in the boot of his car, Becky called Samantha and Ben together as they prepared to set off north to visit Mum's relocated grave.

'Can you move to the left just a little bit, Annie, so I can get the whole of the polar bear in?' Annie and Donny Brooks were having a day out at the zoo accompanied by a photographer from 'Single Mother' magazine which was paying handsomely for the shoot.

Annie's career hadn't looked back since her exclusive story in the Sunday Splash just under a year back. In a masterpiece of fortuitous timing, as soon as the piece had appeared she'd been asked to join the cast of the jungle survival reality TV series *Beating About The Bush* as a last-minute addition. Her inclusion in the two-week run of the show had seen ratings return almost to series one proportions. Annie didn't win, but did net £100,000 for the gig (£25,000 of which was for her agreeing to wear a bikini wardrobe). On top of the money she received for her newspaper exclusive it wasn't a bad return and at least she now held the record for doing the highest number of successive trials on the programme.

The offers had continued to come in for photoshoots and personal appearances and she was currently weighing up approaches from two further reality TV formats, one called *Going Commando* where she and fellow celebs would recreate daring raids from WWII, and one called *Deal Me In*, where the contestants would work in a City trading office for two weeks to see who could make the most money, the twist being that they were dealing in actual, not fake, trades.

Her active life meant that the amount of time she could dedicate to her charity had become somewhat reduced, so earlier in the year she'd reluctantly shelved HASTE, consoling herself that she had made a major contribution to the area of road safety. However, her compulsion to help others remained strong, and even now she was considering launching a new charity to help women get a fairer deal from divorce settlements, something she felt very strongly about due to the ongoing battle she was having with Stuart over ending their unhappy nuptial union.

As Annie held Donny up high so he could see the crocodiles more clearly, she knew, just knew, that all of her hard work had been justified, not only to secure a happier future for herself and her son, but also to create a better world for others.

Nigel and Emma Adlington had enjoyed a romantic long weekend in Paris and, determined to make the most of their final day before heading off to the airport for their return flight to Manchester, were lunching at L'Atelier de Joël Robuchon in St-Germain-de-Prés.

Nigel had suffered, in his own words, an *annus horribilis*, what with his forced resignation and the humiliation of having a succession of tawdry fabrications about his so-called relationship with Annie Brooks printed in the newspapers. It had been a bleak period in his life, and Emma had not reacted as well as she could have. Time, though, is a great healer, and having endured the darkest of days, things were once again looking up for Nigel.

After the 'fall', as Nigel now referred to it, he had in fact become a somewhat unlikely hero among the male colleagues and clients at his law firm for having bagged the attractively built Mrs Brooks. They, too, 'wouldn't have kicked her out of bed.' Despite everything, business was doing well, and he now regularly appeared on current affairs programmes and news broadcasts where his unfettered views and self-deprecating style were a welcome relief to the party-liners who barked 'turn right, turn left, straight on' exhortations with the urgent insistence of a Sat Nav device.

Nor had Nigel's dedication to the cause been forgotten by the Party. He'd taken his punishment like a man, done the decent thing, and hadn't bellyached – they could do with more like him. After his spell in the political wilderness, Nigel had just been invited to chair a select committee looking into the legal aid system. He was on his way back.

All of this had, he knew, been easier to achieve than his struggle to persuade Emma to stand by him. A year ago on PRD, as the world crashed about his ears, he had consoled himself that he still at least had Emma and the children to help see him through it. Then, a week later, the Sunday Splash ran Annie's story, resulting in Emma leaving the family home with the two boys, and vowing to 'take him for every penny he'd got.'

Nigel didn't give up. He grovelled, crawled and beseeched her forgiveness for his momentary lapse, promising eternal fidelity if they could only get their lives back on track.

Unlikely assistance to his cause, unbeknown to Nigel, had come from Emma's mother who, despite never having liked him, warned her daughter that Nigel would make sure she got the thin end of the wedge in any divorce deal going. 'He's a tricky one, that Nigel. His money will be hidden all over the place, you mark my words.'

Over the spring and summer months Nigel and Emma had virtually made up their differences and got back to normal as their Parisian excursion demonstrated. Emma would never forget Nigel's misdemeanours and the memory of them would always be there in the background but hopefully, like a nuclear deterrent, deployment of the arsenal could be avoided. On this beautiful Paris afternoon neither Nigel nor Emma had mutually assured destruction on their minds. Smiling, Nigel raised his glass of vintage Dom Perignon towards Emma in a witty toast: '*Jours Heureux*.'

Six hours behind on Eastern Standard Time, Smudger was still putting the finishing touches to his first New York show. He'd not been to bed yet, but was determined that every piece of work would be hung to his satisfaction in the vast NoHo warehouse before he called it a night.

Smudger's decision to kick-start the next stage of his artistic evolution outside of the UK had been helped along by external forces. Although styling himself as a rebel and an anti-authority symbol, things had got a little out of hand when it was rumoured that he was behind the desecration of Muriel Bell's grave. That theory, first expounded by @wappinglie, was readily taken up and amplified by other print and broadcast media as a possible line of enquiry the police were investigating, especially given the long list of previous attacks allegedly made on AMOLAD by 'an anonymous, disgruntled and anarchistic street artist'. Smudger had been elated at first, highly amused that he was receiving the credit for something he hadn't done. Plus, it was a pretty good prank, although he'd have carried it off a bit more stylishly he thought. At the time Smudger had decided to maintain his air of mystery and pure artistry by neither denying nor confirming the rumour, and his notoriety rose further still.

The police on the other hand, clearly not art lovers, were determined to eliminate Smudger from their enquiries and this had led to a desperate wrangle with detectives putting pressure on his agent, Malcolm, for access. Eventually Smudger cracked and consented to an interview as long as his anonymity could be preserved if not charged.

Accompanied by his solicitor, Smudger was able to prove he couldn't possibly have carried out the crime under inquiry as he was actually on a reconnaissance trip to Barcelona, an alibi readily qualified by the passport office. Nevertheless, the heat had got to Smudger and so Malcolm's suggestion of taking a few months away from Britain was met with a positive response.

It had been one of the best decisions he'd ever made. He wasn't attending the actual show that evening but he knew, as Malcolm had predicted, that the new international and global direction he'd adopted for his art over the past year was already a winner. Extensive Stateside media coverage of the latest British art genius to hit their shores had already ignited considerable pre-show sales, all at stratospherically high prices. The end of runs for his old works were selling for double what they were fetching a year ago, in particular his AMOLAD inspired pieces.

Farren parked the small Seat car in the town's main square and, turning to Michael, said: 'We can walk from here.'

They had arrived at the picturesque fishing port of Sesimbra after a short drive south from Lisbon, twenty-five miles away, and now needed to locate the address on the piece of paper Farren had taken out of his wallet.

The autumn sun still provided sufficient warmth for the two travellers to eschew the wearing of jackets, and they took in the views of the bay twinkling in the sunlight before them like a couple of holiday makers.

Both were aware of the date – how could they not be?

Neither had ever thought to experience a year like it. The two never spoke of the events of a year ago, but both knew how far each had gone in the pursuit of their cause. In that they had a bond as irrevocable and enduring as their blood tie.

Until recently, Michael had suffered flashbacks of his night at Duffield cemetery. Had their actions been justified? In the hue and cry of the discovery of the crime, he felt sure that the police would be coming to arrest him at every minute of the day. He had to try to carry on as normal, but whether he was apprehended or not he couldn't shake the guilt that he had committed a sin that brooked no forgiveness.

As matters developed from that day, he began to recognise the method in the madness of the plan Farren had come up with – things began to fall into place exactly as he had predicted. Furthermore, when it became evident that the police looked a long way from having any leads, Michael began to dare to breath again.

Now Michael had cut himself free from the past and only looked to the future. The family firm he'd presided over to the last had been sold to Fond Farewell Funerals; finally, the Morrisons had escaped the clutches of death, until he was due to make his own appointment with it at least.

Would God ever forgive him for that night in Derbyshire? Michael prayed he would; after all, he'd acted partly in his name. But first Michael had to fully forgive himself.

Farren didn't miss AMOLAD one little bit. When he'd called a press conference to wind up his business eleven and half months previously, he'd met with a wave of admiration for having the courage to say 'enough is enough.' While stunned business hacks pointed out that he could have made millions of pounds by simply selling it to someone else, a subsequent leader in The Times praised this high water mark in entrepreneurial morality. After the shock and revulsion felt throughout the country in response to the desecration of Mrs Bell's grave a growing number of commentators backed his decision to foreclose AMOLAD and queued up to congratulate him on his bravery in taking firm action in the face of increasingly serious attacks on his business.

Church leaders and the funerals industry also jumped on the bandwagon, uttering sage pronouncements on how they'd always had their doubts about the role of ostentatious bereavement in our culture. Still, they added, it's refreshing to see a businessman pull the plug on a successful business on the grounds of taste.

Given the admiration Farren's decision to wind up the business received, and the collective cultural analysis and media reassessment that followed on how we should best mourn our dead, any would-be competitor to AMOLAD quickly dropped any plans they may have been hatching to go big on the bereavement services sector.

A few customers expressed dissatisfaction at the closure, complaining that their guarantee of eternity for their online memorials may not be honoured, but AMOLAD even took care of that with a third-party maintenance contract for the next 100 years.

Farren was sad to have to let his staff go, but everybody, from Jon down to the most junior data programmer had their contracts paid up in full in the voluntary wind up. The final account, including the sale of assets, was yet to be finalised but would yield a surplus rather than a negative bottom-line figure.

Farren hadn't been immune from Michael's worries over

detection and knew that they'd taken an enormous gamble, but like his father he had begun to relax slightly when it became apparent that the police had nothing, not even CCTV from the A6 in Duffield, to go on.

@whistleblower's direct message to @wappinglie to look closely at Smudger's list of attacks against AMOLAD had helped to draw attention away from them. Anybody who wanted to could access the world of social media to discover the name of the most likely perpetrator of the desecration. Even in the mainstream media the connection between 'an anonymous, disgruntled and anarchistic street artist' and Smudger was hard to miss.

Agnes never suspected that Farren and Michael had conspired together. She was as upset as any decent person could be over the atrocity that appeared to be targeted at her son's business; she was also indifferent to Farren's subsequent decision to walk away from AMOLAD – after all, it was up to him, and she couldn't blame him. Agnes' main beef these days was the time Farren spent with Michael, the Johnny-come-lately who had turned up out of the blue when all the hard work was done, and who'd never once lifted a finger for his son. Farren avoided trying to get the three of them together as a family too often, and that seemed to suit everyone just fine.

Farren was already at work on his next career move but first he still had one important job to do, which is why he and Michael were in Portugal today. Ever since he'd found his real father, Farren had been determined to discover more background on Linda, his true mother. As soon as he and Michael had felt able, they'd begun to make enquiries about her, tracing her medical history first, before going back to her university days. It had been a long haul, with numerous false leads, not helped by the popularity of her surname.

Finally, they'd had a breakthrough on the University of Manchester Alumni website when a reunion of the English Department's 1970 intake was advertised. There the private detective Farren had hired to make enquiries managed to find a student from the same year who recalled that Looby was, as far as she knew, from Essex, with an English father who'd died when Looby was in her first year, and a Portuguese mother. Boosted by this lead, they eventually discovered that Linda's mother was still alive and now living back in Portugal after the death of her daughter. Having traced her to Sesimbra, the circle was now about to be squared.

As they headed up to the landmark Moorish fortress atop the town, Farren couldn't help but quicken his step as he neared the address he had been given. A whole new life lay ahead of him.

Consummatum Est

Acknowledgements

I'd like to thank the following people for their assistance and support: Mark Beaumont of Dinosaur for cover design; Glenn Jones of Home Design for website creation: Patrick Carroll, Catherine Carroll, Peter Jones, Charles Rose, Brendan Gore, Gerry McLaughlin, Peter Burling and John Kelly for first draft comment and feedback; Liam Ferguson for structural suggestions; David Lomax for proof-reading, and Nina Webb of Brazen PR for social media assistance.

The Author

Leeds born Paul Carroll has worked in the public relations arena for thirty-five years. His highly successful agency, Communique PR, became one of the best-known, independent PR operations in the UK with offices in Manchester and London. Paul exited the business in 2004 after 18 years in charge following its sale to WPP and is currently a freelance marketing and business consultant. *A Matter of Life and Death* is his first novel.